DEADLY MOVE

Truly gripping detective mystery fiction

ROBERT McCRACKEN

THE
BOOK
FOLKS

Published by The Book Folks

London, 2024

ISBN 978-1-80462-208-7

www.thebookfolks.com

Deadly Move is the eighth book in the DI Tara Grogan mystery series.

CHAPTER 1

Tommy Brady

Tommy had a lot of time on his hands and no one to share it with, but he was never bored. Lonely at times, but never bored. There was always work to be done, running programs and simulations, gathering intel on the big players and hacking their systems. Just for the hell of it. He didn't care about the money to be made. If he had cared, he would have been stinking rich years ago. You only had to look at how he was living to realise it could never be about the money. The last eighteen years had been spent trying to prove a point, but he never thought he would have the opportunity; didn't think it would be today.

He sat back in his worn-out swivel chair, his hands clasped behind his head, watching the numbers tumble on the four screens. Give him ten minutes and he could make them all disappear and with them the fortunes of one man. But in the beginning, Tommy had only wanted to help him. He'd turned him down flat. Now Tommy would make him rue the day.

The thumping beat of heavy metal bounced off the walls. It didn't matter if it was AC/DC or Rival Sons so long as it was loud. Music shut out the world and helped him to focus.

Tommy sipped his coffee and winced. It had gone cold hours ago. He'd lost all concept of time. This was too exciting to worry about food, drink, sleep or whether it was time to get to his day job. He couldn't even remember what day it was. Nothing mattered but one decision. Should he wield his newly acquired power or let his nemesis run free? He dropped his fag butt into the cold coffee.

He didn't hear the voice calling from downstairs. He should have paid more heed to locking his doors when he was working in his room. But people seldom came to his house, and besides, this was a safe neighbourhood.

He peered at his screens, his eyes darting from one to another, checking there were no last minute glitches. Almost there, just a few more seconds and he would have the access he needed.

'Tommy? Where are you?'

This time he heard the call above the din. His second interruption of the day, or maybe the previous visitor had been the day before. He had no idea. Didn't care.

'In here,' he shouted, irritated.

Oblivious to any further comment, he fixed his gaze on one of his precious monitors. He was in; he'd breached the last firewall. But he was unaware of his visitor standing by the door of the cramped box room watching him work.

Now he was free to wreak havoc in the finances of his enemy. He sat forward, his eyes taking in the huge numbers appearing before him. They were even bigger than he'd imagined. He didn't hear the words spoken before the blade pierced the back of his neck. Tommy slumped over, his head crashing down on his keyboard, his right hand losing its grip of the mouse, unable to make that final click. And a man's fortune was spared, while Tommy's blood oozed from his wound and dripped to the floor.

CHAPTER 2

Tara Grogan

It was the start of the week, and the sun was shining, a treat for this part of the world. Trees were in bloom, summer wardrobes on show – colourful dresses, sandals, shorts, polo shirts and camisoles. Announcements of forthcoming music festivals were displayed on hoardings, streets transformed by pavement coffee shops, bicycles, and the smell of hot vehicles queuing at busy junctions.

It was a sleepy morning. How could anything bad happen today? Yet, it already had. DI Tara Grogan wasn't on her way to a modern air-conditioned office in the city or even a stuffy Victorian room with paint-jammed windows and buzzing fans. Music she couldn't recall choosing for her playlist blared as the satnav directed her from a roundabout on Breeze Hill into a region of varied housing. Sandfield Road in Bootle was a small estate of red-brick maisonettes with tiny windows, pitched roofs, covered alleys and sporadic parking bays. The address she'd been given was inconspicuous amongst its neighbours. Tara hated these places. Necessary perhaps, but built seemingly without an aesthetic vision. Why didn't town planners aspire to something better than the drab monotony of the modern day and the culture of cheap and practical? There had to be better ways to live.

She pulled up behind a marked police car and watched as a uniformed constable stretched incident tape from a gatepost on one side of the road to a lamppost on the other. Clipping her warrant card to a lanyard and slipping it over her maroon T-shirt, she stepped from her car in sunglasses, looking around for a familiar face. Instantly, she felt the sun's warmth on her back and might have been tempted to just lean against her car and pretend she was somewhere else, Spain or Greece, but selfish contemplation had no place at a crime scene. Suddenly, DS John Wilson stood before her, towering over her slight frame. If she'd been facing the other way, he'd have blocked out the sun completely. Her younger colleague had round shoulders, short blonde hair and a chubby face that despite the harrowing job somehow always appeared full of life's cheer.

'Morning, John. Not how I was hoping to start the week.'

'No, ma'am.'

'What do we have?'

She had yet to identify the precise location of the crime scene. Wilson swivelled his shoulders and gazed towards the house in question.

'One male in an upstairs room, dead at the scene. The body was discovered by a neighbour who noticed the front door lying open early this morning. They'd gone to complain about the noise.'

'What noise?'

'Apparently music was blaring all through the night. Dr Witney is already inside.'

'Better not keep him waiting.'

They donned white coverall suits, and immediately Tara felt the heat build within. It was not the apparel of choice for a hot day. Approaching the house, Tara noticed the paved front garden, weeds spreading from crevices and bird mess spattered on the doorstep. A forensics team was already at work. The glass-panelled front door was open wide, and the floor of the hallway had been covered with plastic sheeting. Tara and Wilson stepped inside. The air felt stale, already warm from the morning sun. Odours of fried food, bacon or sausages, were mixed with the stench of cigarette smoke. The cream-painted walls were browned from years of exposure to someone's smoking habits. Tara noticed a rectangular stain on the wall where a picture had once hung but, at some point, had been removed. A dirty outline surrounded cleaner paint. There were two doors within the hall, one open to a dim lounge with curtains drawn over a single window. The other door was ajar and presumably led to the kitchen. Stairs covered with dank brown carpet stood to the left.

'Hello?' Tara called as cheerfully as she thought appropriate at a crime scene.

When she reached the narrow landing, a bedroom door opened and there stood Dr Brian Witney, medical officer and pathologist working on behalf of Merseyside Police. Close to retirement and looking weary, the thickset man always managed a friendly greeting for Tara. Over the years, he had developed a fatherly countenance towards his favourite detective. Witney empathised with the beautiful young soul charged with the gruelling task of finding murderers.

'Good morning, Tara, or at least it was before I got here. I had been intending to spend a week in the Lakes rather than the post-mortem suite.'

'C'est la vie, Brian. Maybe next week.'

He stepped back into the room, and immediately Tara got her first sight of the victim. The man was seated on a desk chair, his head and shoulders beached on a large desk supporting an array of computer terminals and monitors. The room was cluttered, and the small patch of carpeted floor was stained red with blood.

Tara shuddered as she caught the metallic whiff of spilled blood. She felt the familiar spike of nerves shooting through her spine but knew she had to look, she must see the victim's face. How else could she hope to bring his killer to justice? See the victim and you won't rest until you find the killer. How many times had that mantra flashed in her head at a crime scene?

The man's face, discoloured by death and loss of blood, was pressed into a keyboard. A knife with a black handle and wide blade protruded from the back of his neck.

'I'm thinking that the knife was forced upwards into the neck and then twisted,' said Witney. 'It probably cut the spinal cord just below the cerebellum. Death would have been instantaneous.'

Witney grasped the victim's head, and respectfully but firmly turned it sideways for Tara to view the face.

She gave a sudden jerk on seeing the open eyes, brown yet lifeless. Quickly, she absorbed the gruesome image, if only to hasten the end of the inspection and escape the room. His hair was greying, was unkempt and did little to help Tara guess at his age. She estimated fifty-something but perhaps he was much younger. His navy polo shirt and trousers were soaked in blood. His feet were bare; a pair of flip-flops had been cast off beneath the desk.

'Estimated time of death is ten to twelve hours ago, to be confirmed. I'm sure that SOCO can help with identification. I'll see you tomorrow for the post-mortem. Have a good day, Tara.'

'Thank you, Brian. I'll try.'

The medical officer departed, while Tara remained by the victim, scouring the box room for anything to explain what had taken place. A plate with a bread crust and slice of bacon lay on the desk with a full coffee mug beside it. A metal ashtray overflowed with half-smoked cigarettes. She noticed that the computers were plugged into a socket strip, but all appeared to have reverted to sleep mode. Seeing the victim's hand still gripping a mouse, she nudged it slightly and two of the monitors burst into life. One displayed a screen saver of an Alpine landscape; the other showed only a password prompt.

'This room is full of junk,' said Wilson.

Tara gazed around shelves stacked with computer equipment, some connected with operating lights showing and others looking discarded and covered in greasy dust.

Several games consoles, three televisions and two old and bulky computer monitors lay in a corner beneath a tangle of cables.

The small window held a battered venetian blind, open slightly to reveal a compact rear garden below and a parking area beyond the house. She could see a couple of SOCOs scouring an untidy patch of lawn searching for evidence.

Tara felt the urge to get out of the room, to breathe fresh air and to deal with the harrowing image of another murdered soul in her mind. The bathroom didn't hold her interest: patterned tiled walls and a washbasin in need of cleaning. A bottle of shower gel, a toothbrush and a tube of toothpaste sat on the windowsill. The front bedroom had an unmade double bed and reeked of body odour. Wilson opened a teak-effect wardrobe to reveal an uninspiring collection of shirts, polos, chinos and a dark-grey suit. Beneath the clothes were a pair of black brogues, well-worn trainers and a pair of workman's boots.

'Not such an interesting bloke,' Tara mused.

'Except for all that computer gear,' said Wilson.

'Depends on what he used it for.'

'We'll get the tech team to have a look.'

They moved to a bedroom at the front of the house. It contained a single bed with a plain blue duvet and a chest of drawers. It didn't strike her as a place that was used much except as a dumping ground for more computer equipment. Several dated workstations of various brands were stacked in a corner and a tangle of cables lay on the bed. Tara left Wilson to the inspection, while she ventured downstairs.

As if on cue, a forensics officer emerged from the kitchen.

'Any ID for the victim?' Tara asked.

The young woman, looking flushed beneath her hooded overall, handed Tara a brown leather wallet.

'The medical officer retrieved it from the victim's pocket. We've already taken prints, so it's OK for you to handle it.'

'Thank you.'

Tara looked through the wallet. A driving license stated the name Thomas Brady. She compared the photo with her recent memory of the victim's face. They seemed a match. The date of birth indicated he was thirty-nine. Much younger than she'd first thought. Wilson joined her in the hall, and also showed him the licence

'We'll finish having a look around then we need to get house-to-house underway,' she said.

'Uniform have already started,' Wilson replied.

'Great, no prompting required then.'

She stepped into the lounge.

'Wow! What do we have here?'

The room was far from tidy; cluttered more than dirty. There were several stacks of books, mostly paperback fantasy novels and a few textbooks on computing, dumped on an overly large coffee table in the centre of the room making it difficult to navigate from one side to the other. A television hung from the wall and below it, on a stone fireplace with a gas burner, were several cardboard boxes. One held LP records; old, seventies, she guessed, judging by the Black Sabbath that was visible. Another, larger box contained various electrical cables, USB and HDMI, chargers and a couple of game controllers. A third box – Tara had to lift the flaps to see inside – contained at least a dozen mobile phones, both old and more recent models. There were also several pairs of spectacles. An iPod dock, minus an iPod, was perched on a footstool below the window. Against the wall stood two garden spades, a rake and a hoe. Next to these sat perhaps the source of the loud music, a retro-style jukebox that played CDs. Several items of clothing – jeans, T-shirts and a gilet – were scattered over a worn sofa.

'Interesting items to have in your living room,' Wilson commented. Tara didn't disagree.

When they'd finished with the house, Tara and Wilson stood outside at last breathing fresh albeit warm air. A male constable approached. He looked young and couldn't have been a serving officer for long, judging by the baby face and his apparent discomfort in wearing a police uniform. But at least he knew whom to address first.

'Ma'am, I have the person who found the body.'

'Lead on,' Tara replied with a smile.

They crossed the road and came to a man waiting on the pavement. He looked to be in his sixties, wearing long denim shorts and a vest. There was an array of faded tattoos down both arms and he had a smile on his ruddy face, suggesting that either he found the episode amusing or was simply enjoying his moment of attention.

'This is Mr Barlow, ma'am,' said the constable.

'Good morning, sir,' said Tara. 'Thanks for waiting around for us. Can you tell me how you came to find the victim?'

The man's speech accelerated as he spoke. Scouse was one thing, but Scouse exceeding the speed limit was another and difficult to make out.

'Tommy was always playing that damned music of his, all bloody day and night. Complained hundreds of times but he took no notice. Even complained to the council but they did sod all. I called the bizzies once and do you know what they said? What kind of music? Bloody loud music, that's what. Didn't matter to me whether it was Mick Jagger or bloody Mozart, I just wanted it turned down. Tommy didn't give a toss. He only cared about those flipping computers.'

'Can you explain how you found Mr Brady?' Tara tried again.

Barlow looked incredulous as if he hadn't already explained.

'I went over this morning about half six. The noise had kept me awake all night. Couldn't take much more.'

'And where do you live?'

'In here.' Barlow jabbed a stubby finger at the house behind him. It stood directly opposite the home of Tommy Brady. 'It's been so hot recently, we had to have the windows open during the night but that made the noise worse.'

'So, you went to complain?'

'Too right, love. Tommy's front door was lying open, just a crack, but I could see he'd forgotten to shut it. So, I stepped in and called out to him. It was pointless; no one could hear anything above that racket. You see, he plays his jukebox downstairs on repeat, like, but he spends all his time upstairs on those blinking computers. So, I went into his living room and stopped the music then called Tommy again. Couldn't believe that he'd gone to bed with the music still blaring. I went upstairs giving off and swearing. Then I saw the poor sod. Slumped over his desk with a blade in his neck!'

The story had come as a rant, but Tara understood the man's shock at finding his neighbour.

'Did you touch anything else in the house besides the jukebox?'

'No, I just got myself the hell out and called you lot.'

Tara thanked Barlow, and Wilson gave him a card.

'If you think of anything else, Mr Barlow,' said Tara, 'please give us a call.'

'Right you are, love.'

Only Monday morning: it was going to be a long week.

* * *

The detective's office at St Anne Street station was already muggy with the heat of late morning. Several fans had been strategically placed on desks and bottles of water were at hand. Tara and Wilson were immediately summoned to Superintendent Harold Tweedy's office, the most pleasant room in the station and the only place where the building's air-conditioning functioned effectively. Tweedy, a long-serving officer staving off the prospect of retirement, was ready with his traditional method of collating evidence from a fresh murder case: a flip chart and marker pen.

'Good morning, folks,' he said in his sanguine voice.

A wrinkled, surly face belied his gentle manner. He stood by his flip chart and had been in conversation with DS Alan Murray. Murray was Tara's closest colleague and friend, although their relationship was often strained. On more than one occasion, however, the large-framed Murray had come to her aid when she most needed it.

'Sorry to begin the week on such a sombre note,' said Tweedy. 'I can think of better places to be on such a lovely day. Hopefully, we can draw up an action plan and get things rolling. Alan was just reporting the info from officers carrying out the initial house-to-house enquiries. Hot off the press. The sooner we act on it, the better.'

'Let's hear it,' Tara said eagerly, grabbing a chair next to Murray.

Tweedy was already adding notes to his chart as Murray spoke.

'Not that much, I'm afraid,' Murray said. 'Tommy Brady had lived alone at Sandfield Road for about eleven years. According to a neighbour, a few doors along, Brady moved to the area following his marriage break-up. We're tracing the ex-wife. No kids or siblings and both parents are dead.'

'Any witnesses to strange things going on at the house?' Wilson asked.

Murray shook his head.

'Nothing much heard or seen. When I say nothing heard, that's not quite true. Apparently, several of his neighbours had complained about loud music.'

'Yes, we've spoken to the man who found the body,' said Wilson. 'Do you think Mr Barlow just lost it because of the noise, he goes to have it out with Brady and things went too far?'

'Wouldn't be the first time,' said Tara. 'Most murders are the result of domestic issues.'

Tweedy wrapped up the discussion with his habit of asking challenging questions of his team.

'Not much to go on, folks. Is it a local quarrel that got out of hand, or something more sinister?'

'Maybe the post-mortem will provide something,' said Tara. But she was already thinking beyond medical examinations and lab results. Unless it was straightforward and a neighbour had taken his complaining over loud music a step further, they needed a lot more information regarding Tommy Brady.

CHAPTER 3

Carla Smith

The smoke alarm was going nuts. The smell of burning toast wafted upstairs. Carla knew it was an end to her lie-in. She didn't have to be at work until ten-thirty this morning, but one or both sons had scuppered her me-time.

'Close the frigging door!' she shouted from the landing.

She saw Lee in the hall wafting a tea towel at the smoke alarm. The kitchen door slammed.

'It's Jack,' he called. 'Can't even make toast.'

Carla grunted her disgust and, still in her pyjamas, came downstairs. The beeping stopped as she put one foot on the hall floor.

'What's going on?' she asked, padding into the kitchen.

'It's him,' said Jack, pushing a knife into the toaster.

'My God! Switch it off first, Jack. You'll get yourself electrocuted.' Carla nudged her son out of the way, hit the switch on the wall then turned the toaster upside down. Crumbs and broken pieces of burnt toast scattered over the worktop.

'Mum! Look at the mess,' Jack moaned. 'I can do it.'

'Well next time do it without bringing the whole frigging house down.'

She fetched the kettle, filled it at the tap and switched it on to boil. Now that she was up, she may as well continue with breakfast and then prepare packed lunches for her boys. Lee's head was fixed to his phone, scrolling through nonsense as he sat with a bowl of Cheerios awaiting some milk. His twin Jack had now spread toast crumbs through the tub of butter. Carla shook her head in disgust.

'What would the pair of you do if I left you here on your own?'

'What?' said Lee without looking up.

'We can manage, Mum,' Jack replied. 'It's all his fault, I asked him to watch my toast and he just let it burn.'

'Cry-baby,' said Lee.

'I'll give you frigging cry-baby.' Jack tossed a crust at his brother.

'Stop it, the pair of you. Can you not get ready for school without a war breaking out in this house?'

Carla sat down with a mug of tea and her vape. She lifted the TV remote from the arm of the sofa and jabbed it at the screen on the wall. BBC News appeared when Lee began to eat his breakfast and Jack, having scoffed his toast, left the room to pack his schoolbag. Only Carla, as she puffed on her vape, paid attention to what was showing on TV. She stroked the strands of her blonde, pink-tipped hair and watched as the local bulletin came on; her mind filled with a to-do list for the day ahead.

She had two rinse and set appointments before one o'clock, and three wash, cut and blow-drys in the afternoon. At four, she would head to her sons' school to begin her second job of the day: cleaning classrooms and toilets until seven. A quick stop at Aldi to buy dinner then home to slip it in the oven. It would be too much to expect either teenager to put a wash on or, saints preserve us, clean the bathroom or even tidy their bedrooms. Such is life. Such is my frigging life, she thought.

Thirty-eight, two dull jobs, a council house, seventeen-year-old twin sons and no man. Carla had it all, or didn't, depending on how you looked at it. Life had slipped by, and she had little to show for it. At times, she thought herself attractive, but that only lasted a few hours on the odd Saturday night when she went to the pub with long-time friends Mandy and Diane. She could hardly recall the last time she'd had a boyfriend beyond one or two shags. No man in this city desired a woman with baggage and no money. 'On the shelf' wasn't an accurate way to describe her lot. 'Dangling from a very high one' was closer to the mark.

The recent good weather had set her thinking about a holiday. Not just for herself but with her boys. Hopefully, she could afford a week in Benidorm or Palma Nova. She had a little put by. Mandy and Diane were trying to talk her into going to Vegas in the autumn, but it was too expensive. Besides, she had no real interest in going all that way just to play the slots and get rat-arsed. She could do that in Blackpool and have money to spare. No, this holiday might be the last opportunity for Jack, Lee and her to be together. If all went well with their exams, both would be heading to uni in September. God love them, they'd walk out of school at the end of the month carefree and six weeks later, take on a debt they might struggle to ever pay off. All she could offer by way of help was the cash she'd put by for the holiday. It wouldn't go far. She loved her boys and, despite their bolshy attitude at times, they had never once asked her for money or demanded the latest trainers or football shirts. They'd been raised to know that they didn't have much but at least they had each other.

The final item on the BBC North West bulletin referred to the return of a self-made billionaire to Merseyside. Sebastian Logan-Sharp, the reporter explained, after an absence of almost eighteen years was now keen to invest in his hometown. The man who had made his fortune with online trading then moved into property was now linked with a proposed major development on the Mersey shoreline. Many rumours were circulating regarding Logan-Sharp, reputedly worth 1.8 billion pounds, including the purchase of a football club in the region. Several clubs were mooted as possible candidates, but Logan-Sharp, the reporter stated, was a devout Evertonian.

Carla watched with interest as the bulletin gave a profile of the Scouser made good: his family, his homes and his philanthropic pursuits. Despite his wealth, Sebastian Logan-Sharp, in Carla's eyes, and in the eyes of many Liverpudlians, would always look like the docker his father and grandfather had been. He wasn't tall at five foot seven, weighed 15 stone, had little of his hair remaining, and his head was frequently concealed beneath a fedora. Regardless of the fine Italian suits, he failed to impress those who had known him before the money arrived. 'Plenty of cash, no frigging class' was how he was viewed.

Carla had known him years ago. Now she hated him.

CHAPTER 4

Tara Grogan

Tara entered the recycling yard in Bootle where eight skips stood in a line down one side and four others for green waste were positioned opposite. She'd left Murray to mind their car, with all the windows down and the boot lid raised to help cool the interior. The space at the rear of the yard was taken up with cages for metal waste and discarded electrical appliances. A huge contraption with a heavy roller for breaking up wood was fixed above another skip, and next to it was an enclosed container holding cardboard waste.

Tara approached a small grey building with a flat roof that served as an office. It had a single door and a window with a metal grill.

The man who greeted her at the door paled on hearing the news. 'Tommy? I can't believe it. Wouldn't hurt a soul. Just came in, did his work and went home.'

'When did you last see him, Mr Taylor?'

'Friday afternoon. We finish at four o'clock on Fridays.'

'And how did Tommy seem to you?'

Taylor, the man who had been Tommy Brady's supervisor, was a burly fifty-year-old, with greying whiskers and shrill voice. He considered Tara's question for a moment then shrugged.

'Just the usual Tommy, joking around as he helped himself to stuff from the skip.'

'What do you mean?' Tara gazed around the yard.

'Well, everybody does it. We all keep an eye out for things of interest when someone unloads their car. I mean, it's still getting recycled if one of us can find a use for it.'

'It's fine, Mr Taylor, I'm not judging you. What kind of things were of interest to Tommy Brady?'

'Electronics mostly. Computers, old hi-fis, records, CDs and mobile phones. Some of it he would fix up and sell at car-boot sales, but more than likely, it just piled up in his garden shed.'

'Did he mention anything that was troubling him?'

Taylor shook his head.

'Do you know of anyone who may have wanted to do him harm?'

'Not Tommy. The proverbial gentle giant, except he wasn't that big. A clever bloke though.'

'How do you mean?'

'Way too clever for working in this place, sorting through rubbish. He knew how to fix all those gadgets he pulled out of skips. I heard that at one time he was a real whizz with computers. He could have earned a fortune. But he's worked here for years. Don't know what happened. He never spoke about it.'

'Do you know anything of his family or next of kin?'

'Divorced years ago. He lived alone, not far from here. Can't say much more.'

'Thank you, Mr Taylor. You've been very helpful. If you think of anything else, no matter how trivial it may seem, please get in touch.'

She gave him her card and rejoined Murray by their car.

'Get anything useful, ma'am?' Murray asked. He was struggling with the heat, his shirt open, tie pulled down, red-faced and sweating.

'There's always a story, Alan.'

CHAPTER 5

Beatrice Howard

'How was it, babe?' Ernst grunted as he towered over her panting body.

His Austrian accent grated with her. His question sounded seedy, insincere, gratuitous and somehow menacing. She didn't answer, and despite the heat of the room, she pulled a sheet over her naked body. She knew from her brief experience of the man that he craved something sleazier than straightforward sex. Nowadays, it seemed that young men wanted to re-enact the last porn they'd watched on their phone.

In Ernst's case she was perhaps a little disingenuous. He was a strong and athletic bed partner and frequently took her breath away. This morning, Ernst had been wonderful. She should be grateful. A twenty-six-year-old Adonis more than happy to pleasure a forty-eight-year-old cougar. Of course, she was aware of her own allure. A near perfect body, youthful-looking face and elegant poise could be irresistible to a young horny male.

Lying beside her, he continued to fondle her supple body, while she reached for her mobile on the bedside table. She checked the time.

'Shit!'

Brushing him off, she slid from the bed and padded to the dresser.

'Time's up, sweetheart.'

Beatrice tipped the contents of a small plastic bag on the dressing table. As she pushed the white powder around with a business card, she reached for a short drinking straw. She kept a handy supply in a drawer.

'What does that bastard want?' said Ernst, languishing on the bed. He watched as Beatrice drew the powder into one nostril and repeated with the other.

'It is no business of yours, young man. Just remember that he pays your wages.' Beatrice went to the en suite and turned on the shower.

'Fuck him! Fuck Sebastian Logan-Sharp, I say. Why can't you come with me, Beatrice? I can make you happy.'

She gave a hearty laugh at his frustrated ignorance. His only attractive feature lay between his legs, not between his ears. Beyond that he was merely another contracted security operative. Ernst would claim he was a bodyguard, but she considered that melodramatic. This was England. Surely people didn't need bodyguards in this country. Not even Sebastian Logan-Sharp.

'Time for you to go, sweetheart. We both have work to do.'

'I will shower with you.'

'Oh no you don't. Now clear off!'

By the time she emerged from the bathroom her current bed partner had left. The cold shower had cooled her on this muggy day, and she dressed in her usual silk-and-lace underwear, donned a necklace of twisted pearls and selected a blouse and white linen suit from her wardrobe. Ten minutes later, refreshed from her shower and exhilarated from her coke, she stood immaculate on Jimmy Choo heels in the bright lounge of the house they'd rented for the duration of their stay in Liverpool. She held an iPad in her hand as she worked down a to-do list with her employer.

Sebastian Logan-Sharp was sprawled on a cream leather sofa, his arms outstretched and his watery-blue eyes fixed on the super-sized screen on the wall. He was a man who enjoyed watching his own publicity, but it was a long time since Beatrice had ceased to be impressed by him. His expensive clothes did nothing for him. He looked a middle-aged slob with a growing beer gut.

When they'd first met, more than fifteen years ago, Sebastian was already stinking rich, and she was struggling to make a success of her life. Her career had begun with acting but floundered within four months of moving to London from Bath. A brief dalliance with modelling petered out after several romantic encounters with the misogynist assholes in that particular industry. What drove her on was that she, in addition to her impressive body, also had a brain. Three years of study at King's College in London and a business degree, resulted in her first proper job, secretary to an exec of a PR company. And that's how she came by Sebastian Logan-Sharp. An invitation with her boss to a weekend at the country home of one of Britain's rising entrepreneurs, and by lunchtime on that first day in Surrey, she had Sebastian's full attention.

They spent the remainder of the weekend together in his room. He was no great shakes in bed, but for some reason she didn't care. He'd invited her to come and work for him, and in addition to acting as his PA, all he'd asked was that she share his bed twice a week. Where was the harm?

Fifteen years later, she now earned a quarter of a million a year, lived in the same house as her employer, had witnessed his personal life, learnt to cope with his foibles, and continued to have a working relationship long after the sex had stopped. She organised most things in Sebastian's life, planned his diary, and helped to foster good relations with business associates. That was no mean feat, considering Sebastian's irascible nature. This was an important source of pride for Beatrice because Sebastian, despite his knack for making cartloads of money, was an acerbic prick with a tendency to rile people. How he'd made it as far as marriage was nothing less than miraculous.

'Seven-fifteen at The Pentium,' she read. 'We will leave here at six forty-five.'

Sebastian looked unmoved as if he hadn't paid her any attention. Beatrice was used to it. She continued reciting their timetable.

'The Lord Mayor is doing the meet-and-greet.'

'You still owe me for coffee yesterday,' he muttered.

She glared for a second, but it was Sebastian all over. Worth a billion quid but didn't allow a coffee break with his PA to be chalked up as expenses.

'I have the receipt,' she replied, derisively. 'I'll give you the £7.49 when we're done here.' She returned to the information on her iPad. 'The Boals have requested a meeting when it's convenient.'

'Tossers. Who else?'

'No one for you to worry about. Paul Renfrew, maybe.'

'Who the hell is he?'

Beatrice lifted the TV remote from the coffee table and raised the volume.

'That's him,' she said.

Sky News was presenting a feature about environmental protests on Merseyside in response to proposed development projects funded by Sebastian Logan-Sharp and partners.

'These outsiders need to realise we don't need them showing up in Liverpool,' an irate man in his thirties was saying. The tagline on the screen beneath the bearded and dishevelled-looking male with darting eyes, read 'Dr Paul Renfrew: Campaigner for environmental justice.'

'We don't want their money if it's going to result in irreparable damage to the local ecosystem,' Renfrew stated.

The news camera panned out to reveal a gathering of several hundred people wielding placards, shouting and cheering at the words of their spokesperson.

'Why should I meet with that asshole?' Sebastian scoffed.

Beatrice winced. Her job required patience in everything.

'It might help smooth things over until we get the deal finalised.'

'I'm bringing money and employment to the run-down areas of my home city. I doubt if that guy has spent more than a day in Liverpool.'

'I think he was born here, Sebastian. Just like you. A local lad made good.'

'Good? What bloody good has he ever done? He's nothing but a sponger.' Sebastian jumped to his feet and jabbed a finger at the TV. 'Who are all these people? They can't all be against the project.'

'Well, many of them are associates of Dr Renfrew or members of other environmental groups. Some of them are women's rights campaigners.'

'What have they got to moan about?'

'They don't agree with your treatment of women in the workplace.'

'Fuck them. Anybody else?'

'Football supporters are beginning to rally. It seems that neither Everton nor Liverpool fans want you to buy their club.'

'They won't be saying that when I bring in the best players in the world. Is that it?'

'The rest are people who simply don't like you.'

'I'm away for a kip before the bloody circus begins. You can pay what you owe me later,' Sebastian blustered, and stomped off.

Beatrice watched him leave the room. She was only halfway down her list, but it was normal for Sebastian Logan-Sharp. It seemed to her that with his rapidly increasing wealth he had grown more irritated with his life and those who inhabited it. One day, perhaps, she would join the people baying for his blood.

CHAPTER 6

Tara Grogan

It would be her last call of the day: a return to Sandfield Road in Bootle. Tara wanted to revisit the victim's home and to discuss the situation with Murray who had not viewed the scene earlier in the day. The area had remained cordoned off, and a couple of SOCO personnel were continuing to remove items from the house and from the rear garden. Tara pictured all the junk the victim had accumulated and wondered if any of it would provide her with the answers she needed to find a killer.

She and Murray were required to don the requisite coveralls to prevent contamination of the scene. They entered the house by the front door and were quickly immersed in the fetid air and odour of stale tobacco. She again noted the nicotine-stained wallpaper and the relatively cleaner space where a picture had once hung. It was hard to miss upon entering the hallway. They began their inspection in the kitchen.

'What do you think, ma'am; was it simply a local row?'

'Seems that way, at least in the absence of evidence to the contrary. Even if it was a local killing, the only motive we have so far is that someone wasn't happy with Tommy playing his loud music. We can't say if the perpetrator arrived at the house with murder in their mind or if they merely came to complain and things got out of hand.'

'I suppose not.'

Tara showed Murray to the box room where she had viewed the victim and his collection of computers.

'Ah! They've taken most of it,' she said, gazing at an almost empty space. The computer equipment had gone, and the shelves had been cleared.

'The tech guys will have a job going through it all,' said Murray.

They were interrupted by the same forensics officer Tara had met that morning. The poor girl looked as though she'd been cooped up in overalls the entire day.

'Ma'am, we found similar items in the garden shed.'

'Thank you,' Tara replied. 'We'll have a look now.'

They made their way out to the garden, a tiny overgrown patch of lawn to the left of which stood a flimsy wooden shed, six feet by four, the felt roof torn and in dire need of replacement. Murray opened the door and stepped inside. There was scarcely room for Tara to join him in the dim windowless space. When her eyes adjusted to the darkness, Tara saw the detritus of old electrical appliances piled on a workbench. There were toasters, a microwave, computers, several mobile phones and a plastic lunch box filled with batteries. On the wall behind the bench was a tool board that held various screwdrivers, pliers, snips, rolls of solder, files and chisels.

'Ma'am?'

It was the tentative voice of the young forensics officer. Tara peered out from the shed.

'I found this in the living room.' She held a mobile phone in her outstretched hand. 'It was lying beneath the sofa.'

Tara realised immediately that she was looking at something more than a basic mobile phone. She'd already seen dozens scattered about the house and in the garden shed, but this one looked different.

Murray said exactly what she'd been thinking.

'We should get the tech guys to look at this first. It's not your ordinary kind of phone.'

'Expensive?'

'Very.'

CHAPTER 7

Sebastian Logan-Sharp

The property rented for his stay in Liverpool comprised two houses within the same grounds. They were modern builds, a bizarre clash of US colonial and mock Georgian style. There were four reception rooms and six bedrooms in each. The house occupied by Sebastian, his family, a nanny, and Beatrice, also had an indoor pool, a gym, and cinema. The other house was occupied by Sebastian's support staff – a driver, a security operative, and a personal chef – and contained a cinema and gym but no pool. The houses were connected by a glass walkway at the rear with a huge conservatory that opened to a patio and gardens. The place resembled a trendy wedding venue more than a pair of homes.

Sebastian couldn't care less. It was simply a place to lay his head. Home was a country pad in Surrey and a South Kensington townhouse. At certain times of the year, it was also an apartment in Monaco and another in Las Vegas where he was the current owner of a junior league soccer team. It was mostly London or Surrey for him. His wife Yana preferred Monaco. It had been an effort for her to lower her standards and accompany him to Liverpool. Not for the first time, Sebastian had resorted to threats to have Yana do as he wished. She was extremely tiresome.

He slapped Shelby's naked bottom and told her to get out. He had to get ready for the damned reception at The Pentium, where he would have to pretend to feel proud of his home city. Eighteen years ago, he couldn't wait to get away from the place. His growing success had required that he base himself in London and not some northern backwater still dining out on The Beatles, a football team, and a few cheeky comedians. It was life, a rich life that he craved. And he'd made it, all by himself. He didn't really need anyone. People were expendable and replaceable. He could afford to buy whatever and whoever he needed and that included his PA Beatrice, his stroppy wife Yana and the young piece of ass who was gathering her clothes from his bedroom floor.

'Will I see you later?' Shelby asked in her American Midwest twang.

Sebastian thought that Shelby had the most alluring green eyes he'd ever seen. Eyes that drew you in and led you to crave every piece of her. He employed her to look after four-year-old Surrey, but he had demanded so much more. Shelby was happy to oblige. He realised she was ambitious. Shelby would not spend all her days as a nanny, he reckoned. She might, however, spend many of them on her back but he didn't care about that.

Sebastian looked her up and down as she pulled on her knickers and T-shirt.

'If you're up for it,' he replied sarcastically.

* * *

'Glad you could make it, love.'

Yana sneered at her husband as she climbed into the Range Rover and sat beside him. Beatrice was in the front next to Gavin, their driver.

Sebastian peered through the window as once familiar streets, many transformed through redevelopment, flashed by on their journey from West Derby to the hotel where the function was being held. He wasn't a man for looking back. He thought little about his formative years growing up on the Treadwater Estate. It was ancient history that could lie buried. His return to Liverpool was purely business. Some locals might regard him as a man wishing to pay something back to his home city. He saw it as a chance to make money. Might just as easily have been Leeds, Glasgow or Newcastle, but the opportunity had arisen on Merseyside.

This evening, aside from the niceties of meeting the great and the good of the city, he was attending as a PR exercise to promote his plans and to gather the right people behind his ventures. He'd seen the potential for protest at his visit on the TV news but was still shocked by the barrage of abuse he faced when he got out of the car.

Dozens of people were held behind barriers as the Lord Mayor stepped forward to shake his hand. The jeers and shouted comments were vitriolic. He even noticed Yana baulk at being called a slut. Sebastian, cold as he now was towards his former supermodel wife, thought it harsh. Yana looked stunning in a sparkling McQueen dress slit on both sides to the waist, her black hair pinned up to show off a diamond necklace, the cost of which outstripped the average price of a house in Liverpool. But Yana did not deserve the abuse. She had done nothing to these people except be the wife of the man they seemed to hate.

Members of the local and national press waited by the hotel entrance. Sebastian hadn't expected this much attention, but he couldn't complain about the publicity. Cameras flashed and questions were shouted.

Beatrice, dressed in a black gown with a glittery trim, stepped ahead of Sebastian and Yana. She performed the introductions, but her words were lost amid the noise of the crowd.

'Hey, Bobby! Red or blue?'

'Will you hire a new manager, Bobby?'

'Leave Otterspool alone!' This reference to a proposed development, was chanted by a group of protestors, but it was lost amongst the jeering of football fans.

During a brief lull in the cheering a single voice could be heard.

'Hey, Bobby! Are you a rapist?'

Sebastian grimaced and hurried through the door into the hotel lobby. Immediately, he turned to his PA.

'What's with the fucking Bobby?' he said.

Beatrice shrugged indifference.

'It's your name, Sebastian. Is that the worst thing you took from that? Someone calling you by your original name? It seems that people round here don't forget.'

'About time they bloody did. I'm throwing a fortune at this frigging town and all they can do is slag me off because I've made something of myself.'

Beatrice beamed a forced smile as two men approached. She turned to the Lord Mayor who seemed perturbed at having witnessed Sebastian's exchange with his PA. But her smile was his cue to get things underway. Despite his official position, the Lord Mayor did not appear to be a man entirely at ease with formal gatherings, nor was he particularly well briefed on the purpose of the occasion.

'Sebastian, I'd like you to meet James Boal and his son Cameron. They are looking forward to working with you.' That was all the Lord Mayor had to offer. He'd made little impression on Sebastian.

James Boal, silver-haired and standing proud in a bow tie and tuxedo, reached out his hand. Sebastian retrieved a smile from somewhere within and shook it. He repeated the gesture with Cameron, a stockily built man of thirty who, like the mayor, looked out of place in an evening suit.

'Glad to meet you, Bobby,' Cameron said. 'Sorry, I meant to say Sebastian.'

Sebastian winced. Already peeved by the whole event, he moved on as Beatrice introduced herself and Yana. The Lord Mayor snatched the opportunity to drift away and mingle with other guests, while Cameron Boal seemed to lose the ability to close his mouth when he shook Yana's hand.

'So, tell me what you think of our plans.' Sebastian had launched right in, all social niceties discarded.

James Boal appeared wrong-footed, but he and Sebastian strolled off, glasses of champagne in hand, leaving Yana pouting before the increasingly awkward and staring Cameron. Beatrice caught up with her boss; Sebastian needed watching.

Across the street, one man had observed the scene from his car. He also knew that Sebastian Logan-Sharp must be watched.

CHAPTER 8

Paul Renfrew

Paul Renfrew felt only irritation. This was not going as he'd hoped. It was fine to be jostled by his fellow environmental protestors. After all they were of one mind: Bobby Smith, aka Sebastian Logan-Sharp, had to be stopped. How many of these money-grabbing developers were there going to be before the world woke up to the damage they were inflicting on the environment?

Yes, Liverpool's heritage was industrial, the city reflected that but there were countless opportunities to make things better now. To repair the damage, start afresh. Why invite yet another vandal with a big wallet to leave an ugly mark upon the city? Paul Renfrew had decided that Sebastian Logan-Sharp would be the last. No more. He must be stopped. The plans for the Mersey shoreline, including the Otterspool development, must fail.

But tonight had been a disappointment. He had more than thirty members of his group ready and waiting outside The Pentium and prepared to give Sebastian and his associates a hard time. They would be seen and heard. Logan-Sharp would be made aware of their opposition. But when they'd arrived, armed with placards denouncing the plans for the Mersey shoreline, someone had beaten them to it. They couldn't even get close to the barrier by the hotel entrance. Dozens of women had got there before them. Women's rights campaigners expressing their disdain for the man who'd gained a reputation for shoddy employment policy and overt sexism. That was fine; they had every right to hassle Logan-Sharp, but why choose the same night as him? Their presence and their shrill voices would dilute the effect of his protest. And they were in his spot.

He and several members of the Merseyside Environmental Justice Campaign squeezed their way to the front. The women uttered complaints, but he just smiled and told them that they were all in this together.

Then the bloody football supporters showed up. The trouble with them was that they were well practised in jeering. They did it every Saturday at Anfield or Goodison. His message to Logan-Sharp and the press pack would be lost. Football and the mere rumours that one of the city's big clubs was a target for the billionaire would steal all the publicity, while his legitimate and more pressing issue would be lost.

When the shiny black car drew up at the hotel entrance, the noise level was impressive. Most of it consisted of the popular football chants of 'Liverpool,' or 'Everton,' and 'Who are ya?' In a quieter moment a female voice shouted 'slut' at Yana Logan-Sharp as she stepped from the car. Paul thought it inappropriate. He wasn't there to attack Logan-Sharp's family. He only wanted justice for Merseyside. The poor woman, stunning and yet somehow out of place, looked thunderstruck as the football supporters took up the jibe and began chanting 'slut! slut! slut!'

Paul detected a change in the expression of the billionaire as he tried his best to appear unruffled by the reception he and his wife were receiving. Then Otterspool got a mention. His companions shouted, 'Leave Otterspool alone!'

He struggled to hear the questions aimed at the billionaire from the press, but what did it matter? Bloody football had won the day. He saw the cameras trained on the supporters' banners. The issue of Otterspool was lost. Sebastian Logan-Sharp did not enter the hotel with the protests at his development plans ringing in his ears. The last single voice he would have heard came from a woman standing next to Paul.

'Hey, Bobby! Are you a rapist?'

CHAPTER 9

Michelle Weller

Having been in her spot for over an hour and surrounded by her mates, Michelle suddenly found herself jammed against the barrier when a bunch of scruffy student types pushed their way to the front.

'We were here first,' she said to the man now pressed uncomfortably close beside her.

He smiled and said, 'Free country, love.'

Michelle held her vexed gaze of the scrawny male with straggly hair and bearded face. His eyes seemed friendly, mischievous perhaps, and she immediately felt unnerved. Was he here to disrupt their protest? A male chauvinist turning up to state the case for testosterone? Then she noticed the placard he was holding but had not yet raised aloft.

'Leave Otterspool alone,' she read aloud. 'What's that about?'

'It's about stopping another money-grabbing toerag from destroying the environment.'

'So, you don't like our Bobby then?'

'Nothing personal. I just hate his guts.'

They both laughed and then Michelle looked behind her as the football supporters announced their arrival.

'Bloody hell,' the man beside her said. 'Who invited them?'

'I think we're about to be upstaged,' she replied.

Then he held out his hand. 'I'm Paul,' he said. 'Merseyside Environmental Justice.'

'Michelle,' she replied, loosely shaking his hand. 'Woman.'

He looked at her curiously when she didn't elaborate.

Michelle didn't feel inclined to explain herself. She'd stated the reason for her presence. She was a woman, standing up for the rights of women to coexist with men, not to feel inferior and certainly not to be fearful every time they stepped outside, went to work, sat in the pub or danced in a club and walked home alone.

At thirty-seven, she was a proud woman but sadly no longer felt attractive or inclined to look her best. Not to impress a man anyway. Freedom was the word she embraced most. She paid little heed to her weight or her appearance. Pride came from her defence of women's rights and that she was fighting for a just cause. She could handle the jibes. Sticks and stones etc. Words like dyke, lezzy and even lipstick lesbian, could hurt some people but not Michelle. She was not the person such terms suggested. She was simply a straight woman who had chosen to avoid relationships with men. Any men. All her friends were women. Tonight, they stood with her in expressing their dissatisfaction at the presence in Liverpool of a man they had labelled the Toxteth Trump, even though Sebastian Logan-Sharp had grown up on the Treadwater Estate and not Toxteth.

His wealth had already saved him on several occasions from standing in the dock accused of assault, abuse and rape. The one way to get him, Michelle had decided, was to attack his business practices. The man was so arrogant, you'd think that given the number of times he'd sidestepped allegations of abuse against women in his private life, he would have at least made sure to clean up his attitude to those women who worked for him, but no. Sebastian Logan-Sharp raked in the cash, while the women he employed in his business empire received the bare minimum allowed by UK employment law. Rumours abounded of sexual misconduct.

Michelle and others worked tirelessly to expose men like Sebastian. The fact that the man hailed from Liverpool only added to her disdain. One day he would come unstuck. She prayed that she would be the woman who stood over his defeated body, her stiletto pressing into his heart.

The man named Paul gave her a curious look when she called out, 'Hey, Bobby! Are you a rapist?'

She wasn't moved to explain herself. Besides, before she could speak, a television crew stood on the other side of the barrier. A reporter was asking Paul to explain why he was protesting. She thought she might get the opportunity to state her case too, but the reporter was male. When he'd finished with Paul, he ignored her and moved on to question the football fans.

But as Sebastian Logan-Sharp had walked towards the hotel entrance he'd glanced over his shoulder. It was less than a second, she realised, but she was convinced that his gaze met hers.

CHAPTER 10

Tara Grogan

Tara relaxed on her sofa, a glass of chardonnay in hand. Her best friend and housemate Kate sat cross-legged on an armchair, a Kindle resting in her lap, her latest read of Scandinavian noir holding her interest. Tara had no curiosity for this genre of fiction. She could summon any amount of true crime tales from memory; she didn't have to make it up. A police detective investigating homicide did not need any reminders of the world in which they lived. Tara's god-daughter Adele lay on the floor in front of the television, colouring in pictures of the natural world. The evening news was playing but only Tara paid it any attention.

She'd heard of Sebastian Logan-Sharp, knew something of his reputation but now learnt that he had returned to his home city with enormous development plans in mind. Rumours that he was intent on buying a football club were rife. She listened to the views of fans being interviewed, those in favour of Logan-Sharp taking over and those against. Murray and Wilson, she imagined, would relish the discussion, Murray firmly set in the Liverpool camp and Wilson a true blue Evertonian. No doubt, she would have to endure the debate tomorrow morning at the station.

'What do you think of him?'

Evidently, Kate was not so engrossed in her thriller. She sipped her beer, watching as Sebastian Logan-Sharp negotiated a hoard of protestors outside a city hotel.

'I suppose if he has money to spend, it will do no harm to spend it on Liverpool,' Tara replied.

'But which club?'

'I don't know.' Tara had no interest in football. Kate, however, like the rest of her family, were staunchly red. 'I was actually referring to his development plans for Otterspool and the Mersey shoreline.'

'You think that's a good idea?'

Kate was rising to the discussion she had started. Tara could always sense it. Kate was more opinionated than her, taking a stand on every issue, while she was content at times to let things flow by. There were occasions when her friend began such conversations simply to cajole her into an argument. She wondered also if Kate's habit of wearing outrageous hair colour and eye-catching clothes was done just to provoke reaction. This evening, her habitually short hair was purple. Kate's eyes were keen, but Tara wasn't up for a discussion, particularly one that she regarded as futile. Did it matter what she thought of Sebastian Logan-Sharp's development plans? It was a free country; the man could do what he liked with his money.

'I have no idea, Kate,' she said, hopefully closing the subject.

Kate rose from her seat and padded barefoot to the kitchen.

'I think you need a refill,' she said, returning seconds later with the open bottle of wine and another beer for herself. 'I can tell when you're not switching off from work.' She smiled sympathetically and filled Tara's glass.

Tara smiled back. 'Thank you,' she said. 'You know me too well.'

'Let's find something decent to watch,' Kate said, resuming her seat.

'As long as it's not Poirot.'

Like most days, Tara had difficulty leaving her world of murder behind at the station door. This evening, the name Tommy Brady held sway over Sebastian Logan-Sharp. Why had someone decided it improved their world to kill an ordinary working man? Of course, that was the reason why she was a detective, to find the answer to such a question. Day one of the investigation over, she had no suspects, no definite motive and no witnesses to the murder of Tommy Brady.

* * *

Pushing open the office door, she heard the discussion in full flow. Just as she'd expected. Wilson versus Murray; red versus blue; Liverpool versus Everton. Both men had garnered support. Three detectives, a clerical assistant and a cleaner at the station were taking sides in the argument. The one thing Tara had learnt from the debate so far, was that the participants had already accepted that either Liverpool or Everton would come under the ownership of Logan-Sharp.

Tara had to squeeze by the gathering to reach her desk.

'Good morning,' she piped. It had the desired effect of pausing the discussion.

The cleaner wandered off as did the clerical assistant. Murray and Wilson had more difficulty in dropping the subject.

DC Paula Bleasdale smiled cheerfully. 'Morning, ma'am,' she said. 'DS Wilson and DS Murray will join us shortly.'

Tara smiled. Both men were not letting go.

'Morning, Paula. Anything strange or startling?'

Paula Bleasdale was the youngest detective on the homicide squad. Efficient, well-mannered and the only female member of Tara's small team. Her face held an untroubled expression, but Tara realised that no member of the team remained unaffected by the things they witnessed in their job. Bleasdale was a picture of fitness and healthy living, with shining brown hair and a trim body. Tara used to feel as Paula looked, bristling with vitality, but lately she had begun to feel her age. Hell, she was still only in her thirties. Kate would bite her head off if she even suggested they were getting old.

'We have a report on some of the items retrieved from the crime scene.'

Both women sat down at Tara's desk.

'Let's hear it,' said Tara.

Bleasdale placed several sheets of paper on the desk but ignored them and instead spoke from memory.

'The only prints on the murder weapon belonged to the victim. It's likely that it came from his own kitchen. The post-mortem is at ten-thirty. I can go with you, ma'am, if you need me.'

'Thanks, Paula, that would be great.'

'The tech team are working through the mobile phones and computers taken from Brady's house. There were 41 phones, 11 laptops and 7 desktop computers. It'll take them a while.'

'Yes, and it might be an enormous waste of time, considering our victim scavenged the stuff from council skips.'

'It seems that Brady had been running some very complicated programs on the computer systems that were still live when we found him.'

'Anything on that expensive-looking phone that was found under the sofa?'

'Not much info so far. There was difficulty accessing the device. But they ran a check on the serial number and the SIM card. It's registered to a company called L-SOS.'

'L-SOS? What is that?'

'It's one of the companies owned by Sebastian Logan-Sharp: Logan-Sharp Online Solutions.'

CHAPTER 11

Yana Logan-Sharp

Breakfast was a harrowing affair when Surrey misbehaved, which she was inclined to do when Yana was present. Her mother couldn't understand it. Why was she so precious and lovable when Shelby was making toast for her, spreading jam or peanut butter on it, just the way she liked? But whenever Yana joined them at the table the child just moaned.

'Mummy, can we go to the zoo?'

Yana didn't answer. Her gold-coated fingernail swiped the screen of her phone. Her almond eyes, without make-up at this early hour, were focussed on whatever gossip she read on the screen. This morning it was a text from a friend in Italy.

'Mummy? Please?' Surrey had abandoned her bowl of strawberries and yoghurt and ignored Shelby's attempts to get her to eat.

'Mummy?'

'Mm?'

> *Wish you were here in Portofino with me, my sweet.*
> *Cosmopolitans for breakfast, remember?*

Yana smiled to herself, picturing the last time she'd been there. God, it was only six days ago. She could still smell his scent. Not that she really loved sex. It was such a messy pursuit. She loved the idea of it, but it was only the attention she craved. If she had to endure a man pounding her body for a few minutes to get some decent companionship, then she was happy to oblige. But Malik was an impressive lover. A bit vigorous but she'd had no problem reaching orgasm.

That had never been the case with Sebastian. For Yana, sex was not the reason for them being together. But it was different with Malik. And so what? He was a Saudi prince who spent much of his time in Italy bedding as many women as he could handle. Liverpool versus Portofino, she mused. No comparison. Sebastian versus Malik, she wasn't entirely sure. With Sebastian she had security. After Malik she knew there would always be others. Handsome men were easily drawn to her. But Sebastian provided her with the means to live in luxury, the life she had always dreamed of. This morning, it was merely the thought of being somewhere other than Liverpool that aroused her.

'Mummy!'

'What is it, Surrey? Can't you see Mummy is busy? Shelby, do your fucking job!'

The nanny blushed and smiled lovingly at the child who then swiped her arm across the table, knocking the bowl of yoghurt onto the wooden floor.

'Surrey, that was careless,' Shelby scolded, moving the child away from her mess.

'Maybe you and I can go to the zoo,' she said.

The four-year-old cheered as Shelby squeezed and tickled her. 'Would that be OK, Yana?'

Yana hadn't even heard. She grinned into her phone and swept her long hair behind her as if she was on camera. But her former life as a model, travelling the world, strutting catwalks in Milan, Paris and New York was also behind her now. She'd chosen the riches on tap from Sebastian.

The girl from Székesfehérvár, a backwater town in Hungary, had come far. She wasn't about to throw it all away on Malik or any other suitor. She was married to Sebastian, a billionaire. Everything she wanted was available, including opportunities to bed men like Malik on a whim. And at least Sebastian loved her, she was certain of that. And he loved his daughter. He had even agreed that she be named after the place where she was conceived, their country home in Surrey. Sebastian had no class and no clue.

Despite their frequent spats, she and Sebastian would stay married. Time apart helped them deal with each other when they got together. It was just that Liverpool was not the most romantic place for their latest get-together, but he had insisted, demanded that she and Surrey be with him. It had taken just five minutes to grow bored with a dull house, dull surroundings and the people she detested most – Beatrice and Shelby. Portofino was marvellous. Perhaps Malik would be waiting for her when she returned.

'Will you come with us, Mummy?'

Yana rose from the table, having consumed a half-glass of orange juice and two strawberries. Old modelling habits die hard. She strutted from the conservatory on expensive heels, her long white dress billowing. The child got no reply from her mother.

'Come on,' said Shelby. 'Let's go see if your father would like to come to the zoo with us.'

CHAPTER 12

Shelby Keibler

She moaned fake pleasure. Shelby didn't care that she felt little. She didn't even care whether Sebastian was trying to make her feel good. All she wanted was for him to plant his seed inside her. Soon after they'd begun sleeping together, she'd come off the pill. She'd had an idea. A pregnancy might be just the thing to give her some job security and perhaps even more.

Shelby knew it irked Yana to see how Surrey was happier with her. Yana never seemed pleased at having her around. Was it any wonder? The child got no love from her mother and Sebastian hardly even noticed his daughter in the house. Most of the time Sebastian was busy in London, while Yana flitted from one place to another with her bevy of girlfriends and lovers. That resulted in Surrey being shipped from one home to the other just to suit the schedule of father or mother.

Shelby accompanied the child everywhere. She loved the little girl and worried what would happen come September when she was due to start school. Sebastian's intention was for Surrey to attend the local prep school close to their country home near Weybridge. But Shelby had overheard Yana saying that she wanted Surrey enrolled at an exclusive boarding school in Switzerland. That would suit Yana. It would also mean that Shelby would be surplus to requirements. She couldn't let that happen. She dared to dream that Sebastian would divorce his wife and she could take Yana's place. If that didn't happen, then a pregnancy might give her some leverage once Surrey started whichever school was chosen.

At first, Shelby had felt uneasy about her affair with Sebastian. She'd worried what Yana would do if she ever found out. Not long into her employment she'd experienced Yana's vile temper when she failed to keep Surrey quiet during a meal in a restaurant. Even the other guests were surprised to hear the tirade of expletives directed at the young nanny.

Shelby was only eighteen when she had travelled all the way from a small town in Michigan to work for the Logan-Sharps. That was just fifteen months ago. It had taken less than three days before Sebastian uttered the first of his suggestive comments, saying that he'd never had a girl with freckles before and how sexy they looked on such a cute face. Two days later, he was stroking her long red hair in the back of his Range Rover en route to his private jet waiting at Farnborough Airport. He didn't seem to care that his daughter was strapped into a seat beside them. For most of the flight to Nice, he'd sat with his hand on her thigh while she tried her best to keep Surrey entertained. But Shelby soon realised that Sebastian didn't care; he was a man used to getting whatever he wanted. The first time they shared a bed, two weeks after she'd begun working for him, Yana was asleep in another bedroom of the same hotel suite. Shelby guessed that Sebastian wouldn't even care if Yana watched as he fucked the nanny.

It was a peculiar dynamic for Shelby. Her parents had separated and divorced the moment her father's affair had been exposed. It was all very normal and somehow more dignified. But Shelby was mystified by the relationship between Yana and Sebastian. They seemed to loathe each other, and yet there was something keeping them together.

'Wow! That was great,' she panted as thickset Sebastian rolled off her body.

'I aim to please,' he puffed.

She lay beside him, sliding her hand over his hairy chest. It was too much to expect that he would finish the job. She was coiled like a spring. But before he dropped off to sleep, she dared to ask a question.

'Why do you stay with Yana?'

She felt his body stiffen. To her frustration, he didn't answer. She drummed her fingers lightly on his chest to encourage a reply.

'I'm sorry, it's none of my business.'

'Damn right it's not, sweetheart.'

'I was just thinking that if she was gone, we would have more time to be together. And if you got custody of Surrey, I could still look after her.'

Suddenly he was on top of her again.

She smiled her delight as he took hold of her hair. Then he pulled with such force that she thought her head was coming off.

'Please, Sebastian, that hurts!'

Rising to his knees, he pulled harder, until her hands left the bed, and her naked body slapped against him. His hands grabbed her throat.

'Don't you dare make suggestions to me about my private life. Do you understand?' He squeezed her neck.

Shelby thought she would pass out. She stared pleadingly into his eyes. Her boss was incensed, his expression held only anger. He squeezed harder, rocking her from side to side to ensure she got the message.

'Yes, I'm sorry,' she said, gagging.

When he finally released her, she flopped down on the bed gasping for breath.

'Remember, darling. You're just the hired help. Your kind are two a penny.'

Despite his anger, an inexplicable thought arose in Shelby that now more than ever, she must conceive.

'Yana is none of your concern, understand?'

'I'm sorry, I just thought you wanted to be with me.'

'You don't think, darling. If you want to stay in this job, keep your mouth shut, unless I tell you otherwise. There is no us. Is that crystal clear?'

Shelby sobbed for what seemed like hours. How could she have been so wrong? Her boss had not become her lover. She was merely another woman he didn't care about. But still, quite irrationally she thought, the best way to get even was to get pregnant. Maybe then he would not be so quick to dismiss her.

CHAPTER 13

Tara Grogan

Bleasdale drove on the way back from the hospital morgue where the post-mortem for Tommy Brady had taken place. Tara had learnt nothing that she thought could help find the killer. Dr Witney, as usual, had watered down the medical jargon in explaining how Brady had died. Essentially, death had resulted from a single stab wound inflicted by a kitchen carving knife. There were no other anomalies, regarding the body. No indications of struggle or that Brady had managed to hit back at his attacker. The killer, it seemed, had struck from behind, and the victim had known nothing about it. No other blood types had been identified on the victim's body or at the scene. Several unidentified fingerprints had been taken from various places around the house. The time of death was set at between eight and ten o'clock on the Sunday night.

Reports from the enquiries at neighbouring houses had so far yielded little information.

'If the perpetrator had been loitering in the area,' said Bleasdale, 'surely someone noticed.'

'Seems not,' said Tara. 'I'm just hoping that we're not dealing with a case where the killer lives locally and is under someone's protection.'

'A gang killing?'

'Perhaps. But the information we have so far on Brady, suggests he was a man who kept to himself. He's an unlikely person to be mixed up with gangs. Maybe his ex-wife can shed some light on what he did on those computers.'

Twenty minutes later they drew up in Newlyn Avenue, Bootle, a quiet road of semi-detached homes with gardens and driveways. Esther Mayhew, formerly Brady, answered the doorbell. It was obvious to Tara that the woman had been crying; her eyes were puffy, and she dabbed a tissue at her reddened nose. When Tara had introduced herself and Bleasdale, the door was opened wider for them to enter.

'I'm sorry,' said Esther. 'Can't stop crying since I heard the news.'

The woman was neatly dressed, her short brown hair was stylishly cut, her face quite rosy and, despite her tears, it held a friendly smile.

'We're sorry for your loss, Mrs Mayhew. I appreciate that this is very difficult for you.'

The detectives were shown into a lounge at the front of the house and invited to sit. The room was pristine and contained a luxurious suite, deep-pile carpet and a high mantelpiece of dark mahogany.

'I know it's years since Tommy and I were together, but I still cared about him. Hardly a day went by that I didn't wonder what he was up to, whether he was eating properly and looking after himself.'

'When did you last see him?' asked Tara.

'A couple of months ago. He worked at a recycling centre. Kev, my husband, and I were clearing out the loft and we took some stuff to the dump. Tommy was working, but we had a brief chat.'

'How did he seem?'

'Same old Tommy. Didn't mention there was anything new in his life.'

'Do you know of anyone who may have wanted to harm him?' Bleasdale asked.

Esther had propped herself on the arm of the sofa. The chat seemed to be of comfort to the woman, but she shook her head at the question.

'As far as I know,' she replied, 'Tommy didn't bother with anyone. He just hid in that damn box room and fiddled with computers and stuff. That's what ended our marriage. He never wanted to go out; he never engaged with anyone and that included me. Oh, we were happy together at the beginning, but when it was clear that we were never going to have kids, we just retreated to our own worlds. His had no room for me.'

'You have children now?' Tara felt inclined to ask. She'd noticed the framed pictures on the wall above the mantelpiece of two young girls and a younger boy.

'Yes,' she said proudly. 'Tara is ten, Molly is eight and Neil is five.'

Tara smiled at the coincidence in first names.

* * *

Next, they drove to an exclusive road in West Derby, stopping by an intercom mounted on a brick pillar that supported electric gates. Bleasdale lowered her window, pressed a button on the device and announced their arrival. The occupants of the property should have been expecting them after Tara had phoned earlier in the morning.

It was an impressive location. Before them, beyond a tiled drive, stood two identical houses. Without ceremony, there was a buzz in response to Bleasdale's announcement of their arrival. The metal gates swung open and as they passed through, they had to guess in which of the houses they would be received. Hedging her bets, Bleasdale stopped between the two.

Before they could get out of the car, a young man with a crew cut and wearing a grey suit emerged from the house to their left.

'You police?' he called.

From his brief utterance Tara surmised that English was not his first language.

'I'm DI Grogan and this is DC Bleasdale.' Both women got out of the car. 'We would like to speak with Mr Logan-Sharp.'

'This way, please.'

He turned and re-entered the house. Tara and Bleasdale exchanged amused glances at the man's laconic manner and then followed. He held the door open for them to enter, and it didn't take long for the wow factor to kick in. They stepped into a majestic hall with shiny wooden floors and a central staircase rising in an arc to a galleried landing. From the hall, Tara could see all the way to the rear of the house, through an enormous kitchen and a conservatory, to the gardens beyond. The man indicated a set of double doors to their left and they entered a lounge furnished with rich leather sofas and armchairs surrounded by ivory-coloured bookcases. The lounge stretched from the front to the rear, connecting to an open-plan dining area that merged with the kitchen.

'Wait here,' said the man. He left the room, closing the door before they could respond.

'Don't say it,' said Tara.

'What's that, ma'am?'

'How the other half live. I know you were thinking it.'

'Only natural. I wonder how many people actually live here. I could get my entire family circle in this lounge alone with room to spare.'

'I believe it's a temporary arrangement as far as Sebastian Logan-Sharp is concerned,' said Tara.

'What do they do with the other house?'

It seemed necessary to whisper their comments. A lavish house tended to induce an inferiority complex and self-consciousness. Both officers resorted to silence and paced about the room. Despite the opulence, Tara sensed a lack of personality in the house but supposed that it was due to it being merely a temporary residence for the billionaire. There were no family pictures on the walls, just pieces of art selected, presumably, by the interior designer of the property. Still, it was an impressive house in which to stay even for a short time.

A minute later, the silence was broken when a confident and smartly dressed woman strutted into the lounge.

'Good morning. I'm Beatrice Howard, Sebastian's personal assistant. How may I help you?'

Tara's eyes widened at the woman's manner. She behaved as though she was front-of-house for the Logan-Sharp organisation. Beatrice stood on high heels. She wore a pencil skirt, silk blouse and a healthy tan. A classy-looking woman of indeterminate age. Early forties perhaps, she thought. She and Tara did have one thing in common. Both women had similarly styled short brown hair with blonde highlights. Tara couldn't help thinking of Kate who was always teasing about adding more colour to her hair. And here she was sporting a style identical to a high-class woman. Of course, Tara was unaware that thirty minutes before her arrival at the house, Beatrice had been sprawled on her bed revelling in her latest line of coke.

Tara introduced herself and Bleasdale.

'We would like to speak with Mr Logan-Sharp,' she stated, matching the formal tone of the PA.

'That will not be possible right now. May I ask what this is about?'

Bleasdale produced a gold mobile phone from her bag.

'We understand this phone is registered to Mr Logan-Sharp's company, L-SOS.'

If Beatrice Howard recognised the phone, she didn't show it.

'And?'

'Can you tell us who it belongs to?' Tara asked. She wasn't warming to this woman despite the similarity in hairstyle.

Beatrice took the phone from Bleasdale. She gave it a cursory examination but didn't return it.

'I have no idea,' she said with a shrug. 'It could be any of our employees.'

'Is it normal practice to issue your employees with such an expensive model? It's worth more than three thousand pounds,' Tara countered.

'I suppose it could be one of Sebastian's, he has several.'

'Has he mentioned losing one?'

Beatrice smiled for the first time. Tara thought it one of vexation.

'Sebastian wouldn't know, I'm afraid. He never remembers to charge them and simply goes looking for a fresh one. I'll show this to him. Maybe he'll recall where he left it.'

'I'm unable to leave it with you at this time,' said Tara.

'Why ever not?'

'Are you familiar with the name Tommy Brady?' Tara asked.

'No. Should I be?' Beatrice replied.

'This mobile was found in Mr Brady's home. Have you any idea how it may have got there?'

'As I've told you, Inspector, I can't be sure that this is Sebastian's phone, and I've never heard of Brady. I am happy to pass it on to Sebastian for you.'

Tara wasn't convinced by the sincerity of the woman. Prevaricating was the word springing to mind.

'When may we speak with Sebastian?' she asked.

Beatrice sighed. Tara was glad to see that she was at least causing the woman a degree of irritation.

'That will not be possible today. Sebastian has several business meetings to attend. Please, leave the phone with me, and I will see that he gets it.'

'Is Sebastian in the house at the moment?'

'No.'

'Then please tell him that I wish to speak with him. We will come back at a more convenient time.'

'You do realise who Sebastian is? He is a very busy man.'

'Ms Howard, this phone was found at the home of a man who has been murdered. I want to know how and why it got there. Please tell Mr Logan-Sharp that I called.'

Tara reached out her hand and the PA resignedly handed over the phone without another word.

CHAPTER 14

Carla Smith

The following day, Carla bunked off work having rescheduled appointments for two cut and blow-drys. The house was easier to find than she'd thought. A vague location stated on the morning news mentioned the leafy avenues in West Derby and briefly showed the pair of houses being rented by Sebastian Logan-Sharp.

She took a bus from her home on the Treadwater Estate to Breeze Hill then a second to West Derby. Using Google Maps on her phone to guide her to the quiet road, within a few minutes she stood facing a pair of magnificent houses within the same grounds. Carla couldn't help her gaping mouth. She'd known for years that he was loaded, but she could never grasp exactly what super wealth meant. She couldn't imagine a billionaire's lifestyle. And this place, these mansions, apparently, were merely temporary for the duration of his stay in Liverpool. He couldn't even make do with a hotel. Carla saw no signs of activity within the property. There were no cars on the drive, and she couldn't see anyone moving around.

An argument raged inside her. She should never have come here. Be strong, you're doing the right thing. What's the worst that can happen? He can say no. At least she would have confirmation that he was the animal everyone said he was. At every urge to walk away, thoughts of her Lee and Jack stopped her. She was doing it for them.

She smoothed down her dress. Was it too much? She couldn't decide. It was the best, the most expensive dress she owned. Marks and Spencer. Bright, colourful and disguising a body no longer fit and trim. She patted her hair, realising just how much the style betrayed her. Feathered blonde with bright pink tips. It showed as much class as one of those chavs on *The Only Way is Essex*. He would piss himself laughing at her. Nearly eighteen years and nothing. Not so much as a Christmas card or a phone call to ask if she was still breathing. She shouldn't have come. Stupid bloody idea.

As she finally went to walk away, her toes nipped in her shoes. They were another mistake. Who wears heels like these to ride on a bus and then traipse through unfamiliar streets? But the sudden pain ushered her to the gatepost. She placed a hand on the wall to steady herself, while she removed her left shoe and massaged her foot. As she replaced it and continued to feel uncomfortable, she noticed the intercom. A burst of courage masked her pain, and she pressed a finger on the speak button. Seconds later, a male voice answered.

'Yes?'

Carla couldn't summon words, her tongue stalled in her mouth.

'Allo?' said the voice.

She glanced towards the house and wondered if there was a camera trained on her.

'Hello,' she answered.

'Yes, what do you want?'

The voice was not friendly, sounded foreign. How the hell did she explain herself to a stranger. Daft to think that Bobby would come running out to greet her.

'I've come to see Bobby,' she said, her voice quivering, her toes nipping, her face, she felt, turning very red.

'Who?'

'Bobby.'

'There's no one here with that name.'

'Sorry. I meant to say Sebastian. I've come to see Sebastian.'

'Make an appointment.'

'Sorry, I didn't realise. Can I do that with you?'

'No. I am only the chef.'

There was no further exchange. The man, whoever he was, had gone. She remained by the closed gates, hoping for someone to appear, to tell her it was fine, and that Bobby was happy for her to come inside. Nothing happened. It riled her. She decided that she would not be palmed-off by a bloody chef if that's what he was. For all she knew, he could have been the house teaboy. She jabbed her finger on the button again.

'Allo?'

'Can you please tell Mr Logan-Sharp that Carla Smith is here to see him.'

'Make an appointment.'

'Listen, shithead. Just tell Sebastian that his ex-wife, the mother of his two sons, wants to speak with him. Can you do that, arsehole? Please.'

There was no response. Carla remained by the gate, simmering in the hot sun.

CHAPTER 15

Cameron Boal

Cameron fidgeted with his pen, drumming it on his notepad. His knee jiggled, and he sweated beneath his tailored shirt and tie. Things were not going well. His father was paying this guy too much respect. Yes, they wanted this deal, but surely it didn't require them to crawl up the ass of the twerp seated at the far end of the table in their own boardroom. So far, Sebastian Logan-Sharp hadn't uttered more than two words. His PA was doing all the talking. She was a hot-looking woman, though. Wouldn't mind a piece of her ass. Maybe they could seal the deal by getting a room in a quiet country hotel. He'd even settle for the back seat of his car.

'We already have several major partners on board with the venture,' Beatrice stated in a businesslike tone. 'Can you please explain what attributes you believe Boal Developments can bring to our project?'

Attributes? What the hell did she mean by that? He stared at her chest; her blouse was open to her cleavage with just a hint of her lace bra visible. The vision reminded him of Miss Atherton, his third-form English teacher, all the guys in his class straining to get a peek at her tanned cleavage. He smiled, recalling their blatant attempts to have her lean over them when they asked her to explain a passage of *Henry IV, Part 1*.

Cameron suddenly realised that all eyes were on him. Beatrice Howard was staring. Logan-Sharp was glaring in his direction. Their own long-serving secretary, Joyce, sat waiting. And his father peered over his glasses. He had to say something. This was supposed to have been a formality. But why did he ever think it would be easy?

'Well,' he began, fumbling for an intelligent reply to the PA's question. 'Firstly, we can match the required figure you require for the investment.' Shit! Did he really say require twice in one sentence? Another thought flashed of Miss Atherton and what she would have said to that. 'Secondly, you can see from our portfolio, I mean our brochure, that we can supply the expertise in construction. Our record speaks for itself.'

His father cut in.

'What Cameron means is that we have thirty years' experience of various developments on Merseyside, including the airport, the revamped docklands and several city-centre office blocks.'

Sebastian Logan-Sharp scratched his head. Cameron winced. Beatrice looked at her boss.

'OK,' she said rather tentatively. 'We are aware of your reputation in Liverpool.'

Cameron guessed she was about to say no. He panicked. His father would go nuts with him if they were to fail.

'We can add twenty percent more capital,' he blurted. 'We know exactly how to progress the building work at Otterspool. Building apartment blocks is our bread and butter. Our designs are better than any of your other partners'.'

'Otterspool! Who the fuck is talking about Otterspool?' Sebastian was incensed. He stared angrily at Beatrice. 'I thought you'd explained this.'

'I did, Sebastian,' she replied, sounding less sure of herself, Cameron thought. She was looking expectantly at his father. Suddenly, she didn't seem quite as sexy.

'James, you were provided with a full rundown of our proposals,' she said. 'It should have been clear that Otterspool is only a portion of our plans. As Merseyside Delta Development, we are embarking upon a major restructuring of the Mersey shoreline in Liverpool and on The Wirral. You cannot cherry-pick little portions of the project, James. We require major investment partners for the duration of the entire project.'

Sebastian got to his feet, lifting his phone from the table.

'Think we're done here,' he said derisively.

Cameron felt his father's eyes drilling into him. Beatrice smiled rather sympathetically at father and son. She offered one last opportunity.

'I think you should reconsider, gentlemen. We can give you one more week before we go public with our plans and introduce our partners.' She flipped the cover on her iPad and stood up.

Looking embarrassed, James Boal squirmed a reply.

'Yes, thank you, Beatrice. We'll rejig things and get back to you in a couple of days. Thank you for the opportunity, Sebastian. I apologise for the misunderstanding.'

A grumbling Sebastian was already heading out of the door.

Cameron sensed Beatrice staring at him; he didn't dare lift his head. Sleeping with her was now probably out of the question. Sebastian didn't even acknowledge him as he departed. The billionaire had made him look a fool in front of everyone, but he wasn't about to lick his ass just to get a piece of the cake. They could manage perfectly well without Sebastian Logan-Sharp. If only his father would agree with him. What the billionaire was proposing was too big for them. Too big and requiring too much money when he had little trust in the man behind it. Logan-Sharp's reputation was that he'd cut your throat for a tenner. He would ditch them in a heartbeat if he wasn't happy. His father didn't see it that way, however. He viewed it as his lifelong opportunity pulling into the station. But Cameron didn't fancy the train ride.

'Thank you for your time, gentlemen,' Beatrice said, gathering her bag and slipping her iPad inside it. 'We look forward to hearing from you.'

'Yes, thank you, Beatrice,' said James. 'We'll be in touch.'

'We need to go public with this before we leave Liverpool,' she continued. 'It would be advantageous to know exactly who the main players will be.'

'Yes, I understand,' said James.

'Goodbye, Cameron. I hope to see you soon,' said Beatrice.

Cameron grimaced more than smiled. He had no words. Beatrice and Joyce left the boardroom leaving him alone with his father.

'What the hell were you playing at?' James barked. 'I thought you had this under control.'

Cameron got to his feet. He didn't want a row with his father, but he reckoned if it had to happen then now was the best time. Get it over and done with.

'This is too big for us, Dad.'

'Too big! It's the deal I've been working for all my life, and now you want to scupper our chances. What the hell's got into you?'

'We could do the Otterspool thing no problem. The other stuff requires too much capital spend.'

'You heard that woman. We can't cherry-pick. They want us for the long term.'

'That's what worries me, Dad.'

'You've never worried a day in your life. You were more interested in getting into that woman's knickers than talking business. I saw you staring at her, and you can bet she was aware of it too. Now you've gone and pissed them off. We have one last chance, and you will not mess it up. Do you understand, Cameron?'

He couldn't decide whether his old man was losing it or whether to pity him. He'd never seen him crawl like that before. He had always been a proud man.

'I don't trust him, Dad. We need to protect ourselves. If we jump in with him, he could pull the plug anytime he pleases. It could ruin us.'

'Sometimes we have to take risks.'

'Don't you think it strange that he's even considering us for the deal? The rumours are that he's struggling to attract interest from the big players. Why is he even bothering about Liverpool? A man like that should have enough opportunities in London. Something's not right about him. Nobody seems to like him, and you can see why. He's an arsehole made good. I don't want him in our lives, Dad.'

'We're doing it, Cameron, whether you like it or not. Just don't mess it up for me.'

His father walked out leaving him alone in the boardroom to consider what on earth he could do to get them out of this damn mess.

CHAPTER 16

Beatrice Howard

Sebastian seemed to be deep in thought on the journey back to the house. He was scarcely aware of Beatrice talking to him.

'The police want to speak to you,' she said.

'The police, what for?'

'Seems they found your mobile phone. Why didn't you tell me that you'd lost it?'

'I must have left it somewhere after a meeting. I've been using a spare.' He held out the phone to show her.

'You must tell me whenever you lose your phone, Sebastian.'

'It's just a phone, love. Damn things are encrypted. No one is getting into it. I reckoned it would turn up and it seems I was right. But why didn't the bizzies just hand it over? Why do they want to speak to me?'

'They found your phone in the house where Tommy Brady lived. He's been murdered.'

'Shit!'

Beatrice didn't reply. They both saw the woman at the same time. She was standing by the intercom at the gates to the houses. Their car's tinted windows prevented her from seeing them. The gates swung open for them to enter and as they did so, the woman seized the opportunity to follow.

Ernst jumped out as their driver, Gavin, stopped the car by the front door of their house. Sebastian was already climbing out and stood watching as the woman hobbled up the drive towards him.

'Sorry, boss,' Ernst said, rushing by and making towards her.

'It's OK, Ernst. I can handle it,' Sebastian said.

The security guard turned on his heels, smiling at a rather bemused Beatrice, but he remained vigilant as his boss went to greet the stranger.

Beatrice thought the woman looked awkward in heels, warm and out of breath in the midday sun.

'What do you want, Carla?' Sebastian said dryly.

'A sit-down and a cold drink would be nice to start with.'

Ernst and Beatrice stood agog as Sebastian strolled by with Carla clip-clopping behind him.

'Hiya,' she chirped to them.

Beatrice smiled then followed at a discreet distance.

Sebastian headed to the kitchen as Carla tiptoed on the polished floor of the hall. Beatrice caught up with her and showed her through to join him in the kitchen. He removed two bottles of Stella from the fridge, rummaged around for a bottle opener, eventually spying a wall-mounted device beside the stove. He opened both bottles and handed one to Carla. She had taken to a stool at the breakfast bar and slipped off her shoes. Beatrice kept her distance, sitting at the dining table, but remained within earshot. She wasn't surprised that her boss failed to offer her a beer. He was likely to charge her for it anyway.

'At least you recognised me,' said Carla.

'What do you want?' He took a long slug of beer.

'That's a nice greeting for your ex-wife and mother of your children.'

'I have a daughter now,' he said.

Carla seemed bemused by the information.

'Do you? That must have been a surprise. And where is the beautiful Yana?'

He didn't answer her question.

'Why are you here, Carla? I haven't got all day.'

She slipped from the stool, padded barefoot right up to him and stared into his face.

'Eighteen years, Bobby. Not a frigging word. Not even a Christmas card, or something for the twins' birthday. Money tight, is it?'

'You threw me out, Carla. Or don't you remember?'

She grabbed his tie and pulled him close.

'Because you were shagging everything in your office wearing a skirt, remember? Then you announced that Liverpool was holding you back. I was holding you back. So, off you went. And my, haven't you done well. The boy from the Treadwater Estate is now a frigging billionaire.'

She released him, returned to her seat and drank some beer.

Beatrice was intrigued by the exchange while feigning interest in browsing her phone.

'Is it money you've come for?' Sebastian said. 'I gave you plenty when we divorced.'

'Well, it paid for the nappies, but it was me who had to come begging.'

Sebastian's face became red, and he loosened his tie. Beatrice could see that already, he'd had enough.

'Beatrice! Would you show this woman out. I have work to do.'

Carla drank her beer, folded her arms and smirked at him. He made to walk away.

'Nice seeing you, Carla.'

'Fuck you, Bobby. Why did you ever feel the need to change your name? Sebastian sounds poncy. And what's with the double barrel? I know Sharp was your mother's maiden name, but what were you thinking, eh? Was it because you're ashamed of everything you left behind; your family, me, the boys, Liverpool? What's your daughter like, Bobby?'

He glared angrily.

'Leave Surrey out of it, she's a good kid.'

'A poncy name for a child, too. Your idea, was it?'

'Fuck you, Carla. Is that why you came? To hurl abuse at me for everything wrong in your life?'

She diverted his comment by changing the subject.

'Did you hear that Tommy is dead? Somebody murdered him.'

'I heard.'

'Wasn't you, was it?'

He shook his head in disgust.

'Wasn't enough that you ruined his life,' said Carla.

Before he could leave the kitchen, Carla at last came out with the reason for her visit.

'Lee and Jack, your sons, in case you don't remember, are hoping to go to university in the autumn.'

He smirked.

'I just thought it might be nice if their stinking-rich dad contributed something to their future. It would save them from being lumbered with student debt, maybe help them get jobs and stuff. Don't worry, they didn't know I was coming. They have no expectations of you. I just thought it would be a nice thing for you to do for your sons, that's all.'

He sneered, said nothing and walked from the room leaving Carla sniffing tears and Beatrice having to deal with her.

When they reached the front door, Carla, holding a shoe in each hand, smiled wearily at Beatrice.

'I hope Bobby treats you better than he did me and my boys.'

'Please, Carla,' Beatrice whispered. 'Leave it with me. I'll see what I can do. He's just in a bad mood today.'

Carla studied Beatrice's face.

'Why would you help me? You don't even know me. And I have no idea who you are, love.'

Beatrice smiled and placed her hand on Carla's arm.

'I'm Sebastian's PA.'

Just then a car swept to a halt in front of them. Two people, a man and a woman, climbed out and came towards them.

Sebastian hadn't quite reached the top of the stairs.

'Good afternoon, DI Grogan,' Beatrice said.

Carla chuckled, then called out.

'Hey, Bobby! The bizzies are here. What have you done?'

CHAPTER 17

Tara Grogan

As Tara and Murray approached the house, two women were standing by the front door. One was the PA who Tara had met the day before. She didn't know the other woman who was announcing their arrival to someone named Bobby.

'Good afternoon, Ms Howard. We'd like to speak with Mr Logan-Sharp now. I telephoned earlier to check he would be available.'

'Yes, Inspector,' Beatrice replied. She smiled, although Tara got the feeling it was directed towards Murray.

The other woman, holding a pair of shoes in one hand, looked on with interest. Tara thought she looked as if she'd been crying; her eye make-up was smudged, her face and neck blotchy red. Beatrice retreated inside and headed for the stairs.

'So, what do you want Bobby for?' the woman asked.

'And you are?' said Tara.

'I'm his ex-wife, love.' The woman stepped from the doorway then turned around. 'When you're done with him, maybe you could get him to fork out some money to help his sons.' She hobbled away still barefoot.

'Strange,' said Murray.

'Indeed,' said Tara.

They stepped into the house in time to see a stockily built man they assumed was Sebastian Logan-Sharp coming down the stairs behind his PA. Before Tara could introduce herself, Sebastian barked an instruction.

'In the kitchen. I could do with another beer.'

He marched on, leaving Tara and Murray to follow, seemingly indifferent to having two police detectives waiting to question him. He took a beer from the fridge, searched several cupboards then finally pulled out a large bag of tortilla chips and tore it open.

'Bloody starving,' he said, pushing some chips into his mouth. 'You'd think a billionaire could afford better service than this.'

Tara noticed him glaring at his PA, who stood with an iPad as if awaiting instructions from her boss.

'Did Ms Howard explain the reason for our visit?' Tara asked, having decided that the man would have no interest in formal introductions.

'You found my phone.'

'That's correct.'

'I didn't think the police did deliveries,' he said, grinning.

'Where did you lose your phone, Mr Logan-Sharp?' Murray inquired.

Tara could see the billionaire adjusting. Without the introductions, he didn't know which of them was the more senior.

'I must have left it somewhere.'

He opened his bottle of beer and took a long swig.

'And when did you lose it?' Murray continued.

Sebastian shrugged indifference. 'Is this really necessary? You found the damn thing, why can't you just hand it back?'

'We're interested to know why it was found in the home of a man who had been murdered,' said Murray.

'I have no idea. I lost it and then you found it. That's all I know.'

'I'm sure your secretary has already explained,' said Tara, looking at Beatrice. 'Can you tell us if you were acquainted with Tommy Brady? He is our murder victim. Any idea why he would have had your phone?'

'This is ridiculous.'

Tara persisted. 'Did you know Tommy Brady, sir?'

Sebastian frowned. 'Yes, I knew Tommy from way back. But I have no idea why he had my phone.'

Murray cut in again. 'When did you last see him?'

'About eighteen years ago, before I left Liverpool. We were mates at school.'

'How long have you been back in the city?' Murray asked.

'We've been here for two weeks,' said Beatrice.

'Had you met Mr Brady since you've been back?'

Tara noticed a brief exchange of glances between Sebastian and Beatrice.

'No. Haven't clapped eyes on him,' Sebastian replied, returning to his beer. 'When do I get my phone back? There is sensitive information on it that I need.'

Tara's eyes widened. She wondered about the nature of the information. Incriminating perhaps, or merely pertinent to his business. Ignoring his request, she instead asked a favour of the billionaire.

'It would be helpful if you could assist us in accessing your phone,' she said. 'Our technical department have had some difficulty. Seems there is a high level of encryption on the device.'

'Too bloody right there is. You try to break into that thing, and it'll self-destruct like frigging *Mission Impossible*.'

'In that case we'd appreciate your help.'

'But why do you need to get into it? There's nothing on it that has anything to do with Tommy.'

Tara explained again. She was growing weary of the man's attitude. 'Nevertheless, Mr Logan-Sharp, it was found in the home of a murder victim, and we must check if it has any relevance to his death.'

'Beatrice will deal with it,' he said dismissively and bounded from the room.

Beatrice provided the information Tara had requested then wasted no further time in showing them out.

* * *

Murray puffed air as he started the car.

'What a prick.'

'You'd think with all his money he could buy himself some manners,' Tara said.

'What do you think, ma'am? Are we going to get anything useful from his phone?'

'Can't be just a coincidence that it was found in the house of our victim and for the billionaire to be acquainted with the deceased. We might not get much from the phone, but we haven't finished with Sebastian Logan-Sharp. There's an explanation for that mobile being in Brady's house.'

'What if Brady just picked it out of a bin at the recycling centre? His supervisor told us they all did it. He had plenty of other phones in his house?'

'Like I say, too much of a coincidence. Besides, is it not strange to you that neither Sebastian nor his PA even asked how or where Brady died?'

CHAPTER 18

Beatrice Howard

Beatrice scurried from the house used by Ernst, driver Gavin and chef Patrice. Sex with Ernst and a snort of coke perked her up for having to deal with her increasingly tetchy boss. She was aware that he'd spent the day on his phone to his various backers who were growing impatient waiting for him to confirm his partners for the Merseyside development. She could see he was on edge. The Boals hadn't helped matters, thinking they could just break off a piece of the pie for themselves with very little risk.

Beatrice marched into the kitchen trying to appear on top of things. She helped herself to prosecco from the fridge. Sebastian tossed his mobile on the counter, looking fed up with talking.

'Have you seen the news?' she asked.

'Why, what's up?' he replied sounding disinterested.

She lifted the remote and pointed it at the TV. Sky News and BBC were covering a speech in the House of Commons by the leader of the opposition.

'Not that,' she said. 'It's on the local bulletin.'

'Never mind. Just tell me.'

She joined him at the breakfast bar, but he gazed vacantly across the room. She could see he was preoccupied.

'Sebastian, are you listening?'

'All ears, love.'

'So far, this venture has been a PR disaster. We must get people on board with the project,' she said sternly. 'I'm sure the Boals will deliver, but we're still coming up short.'

'So, what do we do?'

'MCM and Northwest Horizons will hopefully agree to join, but they're nervous about these damn protests.'

'Which protests?'

'All of them!'

Beatrice was aware she had just raised her voice at her boss, but he had to take heed of what she was saying.

'This guy Renfrew is threatening court action to stop any proposed land clearance at Otterspool. Even if he's not successful, it's enough to hold us back for months and put companies like MCM right off. And now the conspiracy nuts are making allegations on social media about your past.'

'My past?'

'The data harvesting stuff, the business that got you started. That'll turn the public against us. And then there's this women's group calling you a rapist. Now the police are snooping around asking about Tommy Brady.'

'So, everybody hates us.'

'Not us, Sebastian. Just you.'

'What can we do about it?'

'We need to get them onside.'

'Yes, I realise that, but how do we do it?'

'Everyone has their price; you should know that. We bring them here, listen to their concerns and, if we have to, present them with a lucrative sweetener.'

'I know people who could sort the bastards out, no questions asked,' he said.

Beatrice glared.

CHAPTER 19

Tara Grogan

By the next day, thanks to Beatrice Howard they had accessed Sebastian Logan-Sharp's encrypted mobile phone. The information within, however, indicated a high volume of calls but little else. There were a few texts, mostly exchanges between Sebastian and Beatrice, several to his wife Yana and a few to someone called Shelby. If she hoped to find a link to Tommy Brady, then all the numbers in the call list would have to be checked. The usefulness of Sebastian's phone did not rule out Tara's suspicions of its owner. Something in what he'd told her didn't feel right. She reckoned he was lying about when he'd last met Tommy Brady. How else would his phone have ended up at Brady's house? She didn't feel it likely that Brady would have randomly found such an expensive device at the council recycling centre.

Wilson had brought her even more news of mobile telephones. Among the other devices gathered from Brady's house, they had eventually identified his personal phone. The bad news was that so far nothing of interest had been detected. The call list was short and consisted mainly of communications between Brady and his colleagues at the recycling centre. No calls had been made to the phone belonging to Sebastian Logan-Sharp, although online communications were still being evaluated.

Bleasdale reported that the computer hardware taken from Brady's home had been sent to a specialist cyber-crime unit at the Met for investigation. The tech team of Merseyside Police had found intricate computer code with the potential to perform complex tasks in financial transactions. It was too specialised for them to handle. There were, however, some unsavoury images found on a laptop, but the IP address linked to the downloads did not match anything registered to Tommy Brady. It was likely to be from one of the devices that Brady had retrieved from a council skip.

With a mountain of disappointing information regarding her murder victim, Tara was frustrated by the lack of progress. One idea, however, had edged to the fore as the day went on. She was waiting for Murray's return from the station canteen before acting on it.

* * *

On the Treadwater Estate, the next-door neighbour of Carla Smith directed them to the Heads, Shoulders, Nails and Toes salon. It sat within a row of five stores on Bridle Road in Bootle. When Tara entered the shop, she was faced immediately with the woman she'd last encountered on the doorstep of Sebastian's house. The woman had told her that she was Sebastian's ex-wife, and Tara had soon learnt that the billionaire was formerly known as Bobby Smith. Further enquiries had yielded Carla's home address. The shocked look on the woman's face, seeing the same police officers entering her workplace, raised an amused smile with Tara.

'I'm DI Grogan and this is DS Murray.'

Carla's hands that had been snipping at the shoulder-length hair of a teenage girl dropped to her sides.

'What do you want? I don't think I broke any laws going to see my ex-husband and the father of my children.'

'Is there somewhere we can talk?' asked Tara.

Carla excused herself from her client then led the detectives through the salon to a small, cramped staffroom. There was space for a fold-up table, three chairs, a sink, a kettle, and a microwave oven. She turned to face them with her arms folded.

'Has this got something to do with Bobby? Has he complained about me?'

'No, Carla, we're investigating the murder of a Mr Thomas Brady.'

'I used to know Tommy. I was very sorry to hear about him.'

'Your ex-husband said he knew him from years ago but hadn't seen him for a long time.'

'So? What's that got to do with me?'

Tara thought the woman rather abrasive which she didn't need to be. She had gone on the defensive straightaway. Perhaps, Tara thought, she should explain herself a little better.

'I'm sorry, Carla. We're not accusing you of anything. Sebastian was reluctant to tell us much about Tommy Brady. I just wondered that if you had also known Tommy from years ago, maybe you could fill in some background for us.'

'Background on what?'

'How did you know each other?'

'There was a whole bunch of us from school. Me, Bobby and Tommy hung out together. Tommy was smart, like really smart. He could have gone to uni but didn't.'

'Do you know why?'

'My Bobby was to blame. Well, he was my Bobby at the time. Calls himself Sebastian these days.' She scoffed at her own remark. 'Bobby was always full of daft ideas on how to make money. The Del Boy of Treadwater we called him. He used to say, "this time next year, Carla, we'll be millionaires." Tosser.'

'What happened?'

Carla's face clouded over, and she slumped down on a chair.

'Tommy also had ideas but his were clever ones. Computer stuff that I never understood. He wanted to go to uni, get a degree then set up his own company. Bobby liked the idea of a company and somehow persuaded

Tommy to forget about uni and start the business straightaway. So, he did, but he allowed Bobby to join him. Big mistake. They did something like trading in web names. I don't understand all that nonsense, but very quickly they were making loads of money. I worked in their first office for peanuts, answering phones, opening mail and making coffee.

'Tommy was only happy tinkering away on a computer, but I could see Bobby growing restless. He wanted more and he wanted it fast. We were married by then, and their company was branching out into all sorts of stuff. The pair of them used to natter away about data and how they could make a fortune selling it. Then suddenly it all went belly up. Before I knew why, Tommy was out of the company and Bobby was making plans that turned out not to include me. He cleared off when I was pregnant with my twin boys. I hadn't clapped eyes on him until yesterday.'

Tears rolled down Carla's face. Tara was close to joining in sympathy.

'Do you know what caused the split between Bobby and Tommy?' Tara asked.

Carla shook her head then pulled a tissue from a box on the table and blew her nose.

'No,' she said. 'I didn't understand computers, but neither did Bobby. He just had a knack of attracting money, I suppose. When he'd made enough and had established loads of contacts, he no longer wanted Tommy around. The really bad thing was that he managed to ditch him without paying him a penny. Sleight of hand. Tommy had no head for business. It was easy for Bobby to cheat him out of everything. Then Bobby cleared off, and a month later I got turfed out of our luxury flat. I ended up back in Treadwater and have been there ever since.'

Carla dabbed her eyes and sniffed more tears.

'One more question,' said Tara. 'When did you last see Tommy?'

'Not for years. He used to drop by with birthday and Christmas presents for the boys. That stopped around the time he got divorced from Esther. I suppose he had enough problems of his own without worrying about anyone else.'

Tara thanked Carla once again and left her attending to the hair of her young customer.

As they returned to their car, Murray asked his habitual post-interview question.

'What do you think, mu'um?'

'I don't believe the woman had any reason to lie. Like I always say, there is a backstory to every murder. Tommy Brady seems to have had an unfortunate life when he could have achieved so much.'

'And everything points to this rich guy Logan-Sharp.'

'Our only lead so far.'

CHAPTER 20

Yana Logan-Sharp

Yana was restless and bored. So bored that she'd even gone to an adventure play park with Surrey. Shelby came too, of course. Yana did not do parenting on her own. The activity had consisted of Yana sitting alone as Shelby led Surrey through a soft play area, the child screaming and giggling in a ball pen.

Yana was engrossed in her phone, anxious to receive a text from Malik. She'd heard nothing for two days and had to make do with chat between her girlfriends in Monaco. She was coming to realise that Malik, apart from his sexual prowess, was no different to Sebastian. He was a busy man. If she were with him right now, she might be just as bored as she was here in Liverpool. The memories of sun and sex in Portofino were fading. For all she knew, Malik could be home in Riyadh, currently attending to his wife with no thought for his lover.

As her daughter played with the nanny, Yana's frustration worsened. In her mind, she gathered points to use against Sebastian and rehearsed her threats to leave him for good. She pictured an exciting life in Monaco where she could resume her role as a socialite and perhaps even consider a return to the catwalk. It had been hard work, but she missed the attention that came with it. When she thought about it, she didn't really need a life with Sebastian. Just his money. With no word from Malik and as the conversation with her girlfriends faded, her mood descended to her darkest place. She was itching for a fight.

Returning to the house, she could hardly wait for the car to stop before undoing her seatbelt and pushing the door open. Shelby was helping Surrey to get out, but Yana was already in the house clopping down the hall in platform shoes to the kitchen. She found Beatrice and Sebastian, as usual, deep in discussion.

'Sebastian! We need to talk.'

'I'm busy at the minute, Yana. Come back later.'

Her face had violence all over it. She slammed her Gucci bag to the floor in a perfect tantrum.

'Leave us, Beatrice,' she snapped. She had no wish to conduct her row with such a bitch present to hear everything.

Sebastian hadn't yet risen to his wife's provocation. He sat at the table with a coffee mug in his hand and a supercilious grin on his face. It further incensed Yana, who was aware of Shelby and Surrey entering the kitchen behind her. The damned nanny was another person who had no right to witness the family drama. Beatrice had yet to move from her seat next to Sebastian, but Yana at least waited until Shelby had left the kitchen and taken Surrey upstairs. Before she had the chance to order the PA to leave again, her husband spoke.

'Beatrice is staying put. You either keep it until later, Yana, or you say whatever's in that twisted head of yours to both of us.'

Yana stamped her foot on the floor; her blood was boiling over. This could not wait.

'I want to go back to Monaco. I don't know why you insist on me being here.'

'I need you here because we are trying to go public with this project and it's important to attract favourable publicity. We have to play happy families, you, Surrey and me.'

'It's taking too long. I want to go now. I don't like this city. There is nothing for me to do.'

'It's not all about you, Yana.'

'Fuck you, Sebastian. If you won't let me leave, then I want a divorce!'

'Change the frigging record, will you, love. Every time you don't get your own way you play the divorce card.'

'I mean it this time. And I'll take Surrey with me.'

Sebastian shrugged his amusement.

'She's your daughter, Yana, not mine.'

Beatrice looked on in shock.

Yana tottered on her heels. A slap on the face would have been less painful. He knows, she thought. All this time he has known and said nothing.

'I know you thought you'd got away with it. Insisting we call her Surrey after our home and the place where she was conceived. And she might well have been. I don't know who the father is or where he did the deed, but there's one thing you should have checked before you told me you were pregnant.'

Yana's body trembled. She should have been winning this argument. She was supposed to come away with his permission to leave Liverpool, to return to Monaco. Instead, she was being taken down by a truth she didn't think Sebastian knew. And it was all happening in front of that wretched PA.

'I had the snip years before you and I ever met, sweetheart. There's no way I'm Surrey's dad.'

'The operation doesn't always work.'

'I'm happy to take a paternity test, darling. Just say the word.'

'I want a divorce!' That was all she had.

'Fine, no problem. You can have it as soon as this deal is all signed and sealed. Until then you will stay here and do what I fucking tell you.'

'If we are divorcing then I don't have to stay. Tell him how it works, Beatrice. You know what he's worth, and I will get half.'

Beatrice didn't have to respond. Sebastian had one final arrow to fire.

'I'm afraid not, sweetheart. You signed a prenup, remember?'

'I'll fight it,' she said, but her voice was faltering, and tears welled.

'Go right ahead, but there ain't no court going to dispute it. It was a more than generous settlement. You'll get exactly twenty-five percent of my personal fortune at the time we married. Beatrice, how much was I worth five years ago?'

Beatrice seemed reluctant to become involved. Even Sebastian's PA had had enough.

'Your personal worth, not the value of your companies, was 1.6 million,' Beatrice answered flatly.

Yana screamed.

'No! You're both lying. You're a billionaire, Sebastian. That's not right. I'm entitled to half of everything.'

Her husband smirked in victory. Beatrice dropped her head. Yana stared in disbelief. Just to finally condemn her, Sebastian explained.

'You see, darling Yana, my wife who could not keep her legs closed. Most of my money is well and truly tied up in several companies. Even if I needed to, I can't get to it. When we married my personal wealth was declared as 1.6 million quid. So, take it or leave it, love. Surely for you it's worth hanging around here for another few weeks. It has to be worth 400 grand. Sadly, that won't be enough for you to go on living the high life in Monaco. Maybe some other poor sod will put his money where his dick wants to be. Right up your arse. Now, off you fuck, I'm busy.'

Without another word, and struggling to hold back her anguish, Yana walked unsteadily to the fridge and removed a bottle of champagne. There was nothing to celebrate, but she needed to get drunk.

'Fuck you, Sebastian. I hate you.'

He had already resumed his discussion with that bitch who ran their lives. Yana climbed the stairs to her room and slammed the door behind her.

CHAPTER 21

Shelby Keibler

Despite the size of the house, she'd heard the row as she came through the front door and entered the kitchen. Quickly, she led Surrey to her room and set her down in front of the TV. Then she hurried onto the landing to listen.

Yana had imploded, but Sebastian was having none of it. Divorce was being discussed. She was glad about that, but what could it mean for her? Who would be her boss if the pair of them split up? Sebastian obviously paid her salary, but Yana did most of the ordering her around. Beatrice was the person who had interviewed and hired her. If Surrey was to leave with her mother for good, where would she go? Yana would still need a nanny. She could never cope with a child on her own. But she and Yana hated each other. There was no way she could work only for her. She would have to find another job. Unless Surrey was to stay with Sebastian. Maybe Sebastian had been planning to dump Yana and be with her. Shelby needed to know. Perhaps he hadn't meant to be so cross with her.

That night Shelby ventured to his room, thinking he might need some loving after his row with Yana. It would be the first time since he'd so cruelly warned her to mind her own business. But Sebastian wasn't there.

* * *

Next morning, she found Beatrice and Sebastian in the kitchen, busy with plans for a reception to be held at the house. Shelby needed to speak with him as soon as possible. She couldn't wait. As soon as Beatrice had left him alone, she would try.

But all that day Sebastian and Beatrice were occupied with arrangements for the party. It was clear that they weren't discussing the canapes or choosing background music. Patrice, Sebastian's personal chef, and a team of caterers were taking care of those things. Shelby had instead heard names and deals being discussed. At times it had got heated, voices were raised, and the language was coarse. She was aware that something big was going down; she could never appreciate exactly how big, however, but if it meant more money for Sebastian and one day, hopefully for her, then she was happy.

By six o'clock she had organised dinner for Surrey and settled her in her room with Disney movies on TV and a promise to check on her later. She was supposed to stay with Surrey at all times, but she was desperate to speak with Sebastian. She had to know what the future held.

In her bedroom, Shelby slipped on a white figure-hugging dress, applied make-up and donned a pair of heels. She wore nothing under the dress and her long hair hung loose around her shoulders. Feeling nervous, yet exhilarated, she tiptoed around the landing until she reached his bedroom door. Yana's room was directly opposite across the gallery, and Beatrice's was next to it. She prayed that neither woman would see her. Tapping on the door, she edged it open, breathed deeply and stepped inside.

He was padding around, wrapped in a towel and talking on his phone. He didn't acknowledge her. She perched herself on the edge of his bed with her legs apart. After a minute or so it was clear that he was not about to cut his call just because she'd come to his room. When he stopped close to her, and continued to rant at whoever was on the phone, she reached out, grabbed his towel and pulled. It dropped to the floor, and he stood facing her naked; his conversation didn't falter. If she'd paid attention, she would have realised what was being discussed. But she had her own agenda. Sebastian talking about pressurising his partners did not register with her. When she dropped to her knees in front of him, it was clear that Sebastian didn't care what she might overhear. And Shelby didn't mind that she was regarded merely as the hired help. Worse than that, she was the hired help with a limited future.

But Shelby was proficient at her task, and Sebastian eventually ended his call and allowed her to continue. He moaned then grabbed her hair and pulled upwards. She rose to her feet, matching his height on her heels. They kissed ferociously, and he pulled her dress until it slipped from her shoulders, stretching out of shape. As he bit hard at her neck, she wriggled the dress free of her body and stood before him naked, still on her heels. He thrust her backwards onto the bed. It was all over in seconds. There was no intimacy, no cuddling, and now he was done.

'You need to check on Surrey,' he said coldly.

Shelby sat up, retrieved her dress from the floor and pulled it on.

'Seb?'

He was heading for the en suite.

'Don't call me Seb. What is it?'

He stood with hands on hips, like a footballer waiting for a free kick to be taken.

'I love you.'

'Fuck off, sweetheart. You don't even like me.'

She reached the door, crestfallen, feeling used and worthless.

'You need to look for another job,' he said without apology.

'But why?' She couldn't prevent the alarm in her voice.

'When we're done in Liverpool, Yana and I will be going our separate ways. I don't think you'll be happy working for her.'

'But I could stay with you. I can do other things. I'm not just a nanny.'

'Nice try, love, but I don't need anyone else. Beatrice handles everything for me. Out you go, Surrey should be in bed, and I have more calls to make.'

Shelby had failed miserably, and adding to her despair, across the landing, Yana stood with arms folded watching as she emerged from her husband's bedroom. Bracing herself, Shelby managed a shrug then strutted around the landing to her own room. Closing the door behind her, she leaned back against it. She couldn't decide who she hated more, Yana, or Beatrice, the woman who could do everything.

CHAPTER 22

Michelle Weller

She read the email and for a moment couldn't take it in. Why would Sebastian Logan-Sharp invite her to a drinks reception? Immediately, she called her best chum Francine, a fellow campaigner for women's rights, to check if she had also been invited. It was a no, but Francine couldn't help laughing at the idea. A few more calls to her other friends and finally Michelle realised that she was the only one. Now she was in a quandary. There was an RSVP link on the email. She read the message again.

> *Hi Michelle,*
> *Sebastian would be delighted if you could join him on the 26th of the month at 7.30 for drinks at his home. The event is casual, and Sebastian intends to present a brief introduction to Merseyside Delta Development. It is an opportunity for you to ask questions and express your views on the venture.*
> *We do hope you can be present and look forward to meeting you.*
> *Kindest regards,*
> *Beatrice Howard*
> *(for Sebastian Logan-Sharp)*

Why would he invite me? she wondered. Michelle didn't give a toss about Sebastian's development plans. She simply wanted to bring him down for his treatment of women. They must have got her email address from her group's website, Women Bite Back. Was this merely a PR stunt? Then she recalled the brief encounter a few nights ago outside The Pentium. When her gaze had met his, she was convinced there was true eye contact. Or perhaps it was merely a look of contempt for those shouting abuse at him and his money grabbing slut of a wife. Thinking this way fuelled her mood, sparked a little confidence, and before she'd realised, she'd clicked on the RSVP and hit the 'Yes, I will be there' button.

* * *

A few days later, she took a taxi from her home in Bootle to the temporary residence of Sebastian Logan-Sharp in West Derby. A dozen or more fancy-looking cars were parked in the wide drive as the taxi pulled up at the front door of the house.

She'd gone against her personal ethos of not getting dressed up to impress a man. On the rare occasions when she had made an effort, it had been for her own self-worth and pleasure. Stepping from the black cab, Michelle resembled the carefree young woman she'd been years ago. Despite the directive that the reception was a casual affair, she'd donned her best black dress that sat well above her knees. She'd spent more than she normally would at the hairdressers, and had a fresh colour and style. If challenged by any of her mates in Women Bite Back, she would not be able to explain herself. Hypocrite was the word she'd shoved to the back of her mind. Tonight, she kept telling herself, was an opportunity she had to take.

A confident-looking woman with short hair and dressed in a white trouser suit greeted her at the door.

'I'm Beatrice, so glad you could make it.'

'I'm Michelle Weller.'

'Ah, yes.'

Beatrice checked her off the guest list on the iPad she was holding. 'Please, grab a drink and make yourself at home.'

Michelle stepped into the centre of the vast hallway. A young waiter stood at the bottom of the staircase holding a tray of champagne flutes. She took one and said thank you, as her eyes were drawn upwards to the gallery. It was some house, she thought; brightly decorated with the white walls displaying several striking pieces of abstract art, although she knew nothing about such things. She realised too that it probably had little to do with Sebastian Logan-Sharp.

Already feeling self-conscious, thinking she stood out like the proverbial sore thumb, she ambled towards open double doors to discover an equally impressive lounge. Clusters of people stood around chatting, sharing jokes, and she overheard several guests making bitchy comments on the occasion. Most of the seating was taken up by women in little cliques. Several pairs of eyes fell on her, observing her dress sense, she imagined, but very quickly resuming their conversation. She felt a little easier that she hadn't come over-dressed, but realised too that these women would spot H&M at fifty yards. Suddenly, at a loss over what to do next, she heard a voice addressing her from behind.

'Wouldn't have thought this was your scene,' he said.

Turning to face him, she replied, 'Nor yours.'

He looked her up and down, his smile touching on the amorous.

'And you look great.'

'I see you've made an effort too, Paul.'

She acknowledged his smile with her own then sipped her champagne. His hair had at least been washed and combed since they'd last met, although he stood in a crumpled navy suit, his striped tie already loosened. Michelle reckoned Paul Renfrew felt every bit as awkward as she did.

'What do you think is going to happen?' he asked.

'I have no idea. Don't really care. I just want to stand face to face with Sebastian.'

'You're not one of those paint throwers, are you? This is my only suit.'

She laughed.

'Would be a waste of good paint,' she replied. 'It'll take more than a pot of emulsion to bring Sebastian to his knees.'

'Sadly, you're absolutely right. I'm thinking we've been invited so that he can disarm the protestors, not the other way around.'

'I wonder if the football hooligans will put in an appearance.'

'Already here,' said Paul, swinging his shoulder round to indicate a group of men in suits who seemed to be knocking back the free drink. 'Supporters and several board members from Liverpool, Everton, Tranmere, and I think Wigan, too.'

'I still don't understand why we're here,' she said.

'Don't accuse him of being a rapist again until we find out.'

Michelle scanned the room. She was getting nervous. Where was Sebastian?

CHAPTER 23

Tara Grogan

Tweedy's flip charts stood at one end of her office next to a whiteboard. Murray was slouched in his seat munching cheese and onion crisps, Wilson chewed a Mars bar and Bleasdale took frequent sips from a water bottle. Picnic time at St Anne Street, except it was well after seven and they all should be relaxing at home instead of chucking around ideas on their latest case. Tara was starving but was steadfastly avoiding the snacks, thinking of the meal Kate would have ready when eventually she made it home to Hoylake. She was the only one on her feet and felt rather like a teacher before uninspired teenage students.

'We estimate that Brady died between eight and ten o'clock,' she repeated wearily. 'He appears to have spent his entire weekend indoors, despite the hot weather, and probably working on his computer. Any news from the tech guys at the Met on what he was doing?'

'Nothing yet, ma'am,' Bleasdale replied.

'So, we know that it was something too complicated for us to decipher. It may be relevant, or it may have nothing at all to do with Brady's murder.'

'The man was just a geek,' said Murray.

'Anything more from the mobile phones taken from his house?' asked Tara.

'Nothing that seems relevant,' Wilson replied. 'But the work is ongoing. Think of the number of phones we found and multiply that by the number of people in each list of contacts, times the online communications.'

'OK, John, we get the idea,' said Tara. 'But the mobile device of particular interest is the gold one belonging to that thoroughly rude man Logan-Sharp.'

'We didn't find much on it to incriminate anyone. There were several calls made to numbers we have yet to identify. Maybe there will be a match to one of the other phones found at Brady's home. I'll keep you posted,' said Wilson.

'Ma'am,' said Bleasdale, 'do you think that Sebastian Logan-Sharp lied to us? That he *had* met Tommy Brady recently.'

'Quite possible,' Tara replied. 'Let's see what else we get from analysing his mobile phone.'

'It is suspicious though that the two men shared such an interesting past,' said Bleasdale.

Tara had had enough. They were getting nowhere. Her head was pounding; she imagined her colleagues felt the same.

'Let's wrap it up for now. Tomorrow we can review all the info from house to house inquiries, revisit the forensic and post-mortem reports and go over what we have gleaned from the people who knew Tommy Brady.'

CHAPTER 24

Sebastian Logan-Sharp

Before leaving his room, Sebastian checked his phone. There was a new text message. It sent shivers down his back and legs. The bastards had no patience. Why couldn't they at least wait until after tonight? He had assured them that everything was in hand. As soon as the Boals got their frigging act together and he got one of the football clubs to jump, then all would be well. If they kept giving him hassle, he would lose his cool and the whole thing would blow up in their faces. Sure as hell, he wouldn't take the fall.

He stepped into the garden and a stuffy evening. The patio doors had been slid back to allow air to circulate through the kitchen and into the lounges in preparation for the arrival of guests. The man he'd come outside to see was smoking, pacing on the lawn thirty yards from the houses. If he was trying to appear inconspicuous, he had failed miserably. He watched as Sebastian strolled nonchalantly across the lawn.

'They want an update, Sebastian.'

'And I've told them not to get their knickers in a twist.'

Ernst didn't seem to get the British turn of phrase.

'I'm having to deal with investors, football clubs and all the scum protestors coming out of the woodwork to have a go at me. Now the bloody conspiracy theorists are suggesting our money is dirty. I've told you; the whole thing must be squeaky clean, or it won't fly.'

'I have been told to say this.' Ernst sounded hesitant.

Sebastian grimaced. 'Spit it out, sunshine.'

Ernst moved closer, his tobacco breath on Sebastian's face. 'If you fuck up, you'll pay for it.'

'Are you threatening me?'

'Not me, Sebastian,' he said. 'I will simply carry out orders.' Then he clapped Sebastian on both shoulders. 'Better that you don't, eh, boss?' He laughed then strolled away.

Sebastian couldn't prevent his fear rising, but his life had always been one of defiance. They wouldn't get to him. He wouldn't let them.

When he returned to the patio, he saw Beatrice in discussion with the bodyguard who had just threatened him. He would speak to her later and find out what she was up to. His attention was then drawn to the vision of his wife stepping from the house, a champagne flute in each hand. She flopped into a garden seat, holding her drinks aloft to avoid spillage.

'Hello, my husband,' she slurred, 'do I look good for you this evening? Do I look a billionaire's wife?'

Yana looked ravishing. He may loathe her, but she was still a woman he'd take to his bed in a flash. A silk dress of cornflower blue barely covered her tanned frame. Her long legs were outstretched and open. He felt a flicker of arousal. But he wouldn't give her the pleasure. Besides, she was already well pissed. He leaned over her, his hands clasping either arm of the chair.

'You're bollocksed, sweetheart. Why don't you fuck off to bed? You're no use to me anymore.'

'Fuck you, Sebastian. My friends will look after me, and you will have to answer for the way you have treated me.'

She took another drink then slid further down the seat.

Beatrice was trying to attract his attention.

'You're needed inside, Sebastian,' she said, whilst looking with concern at his wife.

He left Yana to her alcohol-soaked wonderland and went to greet his guests.

James Boal, his insipid son Cameron in tow, bounded through the dining area of the kitchen laid out with buffet food. Sebastian selected a prawn vol-au-vent and shoved it into his mouth as his potential business partners approached.

'Sebastian,' said James cheerfully, his hand outstretched.

Impishly, Sebastian used his greasy hand to greet the man.

'Just wondering if you've had a chance to consider our revised proposal?' James asked.

Sebastian showed no indication of knowing what James was on about. He enjoyed seeing people like him squirm and made to crawl. Looking at Cameron, though, he didn't think him to be a man who would lower himself. But then Cameron had already shown himself to be an incompetent prick. He seemed of little use. In fact, Sebastian was considering making Cameron's exclusion a proviso for James's participation in the deal.

'Yes,' he replied. 'I've talked it over with Beatrice. But you should know that things have moved on since our last meeting.'

'How so?' James Boal was flushed and sweating. He looked like a man heading for a heart attack.

'The starting price has gone up. These things change quickly, you know. The banks mess us around. They want more before they will underwrite the project.'

'How much?'

'Thirty percent.'

'Shit!' It was the first word uttered by Cameron, who looked eager to walk away from the deal.

Sebastian didn't baulk. These guys were there for the taking. Another thirty percent from them, and his backers would be delighted. That might get Ernst out of his hair. He didn't want to admit it, but he feared the Austrian.

'I was hoping you would be agreeable,' Sebastian continued, sounding apologetic. 'Cameron did offer twenty percent more last week. I'll leave it with you for an hour or so. There's a couple of other guys we want to bring on board, if you decide that you can't manage it. Enjoy the evening. Help yourselves to the grub.'

Sebastian could hear father and son grumbling as he wandered off to greet other guests.

* * *

When the presentations for the Merseyside Delta Development project were finished and awkward questions professionally sidestepped, Sebastian and Beatrice continued to mingle. At one point, she came over and squeezed his arm, whispering that she'd thought the event was going well.

'All we need now is to buy us a nice football club,' she said.

'Yeah, we'll need the money to pay for all the shit you're sticking up your nose.'

Beatrice stopped dead. Her face reddened. She couldn't find words to hit back. Then, seemingly composing herself, she directed her boss into the path of Paul Renfrew. Evidently, the environmental campaigner had been enjoying the free booze.

'You can't do this to Otterspool, Sebastian,' he spouted. 'You're destroying parkland and squandering the chance to do some real good for the environment.'

'I think you'll find that I can. You people can't just shout for the environment every time a bulldozer moves some dirt. It's not like Otterspool is even a greenfield site. But here's something else you should know, Renfrew. My organisation is your fucking pay-packet.'

'What do you mean?'

'Well, your puny operation gets its funding from a big environmental consortium in London. They look at various ways to improve and protect our environment: clean energy, better transport, avoiding pollution. My company puts millions in their bank account and they in turn fund various environmental groups around the country, just like yours. So, you see, Renfrew, you kick up a fuss over my plans and you're biting the hand that feeds. So, off you fuck, lad. Stay out of this, or you'll be counting blades of grass in Stanley Park for something to do when you're out of a job.'

A woman standing next to Renfrew had listened to every word but said nothing. Her face was somehow familiar to Sebastian, but he couldn't place it. She looked a bit dour and hadn't returned his smile.

'Do I know you?' he asked, turning away from Renfrew who seemed grateful for a passing waiter and another drink.

Beatrice intervened. 'Michelle Weller? Isn't that correct?'

The woman smiled at Beatrice then looked coldly at Sebastian. He processed the name in his head. Faint memories began to stir.

'Hello,' he managed. He held out his hand, but she didn't take it.

'Hello, Bobby,' she said dryly. 'It's been a very long time.'

Honestly, he couldn't recall if it had been years or just last month. He had no clue who she was.

'So, why are you here?' he chirped. 'Not one of Renfrew's cronies, are you?'

'No. I campaign for women's rights.'

'A bra burner, eh?' He laughed at his own quip, but neither Michelle nor Beatrice joined in.

'Things have come a long way since women did that, Bobby. It's sad though.'

'What is?'

'That we are still fighting for the right to be treated decently by men like you.'

He couldn't be arsed reminding this bitch that his name was Sebastian. She wasn't worth his breath, but he was still dying to know where they'd met before.

'Just tell me, darling. How exactly do we know each other?'

Michelle glared icily. He felt her eyes piercing his. If he believed in the supernatural, he'd swear she was the Ghost of Christmas Past come to spoil his night. Finally, she smiled, but it was far from friendly.

'A billionaire with no memory; just what Liverpool needs.'

'What the fuck?'

'Just tell the world, Bobby. Are you a rapist?'

'Listen to me, you fat–'

Beatrice grabbed his arm and jerked him away. 'No, Sebastian!' she hissed.

Michelle grinned as Beatrice ushered him from the room.

* * *

Sebastian and Beatrice stood in the garden, thankfully alone.

'What did you do that for?' he said.

'You start a fight with that woman, and you'll blow everything,' Beatrice scolded.

'Then why the hell did we even invite the likes of her?'

'Because you were supposed to get these people on side. You were supposed to improve your image in this city. Instead, you verbally abused a women's rights campaigner, and that was after you'd torn strips off an affable guy who just wants to protect the environment. The Boals look like you've screwed them over too. Why didn't you tell me you were going to up their price? We hadn't discussed it.'

'You wouldn't understand, sweetheart. I don't tell you everything, you know. You just look after that coke habit of yours, and I'll tell you what you can know and what you can't.'

'Maybe you and I have gone as far as we can go, Bobby.'

'Don't fucking call me Bobby! You should know better. Besides, you can't quit on me. I'd sack you first. I'll send you and your bed buddy packing as soon as I'm finished in Liverpool.'

He lifted an open bottle of champagne from a table and put it to his mouth.

Beatrice, stood upright, remaining calm.

'You're an asshole, Bobby.' She turned to walk away.

'I know! I know. Everybody fucking hates me. And don't call me Bobby. My name is Sebastian. I'm the guy who pays for your coke and don't forget it.'

She gave him the finger over her shoulder and went back indoors.

CHAPTER 25

Carla Smith

It was Carla's second visit in a week, but she didn't know why she was here. That woman who worked for Bobby was insistent that she should come, and she had to be sure to bring her two sons along. Beatrice had greeted them by the front door when they stepped from a minicab. She seemed genuinely delighted to see her again and had even, without sarcasm, complimented her on the dress she was wearing.

'Please, enjoy your evening,' Beatrice had said. 'You have a right to be here.'

Carla winced at the remark. She suspected that Beatrice had invited them without Bobby's knowledge. She didn't want to cause any trouble. Her ex-husband had made things clear on her previous visit that he wanted nothing to do with them. It was Beatrice who had suggested that she could persuade Bobby to change his mind. Carla remained puzzled by the invitation.

The boys flanked her as she meandered through the lounge filled with strangers. They all seemed to be acquainted and have something to say to each other. She allowed Jack and Lee to have champagne and to look all grown up for the moment in the evening when they would stand before their father. Jack was nervous about it, while Lee displayed his usual indifference at having anything to do with a formal gathering. It wasn't cool. He wanted street cred.

An hour passed of sitting around, sipping champagne and people watching. There was no sign of Bobby until he'd stepped up to a lectern to make a speech about his business plans. Carla paid little attention except to inwardly gasp on hearing the sums of money in play. Her ex-husband really had hit the big time. She recognised his wife Yana who strutted around, ignoring just about everyone. She looked every bit the billionaire's wife. Her dress was probably worth more than everything Carla owned. What Yana spent on getting her hair and nails done would be enough to see her boys through their first year at uni. And yet, Carla thought, the woman did not look happy. She looked pissed. Carla had no sympathy. Try living my life, darling, she thought.

As the woman tottered around wielding a bottle of champagne and snarling at those who dared speak to her, Carla's contempt grew. There was still no sign of Bobby coming to greet them and therefore no opportunity for Jack and Lee to meet their father for the first time. Carla's frustration soon turned to seething anger. She had never felt envious of the woman who now shared Bobby's life. She had no unspent love for her ex-husband. All she desired was some recognition that she was the mother of his sons. But as she watched this bitch strutting around, being rude to her guests and struggling to stay upright on giant heels, she felt inclined to scratch her bloody eyes out.

Carla prayed that when they were at last confronted by their host, his assistant would be at his side. It might help ease the tension. She hoped too that the dreadful woman who passed herself as his wife would be well out of sight. But none of her wishes played out as she'd hoped.

'I know who you are?' Yana slurred.

'Is that right, love?' Carla looked critically at the woman swaying in front of her. She noticed Jack and Lee's mouths agape at the sight of the stunning woman. Don't be impressed by the likes of her, she wanted to tell her boys, but the woman had more to say.

'So, you are Sebastian's sons?' She held her hand out in greeting, as if expecting both boys to bow and kiss it, but Carla swiped it away.

'I don't think so,' Carla said. 'We have nothing to say to you.'

'Ooh! Sebastian always said you were feisty. Is that the correct English word, feisty?'

Yana pouted at the boys who looked mesmerised by the flirtatious beauty. Then she glowered at Carla who responded in similar manner. Eventually, taking the hint, the drunken wife of her ex-husband strolled away. Carla realised then just how big a mistake it was to have come.

Despite their long wait, Bobby's approach was unnoticed. He suddenly stood before them.

'This must be Beatrice's idea of a sick joke.'

Carla stared at the man she had once idolised. But time was a great healer.

'Hello, Bobby. Thought you might like to meet your sons.' She turned to Jack and Lee. 'Say hello to your dad, boys.'

CHAPTER 26

Beatrice Howard

At least when she was snacking on cheese and biscuits, she wasn't snorting an expensive powder up her nose. Beatrice sat alone in the kitchen. It was nearly three in the morning, but she didn't feel like going to bed. Nor did she feel like sharing it with Ernst. He was becoming tiresome, assuming that he could have her when he pleased.

From what she'd witnessed during the party, it appeared that the Austrian was more than a mere bodyguard to Sebastian. She'd observed, but hadn't heard, their discussion in the garden. It hadn't looked friendly, and it didn't seem like a casual employer-employee chat. As the evening wore on, she sensed unease in Sebastian. He was more on edge than usual, more acerbic, if that were even possible. Despite the presentations having been well received by the guests who mattered, several others had departed the house having endured a litany of abuse from Sebastian. Sadly, that had included his two young sons. What kind of man does that, she thought. Those boys had done nothing wrong. And yet Sebastian had torn strips off their mother. Surely, they had not deserved to be treated in that manner.

On the business front, the Boals hadn't deserved to be double-crossed in this project. Of course, they were big boys and didn't need her sympathy. It was business, but she realised Sebastian was playing dirty. And several board members of the football clubs around Merseyside had not exactly been embraced by her boss. As far as buying into their clubs was concerned, he'd presented them with a take it or leave it scenario. From what she'd gleaned as she bid each of them goodnight, Sebastian had treated them with indifference bordering on contempt. He was not making it easy for any of them to accept his offer. Because of his bolshy attitude, his otherwise lucrative proposals had been lost on them. None of this aggressive posturing had been discussed when they had planned the event.

But Beatrice's disgust was reserved for the way Sebastian had dealt with those people who already had good reason to despise him. The environmentalists and the women's rights campaigners had little to be pleased about as they left the party.

The spacious house was deathly quiet. There wasn't even a sound from outside. Beatrice opened a bottle of red wine and poured a generous glass. She resumed her seat at the breakfast bar and nibbled on the last piece of classic Gruyère, savouring its nutty flavour. Before this night became another day, she told herself, she would decide her future. Her life was spiralling down through decadence and toxic living with Sebastian. This had to be the right time to move on, to do something different, something better. The large salary was important, she couldn't deny that. But first she had to get clean, no matter how long it took, and then she could focus on getting rich, rather than helping Sebastian Logan-Sharp get richer. Something had to give. Her boss had a lesson to learn. She would be the person to deliver it.

CHAPTER 27

Tara Grogan

Her browsing was providing information, but she couldn't say how useful any of it would be to her case. She'd read how Tommy Brady was once hailed by a local newspaper as the Steve Jobs of Merseyside. This, of course, had been an exaggeration. Tommy Brady's career with computers had floundered. What puzzled Tara was why Brady hadn't continued alone after his breakup with the man who, back then, was known only as Bobby Smith. From what Carla had told her, Brady had been the expert, while Bobby Smith perhaps had the financial nous. Brady, however, had disappeared from the business and computer world within days of his split with Logan-Sharp.

There was little information on what Brady had been up to since then. Tara's online search had found only a single press reference and one colour photograph of Tommy Brady's wedding to Esther. At some point, long after their wedding day, someone had posted it on social media. Tara selected the image and zoomed in on the wedding party. Tommy and Esther were bracketed by a couple who Tara presumed were the parents of the bride and groom. She couldn't be certain that the best man in the grainy picture was Logan-Sharp. It may just have been a relative of Tommy's. There were also two bridesmaids in the shot. At a pinch, she thought one of them may have been Carla Smith, but it was such a long time ago and not a distinct image. She couldn't be certain but made a mental note to check it with Carla. The other bridesmaid did not look familiar at all.

Murray entered the office handing out ice cream lollies to colleagues. It was most welcome in the stifling heat of their room. Tara had spent her morning beside a whirring desk fan trying to stay cool. She continued to browse for information on the life of Tommy Brady as she savoured her ice cream. Most of the articles appearing were recent posts relating to his murder. It seemed nowadays that people had nothing better to do than present preposterous scenarios as to why someone had been killed.

Several of the posts were extensive and included pictures of Brady's home and street, his workplace at the recycling centre, and one even included a photo of the house where his ex-wife Esther lived. The wedding picture she'd discovered earlier also featured several times within the discussions. Theories on the killing ranged from a gangland feud, to robbery, to alien interception of Brady's computer apps, but the worst were the suggestions that he had been targeted by a group of paedophile hunters. Did no one ever stop to think how damaging to a police murder inquiry such futile speculation could be? In truth, speculation was all that Tara currently had on the murder. She had a connection to Sebastian Logan-Sharp and his expensive mobile phone found at the scene. But she still had no witnesses or motive to the murder, unless she was to consider the complaints of neighbours about Brady playing loud music.

'Ma'am?' Wilson shouted from the far side of the office. Usually, he came to her desk if he had some news.

'What's up?'

He hurried over.

'Take a look at the police bulletin board. There's a unit responding to an incident at a house in West Derby. I think it's the place where that billionaire bloke is staying.'

Tara navigated to the latest news page on the Merseyside Police portal and read the report.

'It refers to a sudden death,' she said. 'No mention of anything suspicious. Find out who's dealing with it.'

'Ma'am,' Bleasdale called. 'A uniform patrol was despatched from St Anne Street. Seems to be a routine response.'

'Is the address confirmed as Logan-Sharp's?' asked Tara.

'Yes, ma'am.'

'I wonder who has died.'

CHAPTER 28

Paul Renfrew

Paul's shoulder ached; his tongue rasped in his throat. Turning his head to the side, he watched her sleep, the duvet wrapped around her, despite the heat of the room. Well snuggled in, or an attempt to keep him away? Probably the latter.

It was an unexpected end to their evening spent at the home of the man they hated. At least they'd made the most of the free drink after Logan-Sharp had been scathing of their opposition to his plans. Paul had never got drunk on champagne before. Just as good as anything else when you don't have to pay. Well drunk, they'd shared a taxi. Michelle's home was further away than his, but he thought it polite to ensure she got there safely. When they arrived, he had simply climbed out to see her to her front door. It seemed mannerly to kiss her goodnight. Then somehow, she'd waved the taxi away and he was tugged inside. They fumbled with each other on the stairs, and by the time they'd reached her bedroom, she was minus her dress, and his trousers were around his ankles. But that was it. In seconds, she was out cold on the bed, and he only felt capable of flopping down beside her. Nothing had happened and he doubted that anything would.

'Sorry,' she mumbled as her eyes opened.

He smiled. Didn't really matter, did it? They'd both been pissed, although she hadn't seemed quite as drunk as him when they were leaving Logan-Sharp's house. But he supposed that not everyone reacts the same way to an excess of alcohol. Perhaps the fresh air had got to her.

'What time is it?' she asked.

He had slept in his jacket. He retrieved his phone from a pocket and checked the time.

'Nine twenty-five.'

'Shit! I'm going to be late for work.'

'Me too.'

She sat upright, the duvet coming loose exposing her bare shoulders. She quickly covered herself as he stared.

'Sorry,' she said again. 'I must have passed out.'

'No problem, we both had a skinful.'

She smiled weakly and ran a hand through her hair.

'Can you get out now, please. I have to get dressed.'

'Yes, sure.' He rose from the bed, retrieved his trousers from the floor and went in search of his shoes.

'Make yourself coffee in the kitchen.'

He pulled on his trousers, found his shoes and slipped out of the room. His body ached in protest as he descended the stairs. Had she spent the entire night kicking him up and down the bed? He located the kitchen and boiled water in the electric kettle to make coffee and found a jar of instant in a cupboard. It didn't look particularly fresh; the granules were clumped together, and he had to poke some out with a spoon. Her kitchen didn't look the tidiest. There were unwashed dishes in the sink and a tub of butter abandoned on the worktop beside a cutting board covered with crumbs. He sniffed the milk he'd taken from the fridge, just to be sure, then poured the hot water into a mug he assumed was clean and stirred the coffee. He added some milk and rested his body against the worktop as he sipped. It was better than nothing.

He heard her stirring upstairs, a shower going on and the faint sound of her singing. For a while he tried to recall the previous night. Sebastian Logan-Sharp was a nasty piece of work. It was one thing for him to belittle the environmental protests, but he would have really laid into Michelle if his PA hadn't dragged him away. Michelle hardly spoke after the encounter.

He checked his phone for messages. Remembering that he had a lecture to give to second-year undergrads at twelve, he pondered if it was worth hanging around for Michelle to come downstairs, just to bid her goodbye. It was probably best that he was gone. She'd seemed so uneasy when she awoke beside him, despite her awareness that nothing had happened. He managed a few more sips of coffee and continued to browse on his phone. Opening his social media notifications, he could scarcely believe what he was reading. He hurried to the foot of the stairs and called up to Michelle. She didn't answer. The shower was still going. He tried again.

'Michelle?'

'Yes, what is it?'

'I have to go now but check the news.'

The bathroom door opened.

'What's up?'

'Something's happened at Logan-Sharp's house. I have to go. Thanks for the coffee.'

His head pounded as he closed her front door, and he was struck by an uneasy feeling in his gut.

CHAPTER 29

Tara Grogan

Speculation on social media was rife all morning. It was astounding how a news story could spiral out of control when there was little accurate information forthcoming. Sebastian Logan-Sharp was dead, was the most popular claim, or his wife, his PA, another member of his staff, a houseguest and, ultimately, there had been multiple fatalities in a bloodbath. But the only juice to be had was in discussing the death of a billionaire. One remark fuelled another in a polymeric chain reaction of fake news and misinformation.

Tara, at least, knew for certain that Sebastian Logan-Sharp was not dead. Uniformed officers from St Anne Street responding to the incident had clarified that point as soon as they'd arrived at the house in West Derby. Thirty minutes later, Tweedy had called Tara to his office. He'd just been informed that police detectives were required to attend the scene of a suspicious incident.

'A locum GP was called to the house,' Tweedy explained. 'A woman has died, and not by natural causes, it seems. We need to get over there.'

In her mind, Tara ran through her recent experience of the Logan-Sharp entourage.

'Just a word of warning before we go,' said Tweedy.

'Sir?'

'Despite the fact that it is not the death of Sebastian Logan-Sharp we're dealing with, it is still big news. This will attract major publicity. Please be careful what you say to anyone, particularly in the media. Our work is about to be cast in the spotlight.'

'I understand, sir,' Tara replied.

Already, she felt pangs of nerves and a queasy feeling developed in her stomach. But she'd switched attention immediately to the forthcoming task. She gathered her team of Murray, Wilson and Bleasdale and briefed them en route to the apparent crime scene.

* * *

Alighting from the unmarked car driven by Wilson, Tara saw several uniformed officers moving around the exterior of the twin houses. At that point she did not see any of the residents. She followed Tweedy inside the house that, as she already knew, served as the main residence for the billionaire and his family. It was eerily quiet inside the hall. A constable was stationed at the foot of the grand staircase. He said nothing, and merely pointed upwards.

On reaching the landing, they were met by a man who introduced himself as Dr Shah. He explained that he was the GP who had been called to the house earlier in the morning. Around forty, he managed to sound pleasant yet professional.

'I've reported everything to your medical officer,' he explained. 'These are my contact details if you have any questions.' He handed a business card to Tweedy. 'I really must get back to the surgery, I have a lot of patients to see this morning.'

Tweedy thanked the GP and proceeded around the landing to the first room with an open door. It was an accurate guess. When they entered, Tara felt the space was quite serene. She could see a woman lying on a bed. The bizarre image, disturbing the serenity, was of a man leaning over her, while another in hooded white overalls and wielding a camera, skirted around taking pictures of just about everything.

'Good morning, folks.' Brian Witney sounded, as always, in fine spirits. He smiled at Tara.

'Not such a violent killing, Tara, but I think murder nonetheless.'

'What do you believe happened?' Tweedy asked.

'She's been suffocated.' Witney indicated a pillow lying next to the victim. 'Seems the most likely. You can get forensics to check it out.'

'How long has she been gone?' asked Tara. Her eyes scanned the luxurious bedroom with huge windows and a Juliet balcony overlooking the front drive.

The woman she had never met but recognised from fashion magazines as Yana Logan-Sharp lay on her back, her purple-blue lips dry and slightly parted, her almond eyes open and looking to the ceiling. A beautiful woman, even now in death.

'My estimate is around twelve to fourteen hours ago,' said Witney. 'That would suggest between ten and midnight.'

Tara noticed an open champagne bottle on the bedside table.

'Had she been drunk? No possibility that she has just died in her sleep?'

'I'm afraid not, Tara. There are the telltale signs of suffocation, the bloodshot eyes, blotches on her neck and some foam in her airways, and there is one more thing. The GP hadn't noticed it.' Witney pulled down a satin sheet to reveal the tanned midriff of the former model. She was completely nude. To the left of her navel was a single puncture wound with some blood surrounding it.

'What's that?' asked Tara.

'I found this on the floor next to the bed.'

With a pair of tweezers, Witney held up a thin wooden skewer about 20 cm long, one end of which was stained red. 'It's certainly didn't cause her death, but I reckon she was stabbed with it and then smothered.'

'I don't understand, it seems so ineffectual to do that if you're intending to suffocate someone.'

Witney shrugged.

'Yours is to reason why, Tara. I'll let you know the arrangements for the post-mortem.'

'Thanks, Brian,' Tweedy said. 'As you can imagine there'll be a lot of media interest in this one.'

'To be expected, I suppose. I'll get to it as quickly as possible.'

Tara remained at the bedside as the medical officer continued his work. A plethora of questions tumbled through her mind, and several spilled out.

'Did she sleep here alone?'

Witney closed his case, preparing to leave. He looked down at the bed.

'I don't think anyone has moved her since death. She's lying in the centre of the bed; no indentations to suggest that someone had lain beside her. Perhaps that's a question to be asked of her husband. No indications of sexual intercourse or indeed a sexual assault, but I'll confirm all that at the post-mortem.'

'Yes, of course.'

Her colleagues had already left the room, and when Brian Witney bid her goodbye, Tara was left alone with the victim. The questions kept on coming. What age? Where was home for Yana? Her family? What perfume had she been wearing? Tara could smell it, the only pleasant aspect of the scene. She noticed a light-blue fabric draped over a chair at the dressing table. She avoided lifting it to prevent contamination, but it appeared to be a dress, perhaps discarded by the victim before climbing into bed. Then Tara was struck by the thought that the woman's child was now without her mother. A husband without his wife. Money couldn't buy everything. Why had a young mother been murdered? Finally, she placed her hand on Yana's bare shoulder. It wasn't completely cold, perhaps due to the warmth of the room and the bed.

Her musings were interrupted when three men in dark suits appeared with a trolley and a body bag upon it. Swallowing hard, Tara took her leave from yet another victim crying out to her for justice.

CHAPTER 30

Tara Grogan

Bleasdale was standing in the centre of the hall when Tara came downstairs.

'Ma'am, Superintendent Tweedy has gone back to the station. He wants an update by this evening.'

'Fine, no pressure then.'

'DS Murray and DS Wilson have started interviewing the occupants. Everyone has been moved from here to the house next door.'

'Very handy, having a spare house.'

Before joining their colleagues and the interview process, Tara and Bleasdale walked around the main residence. She felt that the layout had changed since her last visit. The furniture in the lounge had been moved around, sofas had been pushed back to the walls and dining chairs were set in a row by the front window. They walked into the expansive kitchen-dining area where dozens of drinking glasses were laid out on the main table and several platters of food covered with clingfilm sat on the breakfast bar.

'Preparing for a party?' Tara suggested.

'Already happened, ma'am. Last night.'

'Ah, that's a complication we don't need. I was hoping the truth could be found within the group of people living here. But perhaps not. How many visitors?'

'That is being checked, ma'am.'

Tara opened one door of the double fridge and immediately noticed a platter of chicken kebabs and king prawns, a source perhaps for the skewer found by the victim's bed.

Returning to the first floor, Tara and Bleasdale cross-checked each bedroom with the name they had for its occupant. Bleasdale opened the door of the first room to the right of the stairs.

'This is Beatrice Howard's room, ma'am.'

They wandered around a space of the same dimensions as Yana's bedroom. The décor was neutral in colour with the continuing theme of bright abstracts on the walls. A cream silk nightdress lay on an unmade double bed. Tara noticed a trace of white powder on the otherwise tidy dressing table and recognised the signs of drug taking.

The room to the other side of Yana's was equipped as a child's playroom. There was a multi-coloured playmat on the floor with LEGO bricks scattered around, a small desk, a wall-mounted TV and several hula hoops beneath the window. Everything appeared quite normal. There were no signs that a killer had skulked in here prior to murdering Yana Logan-Sharp.

Moving to the rear of the landing, Bleasdale opened the door to Surrey's bedroom. Tara couldn't help comparing it with her god-daughter Adele's room at their home in Hoylake. Adele's was a playroom and bedroom combined, while Surrey's bedroom was simply that. There was little to be seen, apart from a pink teddy perched on the pillows of the single bed.

The room adjacent to Surrey's was by far the untidiest they had encountered.

'Whose room is this?' Tara asked.

Bleasdale checked her notes and Tara saw that her DC had sketched a layout of the house.

'This is the nanny, Shelby Keibler's room.'

Dresses lay on the bed, underwear on the floor and unpaired shoes were dotted about. Several plates of unfinished food and opened cans of soft drinks sat on the dressing table.

'Not such a tidy girl,' Tara mused.

'A bit like me,' said Bleasdale with a giggle.

The last bedroom belonged to Sebastian Logan-Sharp.

'So, Yana and Sebastian had separate rooms.' Tara gazed around at what was the master suite. It contained a super-king-sized bed, and a solid-oak desk stood by a full-length window. A laptop was open on the desk but appeared to be switched off. 'You can't help wondering about the state of the marriage. On television they looked the perfect rich couple.'

'Who knows what lies beneath the surface of any marriage,' said Bleasdale.

'Very true. Are you a fan?'

'Of marriage? Didn't go well for my parents and their experience has put me off the idea. How about you, ma'am?'

Tara smiled wistfully.

'Not on my radar just now.'

Tara had a cursory look around Sebastian's bedroom and the en suite. She saw nothing to suggest anything untoward had occurred. They continued the tour on the ground floor of the house, inspecting the home cinema, gym, and the swimming pool. None of them seemed to have been used much.

'Let's go see the victim's husband and try to find out what went on here last night,' said Tara, bringing their inspection to a close.

The spare house had a similar internal layout to the main one, including the style of furniture and colour of the décor.

'Who would even want to own identical houses side by side?'

'I think it's a one-off situation, ma'am. The houses can be let separately, it's just that on this occasion the occupant is a billionaire, and his needs perhaps are grander.'

Tara didn't dispute her colleague's analysis.

She and Bleasdale carried out a brief inspection of the rooms as they had done in the main house. Only three of the six bedrooms were in use by members of Logan-Sharp's staff, one by the bodyguard Ernst Eder, another by the driver Gavin and the third by Sebastian's personal chef Patrice Allard. They saw nothing conspicuous in any of the rooms.

They found Logan-Sharp seated in the main lounge, a whisky tumbler in one hand and holding a phone to his ear with the other. Murray sat opposite on a dining chair. He looked peeved at being made to wait while Logan-Sharp held a conversation with whoever. But Tara was not prepared to be kept waiting. Remaining on her feet, and with an official tone, she spoke to the widower.

'Mr Logan-Sharp, I would like a word please.'

He glared at her momentarily but carried on with his conversation. Tara guessed it was business rather than a consolatory call to Yana's family.

'Now, Mr Logan-Sharp! If you don't mind.'

She had to suppress her dislike of the man, but first impressions were hard to shake off. Her raised voice had the desired result. He cut his call but maintained a disdainful glare.

'What do you want, love? I've already told your mate everything I know. Why don't you just get on with your job and leave me to mine?'

She let the derogatory comments slide for now. She wasn't here for a slanging match. Perhaps his short temper today was due to stress from the death of his wife.

'I am very sorry for your loss,' she continued. 'Was it you who found your wife this morning?'

'No, it was Beatrice. She called me and then phoned for a doctor.'

Tara turned her head briefly. She could see into the kitchen where the PA was talking to Wilson.

'When did you last see your wife? I assume that you didn't sleep in the same room.'

Sebastian chortled.

'You assume right, sweetheart.'

Tara sensed that he was trying to provoke a reaction from her, but she wasn't about to oblige.

'I saw her last night. Pissed as a newt. I didn't have the time to deal with her. We had a reception here for our investors.'

'What do you mean, deal with her?'

Sebastian set his glass on a coffee table then rubbed his face vigorously with both hands. Tara could have told him that his troubles would not disappear that easily. Today, he didn't much resemble a billionaire, slouching in an over-sized T-shirt and tennis shorts. He didn't have the legs for them.

'She was moaning about having to stay in Liverpool. Never done bloody moaning. She had no interest in why I'm here, didn't care about business. As long as she had cash to spend, Yana didn't care about anything. She couldn't wait to get back to her lover boy.'

'Did you kill your wife, Mr Logan-Sharp?'

His eyes bulged as he spat his reply.

'Of course I didn't bloody kill her!'

Tara allowed her question to sink in. Being regarded as a suspect would give him something else to think about. She moved on when Sebastian had finished his rant.

'I will need a list of people who were present last night, and of those who reside here. That includes your guests, catering staff and contact details for your wife's lover boy, as you describe him.'

'Beatrice will get that for you. Do you really think someone who came to the party killed her?'

For the first time, Tara detected a concerned tone.

'We must consider the possibility. It's likely to have been either a party guest or someone who is staying at the property, unless we find evidence that there was an intruder.'

'You mean somebody who works for me could have killed her?' He sounded astonished at the thought.

'We will need as much information on your household as you can provide, Mr Logan-Sharp.'

'The press is going to have a field day. How long will this take? I have a major business deal to close. Bizzies crawling all over the place is not going to help.'

Tara ignored his question and his protestations. She had a question to ask that had bugged her since she'd first learnt that Yana Logan-Sharp had been murdered.

'Do you believe that the deaths of your wife and Tommy Brady are mere coincidence?'

CHAPTER 31

Beatrice Howard

Her nausea had not abated. Initially, she'd blamed it on the shock of seeing Yana lying dead. Those wonderful eyes of hers now lifeless and staring to space. They were in the middle of a heatwave and yet Beatrice felt gooseflesh on her arms. From the kitchen, she could see Sebastian looking thoroughly fed up as that young detective bombarded him with questions. How much did he know about what happened? He certainly looked shocked when she'd called him to Yana's bedroom, but that didn't mean he hadn't killed her. He would probably say she deserved it. A thorn in his side; he wouldn't disagree with that. And yet Beatrice detected a rare display of vulnerability in the man.

There were times when she wondered whether if he hadn't made so much money, perhaps he would be a more likeable person. Perhaps not.

Beatrice had thought she could handle the questions asked by the police. She'd described to Detective Sergeant Wilson the recent timeline of events, excluding, of course, her nasty exchange of words with Sebastian, her sleeping with the bodyguard and snorting coke. She expected that DI Grogan would ask her to repeat her story. The diligent cop, however, was taking her time with Sebastian. Beatrice wondered what he was telling her. For the sake of this deal, they needed to be careful. If the media got hold of the wrong message, it could scupper their plans. But thinking about it, she realised that she no longer cared about the deal.

While she waited for DI Grogan, she opened her laptop on the dining table and retrieved the file containing a list of guests who had attended the party. Detective Sergeant Wilson informed her, however, that they would require the names of everyone who'd been in the house the night before, not only guests but staff from the catering company. As she worked at the computer, she kept an eye on the discussion between Sebastian and DI Grogan. What the hell were they talking about for so long? The waiting was making her edgy. She could do with a snort of coke.

'Ms Howard, sorry to keep you waiting,' DI Grogan said eventually, to Beatrice's relief.

Despite having been ready and waiting, the detective's approach still caught her off guard.

'Call me Beatrice, Inspector.'

'Thank you, Beatrice.' Tara sat down at the table. 'If you wouldn't mind running through what happened this morning. I believe it was you who found Yana.'

Beatrice cleared her throat. 'Yes, of course. I went to her room at about seven-thirty to check if everything was all right.'

'Was that usual for you?'

'No, not at all. Yana was supposed to be going out with Sebastian this morning. There was to be a PR visit to some of the proposed development sites in the city. Sebastian wanted her to attend. We were running late, and we'd heard nothing from Yana. I just went to check if she was ready to go.'

'Do you believe that she was dead when you found her?'

'Yes. I knocked on her door at first. When I got no reply, I went in and found her on the bed. I called for a doctor straightaway.'

'Did you touch anything inside the room?'

'I'm so sorry, I realise now that I shouldn't have done it, but there was something like a wooden skewer, poking from Yana's stomach. I just panicked and pulled it out.'

'You really shouldn't have done that; it is vital forensic evidence. But thank you for telling me. When did you last see Yana?'

'It would have been during the party.'

'When exactly?'

'I don't recall the time; it was a busy night for me.'

'OK, what was Yana doing when you last saw her?'

'She was sitting on the patio talking with Sebastian. Then I called him away to meet some guests. I don't remember seeing her after that.'

'How did she seem then?'

'I think she'd been drinking quite a bit. She and Sebastian were exchanging words. I got the impression that it wasn't a friendly chat.'

'Did you often see them arguing?'

Beatrice couldn't help a wry grin.

'Par for the course, Inspector. It was a stormy marriage. There was nothing unusual about their tiff last night.'

'Did you notice anything strange during or after the party, an intruder perhaps?'

'Nothing, Inspector. It was a busy evening, lots of people moving around the house.'

'Did you hear a disturbance of any kind?'

'Nothing out of the ordinary. I was up late, well after the guests had left. I had a snack in the kitchen and then went to bed.'

'Did you notice what time Yana went to her bedroom?'

'I'm afraid not, but come to think of it, I didn't notice her as the party drew to a close.'

'Was anyone else moving around the house when you were going to bed?'

'Ernst was outside checking the gates were closed. Oh, and I saw Shelby on the landing.'

'Shelby?'

'Surrey's nanny.'

'What was she doing on the landing?'

'Can't be sure, Inspector, we just bid each other goodnight. Perhaps you should ask her.'

CHAPTER 32

Shelby Keibler

While the police were speaking to Sebastian and Beatrice, Shelby had taken over a vacant bedroom in the spare house for Surrey. There was no way the little girl could be anywhere near the room where her mother had died. Not that she was asking after her. Surrey had been well used to going for several days without contact with Yana.

Shelby had laid out a plastic sheet on the floor, and the pair of them were getting messy with paints and crayons, colouring in pictures of cartoon characters. Surrey had remained settled throughout the morning, seemingly content with Shelby's company and not pestering her with questions. Shelby thought that when the police had finished, she would ask Gavin to drive them to a park and maybe get some ice cream to pass the time. It might help her get through the day.

She was anxious that no one had updated her with news. She knew it was too much to expect of Sebastian, but she'd hoped that Beatrice would have come with a message. Maybe Sebastian needed her. Perhaps he could do with some comfort after the death of his despicable wife. Maybe now, with Yana dead, her job of looking after Surrey was secure. Sebastian could depend on her. And maybe she could still get pregnant, and she and Sebastian would have a child of their own.

As the morning dragged into afternoon, she thought that she'd been forgotten. Then she heard voices on the landing outside the room. She rose from their painting and went to the door. When she opened it, she was faced by a woman with short blonde hair smiling politely.

'Shelby?'

'That's me.'

'I'm DI Grogan, Merseyside Police. Would you mind stepping into the landing and closing the door. It's better that Surrey doesn't hear our conversation.'

Shelby glanced behind her, but the child was engrossed in her painting and didn't look up.

'Yeah, sure,' she replied, suddenly feeling nerves rise in her stomach as she eased the door closed behind her.

'I'm sure you're aware that we're investigating the death of Yana Logan-Sharp. I'd like to ask you some questions. Can you leave Surrey alone for a few minutes or shall I fetch one of my officers to look after her?'

'No, she'll be fine for a while.'

The detective led the way downstairs into a deserted lounge.

'Please take a seat, Shelby,' said DI Grogan. 'I'll try not to keep you for too long.'

112

Shelby felt on edge, wondering exactly what the police were going to ask. But this detective seemed nice, and she began with an easy question.

'Am I right in thinking that you're from the United States?'

'Yes, Michigan.'

'And how long have you worked for the Logan-Sharps?'

'Around fifteen months.'

'Do you enjoy your work?'

'Sure. Surrey is a good kid. We get on well.'

'And how's your relationship with her parents?'

Shelby's hesitation was palpable. She felt her face warm as the cop waited for an answer.

'Em–'

'Our conversation is confidential. I won't be telling Sebastian what you say.'

Shelby nodded her understanding but still did not answer the question.

'I just want to know if the Logan-Sharps are good people to work for,' said Tara.

'Yana is never, I mean *was* never around much. I mean I travelled everywhere with Surrey and her, but she didn't spend much time with her daughter.'

'What did you think of that?'

'I suppose that's why I'm here.'

'How did you and Yana get on?'

'Not well. I don't think she liked me very much.'

'But she was happy with how you look after Surrey?'

'I suppose so.'

'What about Sebastian? How is your relationship with him?'

Shelby knew she was burning up and realised the cop could see it. Her throat was dry; she needed a drink of water. And this cop was smiling at her, waiting. How the hell did she answer her damn question? Did she admit to sleeping with Sebastian? That she was trying to get pregnant so she could stay with him? That she craved his rich lifestyle.

'We get on fine, I think.'

The cop just stared at her. Shelby guessed that she didn't believe a word.

'Let's talk about last night,' said DI Grogan.

'Last night?' She didn't mean to sound alarmed. This was not going well.

'Yes. When did you last see Yana?'

She couldn't tell this cop the truth. That for the second time in a week, Yana had watched her from across the landing coming out of Sebastian's room after she'd just had sex with her husband.

'I saw her going downstairs to the party.'

'What time was that?'

'About seven-thirty. I was staying with Surrey in her room while the party was going on.'

'And you never saw Yana after that?'

Shelby shook her head.

'Did you notice or hear anything strange later on?'

Again, she shook her head. 'Maybe you should ask Beatrice,' she added.

'Why is that?'

'Her room is next to Yana's.'

'Beatrice told me that she saw you on the landing when she was going to bed. It was very late, what were you doing?'

Shelby didn't think her face could get any hotter. She felt on the verge of tears, but she must hold it together.

'I was using the bathroom.'

'I thought all the bedrooms had an en suite?'

'Sure, but I used the bathroom on the landing because I was on my way back from checking on Surrey.'

'Was she unsettled?'

'No, she was fine. I would usually check on her once during the night.'

'And you didn't notice anything strange while you were doing that?'

'No, mam.'

CHAPTER 33

Carla Smith

Each morning, Carla's colleague and best friend Diane had the radio playing from the moment she opened the salon. Usually, it was Radio City or BBC Radio Merseyside. The music perked them up for tending to the first customers of the day, but this morning Carla quickly zoned out and paid scant attention to the live chat and the latest pop songs. By early afternoon, however, as she neared the end of pensioner Mrs Redman's shampoo and set, Carla caught the tail end of the local news.

'What was that about?' she called to Diane, who was waving a hairdryer around her client's head.

'What's that?'

'On the radio. The name Yana Logan-Sharp was mentioned.'

Diane shook her head dismissively. She hadn't heard and showed no interest. Carla lifted her phone and opened the *Liverpool Echo* news app. She could scarcely believe what she was reading and wondered how she'd missed hearing of it until now. Her mind switched immediately to thoughts of the night before. She and her boys had left the big house hating Bobby Smith even more than they'd ever thought possible. A man she had once loved and adored had cut them down merely for them showing up at his house.

'We were invited, Bobby,' she had struggled to explain.

'Well, it wasn't me who invited you, sweetheart.'

The whole time he hardly took notice of his two sons. They were the innocents in this debacle. Raised solely by Carla, they had never met their father and now were faced with his rudeness and hostility. As her quarrel with Bobby escalated, she had glanced at Jack and Lee. Both had expressions of incredulity as they witnessed this man hurling abuse at their mother.

'I thought it was time you at least met your sons,' she had tried. 'They've done you no harm. You should be proud of them.'

Bobby had scoffed as if she'd just commented on the clothes he wore. But she had noticed that he'd been unable to look his sons in the eye. It was then she knew that she had succeeded. She'd pricked what little conscience he possessed, yet still his billionaire pride suppressed good sense.

'I don't need any of you in my life,' he'd said. 'Especially when you show up here with your begging bowl looking for me to pay for uni fees. So, don't waste my time or yours. Get out now before you lower the tone of my party.'

Jack stepped forward, squaring up to his father. He was slightly taller, although there was little meat on his bones. Their faces were almost touching.

'Don't, Jack,' Carla said, tears streaming down her face.

Lee then stepped beside his brother.

'You're a fucking arsehole!' Jack said, his words delivering spittle to the smirk on his father's face.

Bobby hit back. 'Is that the best you can do, sunshine?'

Jack grabbed him by the throat.

'I wouldn't want to know a man like you as my dad. And I don't want your frigging money.'

Bobby attempted to reply, but his words were stalled in his throat by his enraged son.

'Let him go, Jack!' Carla cried.

A man she didn't know, another party guest, attempted to intervene. 'Come on, lads, break it up.'

Lee pushed him away. 'None of your business, mate.'

Carla pulled at Jack's arm, urging him to release his father. She saw Bobby's face growing red as he struggled to breathe.

'Jack! Let him go! You're choking him!'

'Frigging kill him if he talks to you like that again,' Jack had said.

Jack eventually released his father, swiftly put his hands on the man's chest and shoved him away. Bobby stumbled backwards and was only prevented from falling by the guest who had tried to stop the fight. Jack and Lee stood with clenched fists, ready if Bobby should retaliate. Several guests gathered around their host, but Bobby pushed his way through to confront his estranged family once again. But his rage subsided, it was as if he remembered he had other guests, people who were more important to him than his ex-wife and twin sons.

'Time for you to leave, I think,' he said stretching his neck and straightening his jacket.

Jack and Lee seemed to consider the instruction for a moment, staring coldly at their father. Carla stepped between them.

'Come on, boys, let's go.'

She tugged at Jack's arm, and thankfully her sons did as she asked. On their way from the lounge, most eyes were staring at them. The PA stood by the door, an angry look on her face. Carla met her gaze, and the woman mouthed an apology. It meant nothing. She could be grateful for Beatrice's attempts to stage a reconciliation between a father and his sons, but it had failed disastrously, and they were leaving with greater disappointment in their hearts.

When they reached the front door, Carla glanced around in time to see Yana struggling to remain upright as she left the kitchen, a champagne bottle in one hand and with the other lifting her dress to avoid a trip on high heels.

Now the woman was dead. Karma? For whom, she thought. She cared less. Sympathy was not a word she could place next to Sebastian bloody Logan-Sharp.

CHAPTER 34

Tara Grogan

St Anne Street station was besieged by a posse of photographers and reporters awaiting developments in the investigation of the death of the billionaire's wife. The story had gone viral on media platforms over the course of the day. Only in late afternoon, however, was it confirmed publicly that the death was suspicious and that police had launched a murder inquiry. Tara, Wilson, Murray and Bleasdale had difficulty in getting beyond the horde of press and television crews blocking the station entrance. Bleasdale resorted to the car's siren to clear a path, allowing them to drive through.

Once inside their operations room, Tweedy informed them that a brief public statement was to be made in an attempt to fend off over-speculative reporting and rumour-mongering on social media. Already suggestions were being shared on who might be responsible for the murder. There were no prizes for guessing that the billionaire husband was suspect number one.

Following the reading of the statement, thankfully handled by Tweedy, they gathered in his office to discuss progress and plans for a way ahead.

'OK, who's first?' Tweedy stood by his flip chart ready to make notes.

Murray presented a brief profile of the victim.

'Yana Logan-Sharp was twenty-eight years old. Formerly known as model Yana Bartos, a Hungarian national. Her main residences were–'

There was a ripple of oohs as the others imagined the lifestyle of a former supermodel who became a billionaire's wife.

'Her main residences,' Murray continued, 'were South Kensington, Weybridge, Monaco and Las Vegas. She had been residing in West Derby, Liverpool with her husband Sebastian and daughter Surrey. Her husband alleges that she had, or was still having, an affair with a Saudi prince. He is not currently in this country, so that probably rules him out as our perpetrator.'

Wilson took over from Murray.

'Initial word from Dr Witney is that she died by suffocation, most likely caused by foul play. The people staying at the two houses within the residence were the Logan-Sharps, the nanny, Sebastian's PA, a bodyguard, driver, and a chef. Other catering and cleaning staff come and go as required.'

'Thank you, John,' said Tweedy. 'Any suspicions arising from those people you have mentioned?'

'That's where it might be rather difficult, sir,' said Tara. 'How so?'

'In addition to those staying at the address, a party was held there last night.' Tara read from some printouts given to her by Beatrice Howard. 'Sixty-three guests attended the party plus twelve catering and bar staff.'

'That presents us with a huge problem,' said Tweedy.

'We have contact details for each guest,' said Tara, 'and we will be in touch shortly with both the catering and cleaning companies for details of staff who were working at the house.'

Tweedy grimaced. Tara guessed that all the detectives were having the same thought. That if they could not readily find evidence to strongly suspect any of the residents at the address, they would have an onerous task working through the people associated with the party. But Tara proposed one way ahead.

'Can I remind everyone that we are also investigating the murder of Tommy Brady? However tenuously, his death is connected to Sebastian Logan-Sharp. We still do not have a satisfactory explanation as to why Sebastian's mobile phone was found in Brady's house. I would like to pursue that issue and ask more questions of Sebastian and his staff.'

'That's fine, Tara,' said Tweedy. 'Please try to keep a lid on your lines of enquiry, though. The press and social media will make mincemeat of our case if we let them. Is that us finished for now?'

Wilson had something to add.

'Sir, as we all know, we spent the afternoon interviewing members of the Logan-Sharp household, but two people were difficult to pin down.'

Tweedy looked quizzically at everyone, as if they had missed something.

'The bodyguard fella.' Wilson checked his notebook. 'Ernst Eder. He was supposed to be around the house but none of us managed to have a chat with him. Maybe we all thought someone else was taking care of it and he's slipped through. Then there is the driver. I tried to get him on two occasions. Both times he was sitting in the car outside the house. When I asked him for a quick word, he told me he had urgent business for Mr Logan-Sharp, and he drove off.'

'That vehicle should have been secured by us to preserve potential evidence,' Tweedy stated.

'No one except the driver left the place,' Wilson continued. 'So, why did he say he had urgent business? He's just their driver and all the family were at home.'

'Maybe he was sent to get the fish and chips?' Murray quipped.

'Logan-Sharp has a personal chef,' Wilson hit back.

'I managed to speak with him,' said Bleasdale. 'His name is Patrice Allard. He's French and has two Michelin stars.'

This was greeted by another round of oohs. Bleasdale smiled but continued.

'Speaks good English. He told me he was much too busy to have noticed anything untoward during the party. When he'd finished for the evening, he went directly to his room to play his saxophone and then to get some much-needed sleep.'

'We'll try to speak with the bodyguard and driver tomorrow, John,' said Tara. 'And *you* can be *my* driver.'

They all laughed.

Returning to her desk, Tara found a report in her in-tray regarding the online data retrieved from Sebastian Logan-Sharp's mobile phone that was found at the home of Tommy Brady. When she'd read it, she realised the matter could not wait until the following day.

CHAPTER 35

Beatrice Howard

'Did you kill her, Sebastian?'

'No, I didn't bloody kill her. What the hell's the matter with you, talking to me like that? I'm still your boss, you know.'

'I had to ask,' said Beatrice. 'You did have a blazing row the other night.'

The pair of them were seated on a sofa in the lounge of the spare house waiting for the police and forensics operation to be completed. They'd already lost a day of useful work. Sebastian was drinking whisky, and Beatrice was buoyed by a snort of coke twenty minutes earlier.

'Having a row didn't mean I wanted to kill her. Besides, she'd tried to play the divorce card once too often. I just called her bluff. Reminded her that she gets very little when we split. The silly girl would never have left me. So why would I kill her? Doesn't even make good business sense, does it?'

'Seems like you had it all figured out,' she said, getting to her feet.

'I didn't kill her, Beatrice.'

'So you keep saying.'

He stared coldly at her for a second then changed the subject. 'How is this going to affect us? Will it kill the project?'

Beatrice continued glaring at him.

'Well?' he said.

'Might be that Yana's murder will buy you sympathy from Joe Public. Then again, judging by what's being said on social media, you're getting the blame for it. Those who are already on board with us will hopefully stick with it. Those who haven't signed up have another good reason for walking away.'

'What's that supposed to mean?' he snapped at her.

'You asked me how I see it, Sebastian.'

'OK, OK, go on.'

'Well, for starters, you pissed off the Boals last night by upping the price of their participation. You still haven't told me why you did that.'

'There are some things, darling Beatrice, that you don't have to know.'

She gave him a dismissive shrug. 'You're still an asshole, Sebastian.'

'Fuck you. Where is Ernst? I haven't seen him all day.'

'How would I know?'

Beatrice looked up to see Patrice standing over them.

'Sebastian, the police want to speak with you, sir,' he said.

Beatrice thought Patrice had a rather smug look on his face as if he was enjoying all the excitement the last twenty-four hours had brought.

'Again?'

'Shall I bring them in here, sir?'

Sebastian sighed with exasperation and reached for the bottle of twenty-five-year-old single malt on the coffee table.

'May as well. They're not going away on their own.'

CHAPTER 36

Tara Grogan

'Not this again,' Sebastian groaned.

Tara was not intimidated by the man's mordant attitude. Even at this early stage of her investigation into his wife's murder she had enough evidence to arrest him as the prime suspect. The couple had been seen arguing and it was known that their marriage was in trouble. But she realised the press would just love to see the billionaire arrested and in the long run, the publicity might be counter-productive to her investigation. It could wait until they had him all signed, sealed and delivered. With his huge development plans for Liverpool ongoing, she didn't imagine that he was a flight risk.

'On our two previous meetings you have not been forthcoming about your relationship with Tommy Brady. I now have proof that you and Brady had been in contact more recently than you suggested.'

'So? What's that got to do with my wife's death?'

Tara remained standing. She wasn't tall, and looking down on a suspect slouched on his sofa, she felt, gave her a slight advantage.

'Two WhatsApp calls were made from your device to another found in Brady's home. Would you care to explain that?'

'Just catching up with an old friend, that's all.'

'Why was your mobile found there?'

'I've already told you. I don't know. I lost the damn thing.'

'Did you visit Tommy Brady?'

Sebastian drained his glass and took a deep breath. Observing his discomfort, Tara found it hard to believe that this man was filthy rich. Surely, it wouldn't be long before he screamed for his solicitor.

'Yes, OK. You got me! I called to see Tommy.'

'When exactly?'

'I can't remember. I'll have to check with Beatrice; she's in the kitchen.'

'We can do that for you,' said Tara. She nodded to Murray who strolled off to find the PA.

'Why did you go to Mr Brady's home?' she asked.

'I've told you. He was an old friend. I was just catching up with him since I was back in Liverpool.'

'My understanding is that when you moved away from Liverpool, you and Brady did not part on friendly terms.'

'I don't know where you got your information, love. Tommy and I were the best of pals. We just went our separate ways, that's all. Just business.'

Tara watched as he reached for a whisky bottle on the table, but it was empty. He sat back again, but his eyes were looking to the door. She was surprised at how quickly she'd grown accustomed to his ill manners. It was late and she didn't wish to be there either. Her best friend dinner waiting for her at home. Murray had a wife to get home to.

'What did you talk about?'

'I can't remember, love. Why does that matter?'

'It's Detective Inspector, Mr Logan-Sharp. Try to remember that. Now please answer my question.'

He scoffed at her rebuke and got to his feet, standing uncomfortably close to her. He was several inches taller but if he was trying to intimidate her, it hadn't worked. She held the advantage. She matched his gaze and waited for his reply. He looked to be a man under strain and perhaps his wife's murder was not the sole cause of it.

'It was like I said, *Detective Inspector*, we were just catching up. Hadn't seen each other for years.'

Their exchange was interrupted by Murray's return to the lounge, but he stopped several feet away.

'Can I have a word, ma'am?'

Tara stepped out of earshot from Sebastian to speak with her DS.

'According to the PA, ma'am, Logan-Sharp visited Brady's house on Sunday, 19 May.'

'That was the day Brady was killed,' Tara whispered. Her eyes were fixed on the billionaire who had resumed his seat and was browsing on his phone.

'Yes, ma'am. He called at the house around four in the afternoon and stayed for twenty minutes.'

'Did he go alone?'

'Logan-Sharp, his driver, and his bodyguard were there.'

'Yes, those two. Go and have a word. Wilson has been trying to catch up with them.'

'Yes, ma'am.'

Tara stared at Logan-Sharp. She must decide what to do next. He still had much to explain.

'OK, Mr Logan-Sharp, let's talk again about your wife.'

'Don't you people ever quit for the night? I need another drink. It's been a hell of a day.'

He stormed off, leaving Tara to either wait for his return or to follow. She entered the kitchen in time to see Beatrice exchanging a conspiratorial glance with her boss.

When she saw Tara, she quickly got to her feet and carried her plate and coffee mug from the kitchen. Outside, the chef Patrice Allard, a tall rake of a man with a bony face and silver hair, paced around the patio having been asked to pause his dinner preparations during this latest police visit.

Instead of more whisky, Sebastian had settled for a bottle of lager from the fridge. He took a long drink as Tara waited. She recognised stalling, was well used to it, but always countered it with apparent patience. At times, her attitude unnerved the person she was interviewing even further and very soon they were inclined to end their silence. It was indeed a calmer Sebastian who next spoke.

'What else do you want to know, Detective Inspector?'

'Tell me more about your argument with Yana during the party.'

'Personal stuff.'

'It would help if you could be more specific in answering my questions. I will keep returning to the subject if I don't get your full co-operation.'

'Are you married, Inspector?'

'No.'

'Ever been married?'

'No.'

Sebastian scoffed. 'Then you wouldn't understand. It was husband and wife stuff.'

'As I've already said, please be specific. Were you having marital problems. I gather that you had separate bedrooms here. Was that normal?'

'We were headed for a divorce, is that specific enough? I had told her exactly how much she would get when we parted. She didn't like it much. So, you see, Detective Inspector, we were splitting up. I had no reason to kill my wife if that's what you're hinting at.'

'Can you think of anyone who would wish to harm Yana?'

He took another drink of beer and appeared amused by the answer he was about to give.

'No. Unless someone was trying to get at me. It seems that everybody hates me.'

Tara was not inclined to contradict the billionaire. A rich man and self-pity were an intriguing combination. For now, she decided she had enough to arrest him on suspicion of murdering Tommy Brady. A spell in custody might loosen his tongue, although she was aware of the furore his arrest would create. Tweedy had advised that she tread carefully. An early arrest of the billionaire would create uproar and that would not be helpful. She decided to hold off.

CHAPTER 37

Michelle Weller

They were unsure whether Sebastian Logan-Sharp would make an appearance. Perhaps even a loathsome billionaire was inclined to mourn the death of his wife. His murdered wife. The protests over the proposed development on Merseyside and the opposition to a football club buyout still seemed valid without his presence. But for Michelle and her companions in the Women Bite Back campaign, their protest would have less impact if their target was absent. It didn't help that after nearly two weeks of sunshine the weather had finally broken, and they'd been doused by several showers since their arrival. They stood near the entrance to an adventure play centre on Otterspool Drive. On the far side of the road, parkland and a promenade skirted the Mersey shoreline.

This was the proposed site for a complex of apartments and leisure facilities, merely a portion of the vast Merseyside Delta Development project. This morning's gathering of the interested parties in the scheme – city councillors, developers, investors and indeed various protest groups – was to be the first public presentation of the colossal plans. In the coming days several other proposed sites would host similar events. But doubts had been aired in the media since the murder of Yana Logan-Sharp. Michelle had a morning paper in her bag. The headline read, 'What happens now?' Would the death of the billionaire's wife scupper the plans, or would there merely be a pause in proceedings while the murder was investigated?

Michelle and a dozen companions in the Women Bite Back campaign had nabbed what they hoped was the best spot to have their protest noticed by dignitaries entering the centre. On the opposite side of the road, outside the double gates to the centre, she noticed Paul Renfrew and his environmentalist buddies. Their gaze had met once, and he had smiled. She didn't respond but continued staring at the man until his attention was drawn to something else. For Michelle, it seemed that they didn't share the same objectives. Since that party in West Derby and the night they'd spent in her bed, she wondered what Paul really thought of her. Was he interested in a relationship, or was he just another man who would use and abuse her?

She didn't think that Sebastian Logan-Sharp could sink any lower in her regard of him. But when a black Range Rover sped through the open gates, past the gathering of women's rights, environmental and football protestors, and shed its passengers including Sebastian by the door of the play centre, Michelle realised that the man had no soul, never mind a heart. She had no sympathy for his slut of a wife who was now dead, but surely her husband would at least show some respect following her passing. It seemed not.

She jeered with the others as Sebastian paused by the entrance of the building to greet members of the city council. His fancy PA in her fancy business suit and high heels stood by his side.

'Murderer!' Michelle screamed.

Her mates quickly joined in, and in seconds there was a concerted chant by all protestors.

'Murderer!'

Michelle realised that if Sebastian hadn't heard her solitary call, he sure as hell heard the chants of a hundred people. It made her presence worthwhile.

When the cheering subsided and all attendees at the project launch had arrived, Michelle gazed across the road again at the environmental protestors. Subconsciously, she was searching for Paul. But his eyes were already upon her. He didn't look happy.

CHAPTER 38

Tara Grogan

It seemed that Tara could gain better insight into Sebastian Logan-Sharp from the media than she could from her own investigation. The newspapers had already decided that he was responsible for his wife's death. The tabloids cited examples of the couple's stormy relationship. There were old pictures of Sebastian out on the town in the presence of beautiful women and beach snaps of a topless Yana in Marbella, Antigua, and one of her entering a Paris restaurant in the company of a Saudi prince. The most popular suggestion was that the marriage problems had come to a head on Merseyside. But no one was blaming Liverpool.

Kate had bought two morning papers on her way back from the school run. Tara borrowed *The Echo* while Kate showered. Thankfully, so far, no one in the media had linked the murder of Tommy Brady with Sebastian Logan-Sharp. The Brady murder hadn't featured highly in the news, so until a wily journalist did some digging into Sebastian's early life, the connection would go unnoticed. At least that bought her time to pursue the matter before the public cried out for the head of the billionaire. Innocent until proven guilty did not sell newspapers. Taking down an insolent billionaire was much more lucrative. Tara was relieved also that the press had not identified the detectives engaged in the investigation. She dreaded a horde of photographers outside her recently acquired home in Hoylake all vying for the best picture of the lead detective. Hoylake was supposed to be her haven, her retreat from the horrors of police work. But Tweedy had warned them that they would soon be cast in the full glare of the media spotlight. It was vital that their thinking and their investigation was not dictated by unfounded speculation.

With that in mind, she abandoned her reading of the paper, tidied the breakfast things away, and made some toast and fresh coffee for Kate.

She called to her friend from the hall. 'I've left breakfast for you. See you later.'

'Bye, Tara love. Take care.'

She always said that to her. Friends from schooldays, Kate had always worried about Tara doing the job she did. And it wasn't a baseless fear. On several occasions, Tara had narrowly escaped death or serious injury.

With Tweedy's warning in mind, perhaps, Tara peered from the hall window checking there was not a gang of photographers waiting to pounce. But her normally quiet road was deserted.

* * *

At St Anne Street station there were a couple of reporters and a photographer loitering by the entrance. Tara wondered if something had happened since she'd last checked the news during breakfast.

In the detectives' operations room on the first floor, she scarcely had the chance to place her bag beneath her desk and log in to her workstation when Wilson called out that Tweedy had summoned them.

Murray, Wilson, Bleasdale and Tara filed into the super's office and sat down. Tara expected news of fresh developments, but Tweedy merely requested an update from his team. Wilson kicked off proceedings.

'Sir, we've now collated a full list of contact details for everyone we believe attended or worked at the party in West Derby.'

Tara interjected. 'Sir, we will need extra bodies to conduct interviews with everyone on that list.'

'I'll request some uniforms to help,' said Tweedy. 'It might be wise, though, to prioritise the names.'

'Already on it,' Wilson replied. 'Guests, then staff from the catering and cleaning companies.'

'Tara, I gather you spoke to Mr Logan-Sharp last night?' said Tweedy.

'Yes, sir. Logan-Sharp admitted that he had visited Tommy Brady at his home on the day he died. It most likely explains the reason why his phone was found at the scene. I believe it gives us good reason to bring him into the station for interview under caution. Since this is such a high-profile case, sir, I didn't want to act without your permission.'

'Did Logan-Sharp explain why he had visited Brady?' Tweedy asked.

'He claims that he was merely catching up with an old friend. He visited Brady late afternoon. According to the post-mortem report, Brady died between eight and ten o'clock on Sunday night.'

'Is there anyone to corroborate Logan-Sharp's story?'

'His driver and his bodyguard.'

'And what did they tell you?'

Tara hesitated.

Murray cut in. 'The driver is still a bit shy, sir. So far, he's managed to avoid us. When we called last night, he was nowhere to be seen.'

'Do we have a name for this person? Can we run a background check?' asked Tweedy.

'Gavin,' said Wilson. 'That's all we have. Gavin the driver, sir.'

It might have raised a titter among the detectives, but it seemed that everyone realised it was a shortcoming in the investigation.

'The bodyguard Ernst Eder is proving to be just as elusive,' said Murray.

'You must get that sorted out, Tara,' said Tweedy.

Tara flushed. It was a silly oversight. The driver and bodyguard might be crucial to both murders.

'If that's everything—' Tweedy said, but Wilson interrupted.

'One more thing, sir. I've been going through statements again taken during the house-to-house enquiries at the Brady crime scene. It was something we missed first time round.'

'Yes?' said Tweedy.

'Just further confirmation that Logan-Sharp visited Brady on that Sunday. A neighbour had by chance photographed a black vehicle parked outside Brady's house. The registration matches a vehicle leased by L-SOS, one of Logan-Sharp's companies.'

'OK, John, good work,' said Tweedy.

'Do I have your permission to bring Logan-Sharp here for interview, sir?' Tara asked.

'I think you should tie up some of your loose ends first,' Tweedy said. 'The driver and bodyguard issue, your background checks on Logan-Sharp and the others in his household. We can see what comes out of the post-mortem for Yana. Perhaps we can manage to do those things and remain under the press radar. We don't want to create problems for the investigation by hanging Logan-Sharp out for all to see.'

'Yes, sir.'

Tara left the office feeling despondent. Having met Sebastian Logan-Sharp on three occasions, and despite his rudeness and that he was worth billions, she thought him quite easily rattled. He would be easy to unpick; approach him in the right manner and he might say more than was good for him. She could be getting under the man's skin while her team went about the interviews with people who had attended the party.

She called Bleasdale to her desk.

'Paula, where is Sebastian Logan-Sharp this morning?'

'He's supposed to be at an adventure play centre on Otterspool Drive,' said Bleasdale. 'This afternoon he's due in Birkenhead.'

'That's all I need, thank you.'

She jumped up with aplomb and called to Murray.

'Alan! Let's go speak to Gavin the driver.'

CHAPTER 39

Tara Grogan

Hoping to avoid the attention of journalists who might be following Logan-Sharp's schedule, Tara signed out an unmarked vehicle from the station's carpool. Murray drove them quickly to Otterspool Drive where they soon encountered a crowd of around one hundred people protesting against Sebastian and his entrepreneurial intentions. It proved to be a waste of time travelling in the unmarked car because Murray was forced to use the blue flashing lights to inform the crowd that they required access to the grounds of the play centre. Now everyone could see the bizzies arriving. Eventually, the protestors blocking the entrance made way but not without a barrage of jeers as they began to suspect that something was afoot. There were already uniformed police by the gates, although none of the officers seemed interested in the protestors' movements. They merely watched as Murray drove into the grounds and pulled up beside several SUVs. A cluster of photographers loitered at the entrance to the building.

As she got out of the car, Tara heard the shouts their arrival had rekindled in the crowd forty yards away. She and Murray approached the vehicle parked nearest the building's entrance, a black Range Rover with two men inside. Her sudden appearance by the driver's door seemed to have startled them. Holding up her ID, she smiled broadly and indicated that the driver should lower his window. Murray did the same at the passenger side with the driver's companion.

The man eventually decided it was wise to comply with Tara's request. He had a pleasant face, was well-groomed, and he stared at Tara through lively blue eyes.

'Your name, please?'

'Gavin.'

She raised her eyebrows when nothing else was offered.

'Do you have a surname, Gavin?' she asked.

'Westport.'

'Would you mind stepping from the vehicle please, Mr Westport?'

'Is this necessary?'

'I think so,' she replied.

Tara heard a similar scenario playing out with her colleague. It seemed Murray had encountered Logan-Sharp's bodyguard Ernst Eder.

Gavin Westport stepped from the car and, dressed in a neat grey suit and striped tie, he loomed over Tara. She could smell his pleasant aftershave and noticed he was chewing gum. He smiled bemusedly through thin, purplish lips. There was a question in his challenging expression as if asking her 'what are you going to do now, Inspector?'

'May I see some means of identification, please?' she asked him.

He looked incredulous, shrugged then eventually retrieved a wallet from his inside jacket pocket. He opened it to reveal a driving license behind a plastic window. Tara read the card. It confirmed the name Gavin Westport and below it was an address in West London.

'Thank you,' she said. 'I believe you are a driver for Sebastian Logan-Sharp?'

'Correct.'

'Why have you been avoiding my officers during our visits to your employer's home?'

Westport grinned and stared into her eyes. She felt the need to step back from this man. His behaviour was strange. He hadn't protested, hadn't offered chat and had done everything she'd asked so far. He did not, however, respond to her comment about him being elusive.

'On 19 May, did you drive Mr Logan-Sharp to a house in Bootle, the home of a man named Tommy Brady?'

'I may have. Can't remember.'

'Let's assume for now that you did. Was there anyone else with you besides Mr Logan-Sharp?'

'Might have been. Can't remember.'

'Did you enter Mr Brady's home along with your boss?'

'Might have done. Can't remember.'

'On the night Yana Logan-Sharp died, where were you, Mr Westport?'

'Can't remember.'

She didn't appreciate his smugness. Why be so cagey?

'Perhaps, Mr Westport, you should come down to St Anne Street station. A police interview room can work wonders for the memory.'

'Are you arresting me, DI Grogan?'

He was good. He'd remembered her name from glimpsing her warrant card through the car window.

'I can do, if necessary.'

'On what charge?'

'How about obstructing a police officer in the performance of their duty? Just to start with.'

It was timely that Murray appeared to have finished his conversation with Gavin's companion. The man was already back inside the SUV. Tara beckoned her DS.

'Would you mind escorting Mr Westport to our car, DS Murray. He fancies meeting the gang at St Anne Street.'

She thought he might break into laughter at her quip, but as Murray led him away, she noticed him gazing towards the gates and the melee of protestors intrigued by what was unfolding. The other man looked concerned as Gavin was placed in the police car. Tara decided to have a quick word. Maybe this guy would be more forthcoming. She approached the open door on the passenger side.

'What are you doing with our driver?' the man asked.

'Your name, please?' Tara asked him. She prayed she wasn't about to go through the same rigmarole she'd endured with Gavin Westport.

'Ernst Eder. I have spoken already to your boss.' The man gestured towards Murray.

Tara grinned. Misogyny was alive and well.

'That is DS Murray. I am Detective Inspector Grogan.' The significance of her correction didn't seem to register with Eder. 'What exactly do you do in your work for Mr Logan-Sharp?'

The man shrugged derisively. 'I manage security.'

'So, during the party the other night at Sebastian's home, were you managing security?'

'Yes, yes. I take care of everything.'

Tara examined his gaze. Maybe something could be lost in translation, even in facial expressions. He seemed quite content at the answers he was giving.

'Did you manage security for Yana also?'

Now his face turned surly. She wondered if his ability to speak English would suddenly desert him.

'I do not understand.'

'Well, presumably if you were in charge of Yana's security, you can tell me how someone got into her bedroom and smothered her?'

'I cannot answer your question.'

'Can't or won't?'

He stared coldly but offered nothing. As she returned his stare, she considered bringing him to the station also.

'What were you doing during the party?'

'I was outside.'

'Why were you outside?'

'Security. I told you already.'

'I think you should join Mr Westport in our car. Maybe you can provide me with more details when we get to the station.'

She called to Murray again.

'It seems Mr Eder would also like to join us at St Anne Street.'

'Yes, ma'am.' Murray grinned then indicated that Eder should get out of the car and accompany him.

'You're wasting my time, police lady. When he comes out, Sebastian will be angry that we are gone.'

'You are not under arrest, Mr Eder. Your attendance at the station is entirely voluntary though advisable. I will explain that to Sebastian.'

Eder got into the back seat of their car next to his colleague.

'Are we off then?' Murray asked her.

'Not just yet. I'd like a word with Sebastian before I take his bodyguard and driver away.'

CHAPTER 40

Cameron Boal

Cameron was still seething. He didn't know who to be angry with the most, his father or Sebastian Logan-Sharp. Seated in the second row behind several prospective partners in the scheme currently being outlined by Sebastian, he realised that's exactly what they were: second row and therefore second rate. His father sat to his right, engrossed in the brochure outlining the plans for Merseyside, a leaflet he'd already digested several times.

This morning they were having to listen to the details regarding Otterspool, the only piece of the entire project of interest to Cameron and one he thought they could deliver. Also this morning, Sebastian was to inform them whether their latest offer for participation in his project had been accepted. Cameron prayed it would be rejected but he realised that if they had failed, his father would blame him for being too cautious. He would rather endure his father's wrath than be drawn into a scheme where they would have little control and have to watch as their money drained all the way down the Mersey.

What a callous bastard, he thought as Sebastian switched on what little charm he possessed to present a new vision for Merseyside. Cameron found it hard to believe that people were so easily taken in by the billionaire. But how could a man who'd just lost his wife in tragic circumstances, stand up in public and talk business deals? Had they loved each other? Was Sebastian even capable of loving someone other than himself? He doubted it.

A vision of a dazzling woman in a blue dress floated through his head. He wouldn't have minded a piece of her. And it wasn't for his lack of trying. When he'd spied her at the party, she looked forlorn sitting alone on a patio chair nursing a glass of champagne. No one else was taking any notice of her. He found that strange. A woman who looked as she did, a frigging supermodel, shouldn't be sat on her own at a party. An idea had flickered to life in his head.

'Yana, no mates?' he'd quipped, taking a seat beside her.

She raised her head to look at him, seemed confused by his comment and returned her gaze to the glass in her hand. Perhaps it wasn't a phrase familiar to a European. He tried again.

'These parties not your thing?'

'Parties, I like,' she said, 'but not a party for conducting my husband's business.'

'I know what you mean. I'd rather be somewhere else too.'

She looked towards him with a wry smile, and this time seemed to examine the man who was taking the trouble to speak with her.

'Where would you like to be?' she asked.

He realised his face was giving him away. At that moment he'd be happy with a room upstairs and her lying next to him.

'I don't know, somewhere with a beach, good wine and a beautiful woman next to me.'

He knew it was crass but since Sebastian had already pissed him off that evening, he could think of nothing better than having a piece of his stunning wife if she'd let him. Without another word, she got to her feet and wandered off down a path through the lawn. He saw no reason not to follow. The pathway had several pergolas draped with clematis. When he reached the final one, he found her sitting on a rattan sofa within a patio equipped with a barbecue. She patted her seat, inviting him to join her.

'This will do for now,' she said.

He sat down, and immediately she leaned over and kissed him on the lips. He thought he would faint with his arousal. In seconds she was all over him. Although the patio was hidden from the back of the house, he didn't care that they might be discovered by wandering party guests. Her hand went to his crotch and squeezed hard. He loved what she was doing; he was enjoying himself. And if the husband was to find them, so what? It would put an end to the deal, and he would be free of Sebastian Logan-Sharp. But no one disturbed them. After several minutes, Yana sat upright, smiled drunkenly and pushed him away.

'I'm going to bed.'

He gazed at her, feeling unsure. Was that an invitation?

'You can join me if you like. I don't sleep in Sebastian's bed.'

She rose unsteadily to her feet, and he scrutinised her slender frame perched on heeled sandals. She was way out of his league.

'Give me a few minutes,' she said. 'I will leave my bag by the door so you will know which room.'

He watched her tiptoe back along the path, spilling the remainder of her drink on the way.

CHAPTER 41

Tara Grogan

She didn't believe she had inconvenienced Logan-Sharp too much, although he was not pleased. If only he'd been more abusive, she could have arrested him then and there. Instead, she issued a warning to the billionaire.

'Regardless of what I learn from your bodyguard and your driver, I intend to speak with you again, Mr Logan-Sharp.'

'I'll look forward to it, love,' he jibed.

Tara was certain he'd winked at her as he strolled away. Beatrice, it seemed, was now having to drive them to their next appointment.

Tara urged Murray to get going. She wanted to be clear of the protestors before they closed in around Sebastian's Range Rover. As they exited the gates, she noticed both men in the back seat of the car watching the protestors. There was a vehicle parked on the road opposite the exit. Gavin Westport glanced towards it, and Tara noticed a man in the driver's seat watching as they sped by.

At the station, Ernst Eder and Gavin Westport were placed in separate interview rooms and offered tea. Both men were present voluntarily, although she hadn't explained that to Westport whom she had told might well be charged with obstructing a police investigation and withholding information. She couldn't remember which of the two offences she'd used by way of threat. In truth, she did not wish to detain either man longer than was necessary. Once the press learnt about it, there would be another flurry of online speculation. She simply wanted to extract information in a focussed environment that was not under the nose of their employer.

She and Murray began with Ernst Eder. He had declined refreshments and sat upright at the table when they entered the sparse interview room. Tara guessed he'd quickly grown bored of reading the informational posters dotted around the walls on reporting crimes.

'I would like to deal with events surrounding the party at Sebastian Logan-Sharp's home,' Tara began. 'Please, tell me your recollection of the evening.'

The bodyguard simpered at the question and looked directly at Tara. 'I was outside, watching guests arrive.'

'All evening?'

'No, at the beginning. Then I went inside, to the kitchen, and then out to the garden.'

'Did you notice anything suspicious during the evening?'

He shook his head.

'Did you have contact with Yana at the party?'

Another shake of the head. He already seemed bored of her questions.

'How much longer for this?' he asked.

'Not long, Mr Eder. Did you witness an argument between Yana and her husband?'

'I saw nothing like that.'

'Did you notice any of the guests behaving strangely?'

'I saw nothing.'

'One last question, at what time did you go to bed?'

Eder seemed to consider this question more than he'd done for the others.

'About one-thirty. I closed the gates, checked the doors, then went to my room in the other house.'

They left Eder and went to the adjacent interview room where a rather casual figure was pacing up and down, hands in his trouser pockets.

'Sorry to keep you, Mr Westport,' said Tara, cheerfully.

Gavin smiled thinly.

'I understand, Inspector. You have a busy job.'

Tara thought that the man was sarcastic, although he did sound charming. He was too well-spoken, too confident perhaps for someone who made his living as a chauffeur.

'If you would like to sit, we can get started,' Tara said.

'I'll stand if you don't mind. I'm sure this won't take long.'

Tara felt disarmed by his attitude but didn't object to him standing. She also remained on her feet, leaning against the table where Murray had already sat down.

'Let's start with you driving Sebastian Logan-Sharp to Tommy Brady's home. Tell me what happened?'

Gavin had at least stopped pacing. He faced her, still with his hands in his pockets.

'Nothing much I can tell you, Inspector. We drove to the house. Sebastian went inside; I waited in the car with Ernst. About twenty minutes later, Sebastian returned, and we drove off.'

'Did you go into the house at any time?'

'No.'

'Did Mr Eder?'

'No.'

'How did Sebastian seem when he returned to the car?'

'He didn't say much. He never says a lot to me, anyway. He simply told me to drive home.'

'Did he appear nervous, upset or stressed?'

'I would say that he was fuming. But in my experience fuming is his default.'

Tara switched to asking Gavin about his involvement at the party in Sebastian's home, but she learnt nothing. He told her that he'd spent the evening initially observing guests arrive then later helping himself to refreshments in the kitchen. He had nothing to say regarding Yana, Sebastian or any of the guests. He'd apparently seen and heard nothing. Tara wondered if it had been worthwhile Sebastian hiring security personnel who didn't take notice of things around them. If both men were merely keeping shtum to protect their boss or were under orders to say nothing, then she would have to go directly to Sebastian, and she knew the trouble that would stir up.

CHAPTER 42

Tara Grogan

Murray suggested a way to tackle the list of people they had still to interview. It was hardly rocket science but Tara listened anyway.

'Leaving aside the residents of the houses and given that Wilson has already separated guests from staff, we can subdivide the guests.'

'In what way, Alan?' Tara asked.

'Beatrice Howard told me that among the guests were Sebastian's business associates, those involved in this big deal he's been talking about. Then there were people opposed to the development project. Some members of the protest groups we have seen on the news were invited to the party.'

'Bit strange,' said Tara.

'According to Beatrice, they were hoping to get them onside with the project. The party was intended as a PR exercise.'

'It went a bit awry when the hostess was murdered,' Wilson quipped.

'So, we could divide the guest list along those lines,' Murray concluded.

'OK, sounds like a plan,' said Tara. 'I suppose the protestors would have motive in attacking Logan-Sharp though not specifically for killing Yana.'

'One other subdivision, ma'am,' said Murray.

'And what's that?' Tara asked. 'You certainly had an in-depth conversation with the PA.'

'Yes, ma'am, she's a stunning woman.'

Tara frowned.

'Sebastian's ex-wife and his twin sons were also invited to the do,' he added. 'According to Beatrice, they caused a bit of a scene with the host.'

'Great! I wonder why Beatrice did not mention this to me,' said Tara. 'I can't wait to get started.'

* * *

Tara pulled into her drive behind Kate's red Toyota. For a change she'd hoped to get home first and prepare dinner. Kate always got there before her, and Tara was beginning to feel guilty. It was such a blessing to have her best friend sharing her home. It felt good to have company rather than living in an empty space. The hope of ever having a lasting relationship with a man, getting married and having a family had slipped from the priority list in her mind. Nowadays, the same outlook seemed to apply for Kate. Work and home were their priorities, she at St Anne Street station and Kate at the Royal Hospital. Tara felt relieved also to be living outside the city, across the Mersey in Hoylake.

She climbed from her car and gathered her bags, one containing clothes for the gym that she never seemed to have time to visit, the other, items from a hasty food shop for dinner. When she reached her front door, she gazed at a car parked on the far side of the road from her driveway. There was a man sitting at the wheel. She got that instant sting of alarm, wondering what he was up to. He might have no interest in her, or he could be a threat. Then she recalled the vehicle by the gates at Otterspool. It seemed likely that it was press watching her movements and hoping for a scoop on the Yana case. Over the years she'd endured the beady eyes of serial killers and of rogue police officers. She prayed that the man's presence was entirely innocent. But she would keep an eye on him until he left.

CHAPTER 43

Tara Grogan

The woman was between clients when Tara entered Head, Shoulders, Nails and Toes, leaving Murray to wait in the car. She didn't feel it necessary to drag him into a predominantly female environment. Didn't want him getting over excited.

Carla Smith did not look happy at receiving another visit from a police detective. Rather than greet her, the woman continued clearing her work area, brushing up hair on the floor and dumping a used towel in the laundry bin. Tara was happy to wait until she was finished.

'I'd like another chat please, Carla.'

'You'd better come through,' she replied in a brusque tone.

The salon was much busier than on Tara's previous visit.

When they entered the small staffroom, Carla stood with arms folded and a scowl on her face.

'I can guess why you're here,' she said curtly.

Tara was puzzled by the comment and merely waited for the woman to elaborate.

'You've come about my Jack grabbing his father by the throat at that damned party the other night. Is my ex-husband pressing charges?'

It sounded interesting and, although it was not the reason for her visit, Tara allowed Carla to continue. Maybe she would get all she needed without having to ask any probing questions.

'Jack would have killed him if I hadn't stopped it. Can't say Bobby didn't deserve it. Do you know, he totally dismissed his sons like they were shit on his shoe? Can you believe that? Hadn't clapped eyes on them before and his only words were to tell them they shouldn't have come. Our Jack only grabbed him after Bobby slagged me off about begging for money. I was only suggesting that it might be nice if he contributed a little to his sons' future – uni fees and the like. Not as if he can't afford it. But he didn't have a pleasant word to say to them. How do you think my Jack and Lee felt?'

'It must have been very awkward for them,' said Tara.

'At least they got to see what their father is really like. That it's not just me saying it all the time. And then there was that slutty wife of his.'

Tara's eyes widened at the woman's harshness.

'I know you shouldn't speak ill of the dead, but that bitch probably deserved what she got.'

'Why do you think that?'

Carla paused, realising perhaps that she'd been venting her spleen a tad vigorously in the presence of a police officer.

'I'm sorry. Shouldn't have said that. Aside from what I'd read in magazines I didn't really know her.'

'Did you see Yana during the party?'

'Yes. We exchanged a few words. They weren't friendly and she was drunk.'

'Where exactly did you speak with her?'

'It was in the big sitting room. Don't worry, Inspector, there were loads of people around. I didn't kill her if that's why you're here.'

'I haven't accused you of anything, Carla. I'm just trying to establish a timeline for the last hours of Yana's life. Someone decided that she had to die. Did you notice the time when you spoke with her?'

Carla shook her head. 'Not long after we arrived, about eight I suppose.'

'Did you see her again during the evening?'

'No. Later we had the pleasure of Bobby's company for a few minutes and that's when our Jack grabbed his father. We left a while after that.'

'What time?'

'Don't know exactly.'

'And your sons left with you?'

Carla seemed hesitant. 'To be honest, after the fight with Bobby, we didn't leave straightaway. We got to the front door and that assistant of Bobby's suggested we at least stay and have a drink. I was upset and the boys were trying to comfort me. So, we sat in the back garden and had a few drinks.'

'And during that period were you all together?'

Carla stared obstinately at Tara. 'My boys didn't go near the woman, Inspector. We were all upset, but Jack and Lee wouldn't hurt anyone.'

'What time did you leave the party?'

The hairdresser lowered her head, her face partially obscured by her pink-tipped hair. Tara waited. Carla seemed more concerned with defending her family rather than answering Tara's direct questions.

'I don't remember,' she said. 'I got drunk. The rest of the night is a bit hazy.'

'And your boys?'

'Leave them out of this, they did nothing wrong,' she sobbed. 'All I wanted was for them to meet their dad.'

'I will need to speak with them, Carla. It's probably best if I see them at your home.'

Tara left the hairdresser sipping strong tea at the table in the salon staffroom. She wasn't sure what to make of their conversation. The family certainly had a motive to hit back at Sebastian. Maybe there had been a further exchange between Carla and Yana.

Murray was drinking coffee and munching crisps when she got back in the car.

'How did it go?'

'Interesting. I wasn't expecting to come away with more suspects added to our list.'

Murray set his coffee into a cup holder and started the car as Tara reported her conversation.

'Carla told me about a heated exchange involving her family and Sebastian at the party. All three have motive stemming from that row. And I find it interesting that Carla also knew Tommy Brady.'

CHAPTER 44

Cameron Boal

It was all he needed. His secretary Joyce had just told him that a police officer wished to speak with him. He could see through the glass partition of his office to the desk where Joyce handled most of his daily affairs. But standing beside the desk was a young woman with cropped hair, wearing dark trousers and a white blouse. She didn't strike him as a cop. Maybe she was just the work experience kid and the big round-shouldered bloke with his hands in his trouser pockets was the detective.

He asked Joyce to give him a couple of minutes to finish off what he was doing. This morning and most of the previous day had been spent trying to rustle up sufficient funds in readiness for his father to piss it all away on this deal with Logan-Sharp. His father could not be told otherwise. He wanted the deal, to hell with what his son thought about it. But Cameron had dared to hope that the death of Logan-Sharp's wife would somehow put an end to the billionaire's plans for Merseyside. Quite the opposite had occurred, it seemed. The heartless man had simply carried on as if nothing had happened. He'd agreed to their participation in the project subject to them meeting the financial requirements. And now Cameron was under pressure to raise the extra money to take part in the damn scheme. It was getting to the point where he might have to consider remortgaging his house, not that it would come close to providing the sum he needed.

He saw them staring. He had to consider how to react to their questions. Did they already know? Had someone seen him in the garden with his hands all over Yana? How could he explain himself? He felt the sweat break out on his forehead. He loosened his tie and looked out again. The little work-experience girl was staring right at him.

OK, he thought, if someone had seen them in the garden, he could explain that there had been nothing to it. Yana had been drunk; everyone had seen her. Then he remembered seeing a girl on the landing. She would have seen him going into Yana's room. Had she told the police? He felt his palms moisten as he got to his feet and went slowly to his door. The big cop and the girl saw it as their cue to approach. He was shaking.

'Mr Boal?' said the work-experience girl, quite cheerfully. 'I'm DI Grogan and this is DS Murray. Thank you for seeing us. Hopefully, this won't take too long.'

Cameron Boal felt his face warming. How could he have called it so wrong? Not only was the youngster a real cop but she was the senior of the two.

'Hello,' was all he managed as he stood aside for them to enter his office.

'Please, take a seat,' he said nervously. 'Sorry to have kept you waiting.' He straightened his tie before returning to his desk. 'So, how can I help you?'

Deliberately, he sat with his back straight and his hands clasped in front of him. It should prevent him fidgeting. Hopefully, he didn't appear on edge.

'We would like to ask you some questions regarding your association with Sebastian Logan-Sharp,' DI Grogan explained. 'I take it you've heard about the death of his wife?'

'Yes,' Cameron said, 'it was terrible. Please understand, but I cannot discuss anything to do with our business dealings with Sebastian. There are negotiations at a critical stage right now. I don't want to jeopardise any of them.'

'Perhaps we won't have to touch on that,' she said with a businesslike smile. 'Can you confirm that you were a guest at the reception in Sebastian's home?'

Up close, this woman cop was delightful. She could pout for England, but from the way she was looking at him he reckoned she was a real tough nut. He couldn't see himself getting off with her in the way he had with Yana. She was still staring. Then he realised that she was waiting for him to answer her question.

'Yes, I was. Dad and me. All the prospective partners in Sebastian's Merseyside project were invited.'

'Did you speak with Sebastian at the party?' the other detective asked, his notebook open and pen at the ready.

'Er, yes, I did. But as I've said, I can't tell you anything about our business arrangements.'

'Did you only talk business?' DI Grogan asked.

'Pretty much, yes. Sebastian is very intense. Doesn't seem to switch off. He tends to bypass small talk.'

'How well do you know him?' she continued.

'Not that well, to be honest. Only met him when he came to Liverpool with this project.'

'And how about his wife?' Murray asked.

Cameron felt the bile rising from his stomach. How did they know? *How much* did they know?

'What do you mean?' He felt the tremble in his own voice and realised he sounded defensive.

'Did you meet her at the party?' said Murray.

'Em, yes briefly.'

'How did she seem?' Tara asked.

'A bit tipsy, to be honest. She didn't say much really.'

'At what stage of the evening did you speak to her?'

Cameron shrugged then shook his head. It gave him time to compose an answer.

'I can't remember exactly,' he said. 'Sometime in the middle of the evening, I suppose.'

'What time did you leave the party?' asked Murray.

'Not that late. About eleven-thirty.'

'One final question, Mr Boal,' said Tara. 'Did you notice anyone acting suspiciously or did you witness any heated arguments during the evening.'

'Nothing I can think of, Inspector, sorry.'

As soon as they'd left, he rushed to the bathroom and disgorged his lunch in the toilet bowl. They knew everything. He could feel it. It was daft to think that no one had noticed him with Yana. If they didn't already know what he'd got up to, Cameron felt that the pretty detective soon would.

CHAPTER 45

Tara Grogan

For the first time during this investigation, she saw her name in a newspaper.

'DI Tara Grogan,' the piece stated, 'is the senior investigating officer in the search for Yana Logan-Sharp's killer. The detective has appealed for the public and the media to refrain from speculation over the murder. It is upsetting for the family and could seriously harm the investigation.'

Tara had made no such appeal. It was Tweedy who had delivered the statement to the media. On top of the inaccuracy, the report didn't shy away from criticising the apparent lack of progress from the police. Sitting forlornly over her breakfast in the station canteen, she slid the tabloid to the side. This morning, she couldn't settle to eat at home as normal. She thought she might avoid the reporters and cameras if she got to St Anne Street early while they queued at Starbucks for their mochas and spiced lattes. She stared incredulously at Murray who never seemed to lose his appetite for a full English. A simultaneous tsunami, earthquake and meteor strike in Liverpool wouldn't stop him from enjoying his fry-up. She was struggling to eat a slice of toast with strawberry jam.

'At least they haven't got wind of the connection with the Tommy Brady killing,' Murray said between mouthfuls of fried egg and sausage.

'Only a matter of time, I suppose,' said Tara. 'I still can't believe they are following us around. There's been at least two guys taking pictures at every place we've visited to interview witnesses. Sooner or later one of our suspects is going to cry intrusion when their picture is spread over the tabloids. Innocent people are going to find themselves branded as murderers just because we had reason to speak with them.'

'Most of it is finished with for now,' Murray said. 'All Logan-Sharp's business associates who attended the party have been interviewed. That leaves the people from the protest groups to be questioned. Wilson and Bleasdale are dealing with the staff from the catering and cleaning companies.'

'I thought we would have learnt more by now,' said Tara. 'It's strange how little was noticed during that party.'

'Yes, or maybe people don't want to get involved and risk upsetting Sebastian.'

'We need to speak with Carla's boys this morning. I wonder if the confrontation with their father was bad enough for one of them to hit back at Sebastian.'

* * *

Driving into the Treadwater Estate never failed to induce gut-wrenching discomfort in Tara. On the surface, it was a typical sprawl of council housing, or social housing as they called it nowadays. That was a much softer, almost affectionate term, as if to describe an environment where all the residents were happy with their lot and with each other. Tara viewed it differently. Treadwater sparked memories of killers, drug gangs, and impoverished and lonely people.

Murray pulled up outside a row of terraced houses on Deeside Crescent. As Tara stepped from the unmarked car into a humid morning, she gazed around realising she was only a hundred yards from the flat where she had once lived during an undercover operation – a situation where she had narrowly escaped death. She felt a shudder, and quickly the memory was despatched to the recesses of her mind where lurked all manner of horrors.

Evidently, Carla Smith had been watching for their arrival and stood by her open door as Tara and Murray approached. She had come to recognise the woman's indignant stance, her arms folded and a cold defensive stare.

'Good morning, Carla, I assumed you would be at work.'

'I thought it best that I was here when you came. They're still just kids, you know.'

'I haven't accused them of anything. I'm just trying to discover what happened at that party.'

Looking unimpressed by the assurance, Carla turned and led them inside the tiny space that served as an entrance hall. Tara was struck by the contrast to the house where her ex-husband resided. The living room-kitchen had a smell of burnt toast, poorly masked by the sweet odour of a Yankee Candle. Carla shouted upstairs to her boys. There was a rumble as feet hurried on carpeted stairs before Jack and Lee bounded into the room.

'Morning, guys,' Tara said jovially. Neither of them replied, both standing casually in football shirt and jogging pants. 'Thanks for agreeing to speak with us this morning.'

Her comment was met with blank stares. She had thought initially of interviewing them separately, Murray handling one son while she the other. She quickly realised, however, that Carla was intent on hearing everything. It would cause less friction, she decided, if questions were asked of all of them in the same room at the same time. Murray had taken a seat in a recliner chair by the window and the boys sat together on the sofa, while Tara sat on the remaining armchair. Carla stood by the door, her arms again folded, her expression difficult to read although happy was never going to feature.

Sensing the uneasy atmosphere, Tara dispensed with any further pleasantries with Jack and Lee. She thought they might prefer to get to the crux of the reason for their visit.

'Tell me, what happened between you and your father?'

'That prick's not my dad.'

Tara and Murray had not been introduced to the twins. She asked him his name.

'I'm Lee,' he replied.

She was struck by the resemblance between the boys and Sebastian. They had a busy, rather cheeky look in their eyes. Aside from that, they appeared fit and strong while their father had gone to seed.

'OK,' said Tara, 'I realise you are hurting over this, Lee, but I need to hear your version of what happened between you and Sebastian.'

Jack smirked on hearing the name.

'He was slagging off our mam, so I grabbed him,' said Jack.

'Some bloke tried to stop him,' Lee said proudly. 'I told him to piss off. It was none of his business.'

'Was Yana present when you were fighting with Sebastian?' asked Tara.

'Don't know,' Jack replied with a shrug.

Lee did not add anything, but Carla spoke.

'We met her before that business with Bobby,' she explained. 'I've already told you it wasn't pleasant. She was drunk.'

'Dick teaser!'

'That's enough of that language, Lee,' Carla scolded. 'The woman is dead. It's not nice.'

Lee shrugged indifference.

'What did you do after the row?' said Tara. 'Your mum said that you stayed at the party for a while longer.'

Jack and Lee both laughed and looked to their mother.

'What?' said Tara.

'We decided to stay and to drink and eat as much as we could,' Jack said as Lee sniggered. 'Sebastian was paying for it. We had a great time. Food was great.'

'Did you speak with Sebastian at any point after your quarrel?'

'Nope,' said Lee. 'He stayed out of our way. Knew what was good for him.'

'Did you speak with Yana again?'

Tara detected their hesitation. Jack glanced at his brother then at Carla.

'You may as well tell them, Jack,' she said.

'I needed to go for a piss,' Jack said. 'She was going upstairs, and I followed behind her. I thought she was going to fall; she wasn't too steady on those big heels she was wearing.'

'Why did you follow her?' asked Tara.

'I thought the toilet would be upstairs.'

'You didn't think there would be a downstairs bathroom?'

'Na.' He chuckled as if the idea of a downstairs loo was ridiculous.

'What happened when you got upstairs?' asked Tara.

'I asked her where the toilet was, and she laughed. She waved her hand around like I was supposed to know.

Then she opened a door for me, and it was a big frigging bathroom.'

'Where did Yana go after that?'

'As I went into the bathroom, she was going into a room across the landing, but she left her handbag hanging from the door handle.'

'Did you see anyone else upstairs?'

'I don't think so. I'd drunk a lot of booze too, you know.'

'Anything you can remember might be a help to us, Jack.'

'Tell her about the girl,' said Carla.

CHAPTER 46

Beatrice Howard

Beatrice was relieved that the police at last had gone, and they were free to carry on with their business.

Sleep was difficult. Last night she was awakened by Surrey screaming through a nightmare. She could easily understand the poor child feeling traumatised by her environment, and it was hard to know how much she had absorbed of the recent tragic events. Her screams were followed firstly by Sebastian, from his bedroom door, telling Surrey to be quiet, then by Shelby trying her best to soothe things and – good on her – yelling back at Sebastian, informing him he wasn't helping by shouting at his daughter. To which Sebastian reiterated that Surrey was not his child.

Things had just quietened down when Beatrice heard a knock on her door. She sat up in bed, and in the dimness recognised the shaven head of Ernst edging into the room.

She hadn't been expecting him, and in the past few days hadn't even thought about having sex. Her suspicions of him had been aroused when during the party she'd spied him engaged in a serious conversation with Sebastian. She couldn't imagine what the pair had to talk about unless Sebastian was merely handing out orders or informing Ernst of upcoming activities. But she viewed it as something more sinister when she saw that Sebastian was the one who looked concerned over what was being said.

Ernst slipped beneath her sheet, and immediately they engaged in vigorous and noisy sex. If anyone else was disturbed again from their sleep that was just too bad. She had needs and right now this Austrian brute was tending to them. But when it was finished, and she lay on her back catching her breath, Beatrice's concerns quickly resurfaced.

'What were you talking about with Sebastian at the party?'

In the darkness she couldn't judge his expression, but he ceased the gentle stroking of her breast.

'It's not important,' he replied.

'It is important to me if I have to deal with a boss who has been upset by you.'

'Don't worry about it.' He sat up and quickly rose from the bed. 'Sebastian will behave.'

'What do you mean, he'll behave? He doesn't answer to you. You're just the bodyguard, aren't you?'

Ernst didn't reply; Beatrice didn't wait.

'Aren't you?'

'Sebastian is not my boss. He does what *my* boss tells him to do.'

Beatrice rose to her knees.

'Who do you work for, Ernst?'

Suddenly his hand grabbed her throat. She tried to pull away, but he was too strong. He pushed her back down on the bed. His firm grip moved to her crotch, and she yelped in pain.

'It is not your business, lady Beatrice.'

He squeezed harder. She drew a sharp breath. Even in the darkness she saw the menace in his eyes. Time seemed to pause, and she felt terrified as he pierced her gaze with an evil stare. She truly thought that she was about to die. His hand closed like a vice at her crotch. At that moment, she easily believed that *he* was the beast who'd taken Yana's life, and now was about to take hers. She screamed. His hand pressed down on her mouth for a second then he slapped her hard. At least the pain had moved from between her legs. Then he slapped her bottom in a playful yet cruel manner.

'Get the fuck out of my room!'

He laughed, rose from the bed and pulled on his shorts.

'You and I are done,' she cried. 'Stay out of my way or I will have Sebastian sack you.'

He laughed again. She tried to scurry away as he clambered over the bed towards her. He butted his head against hers and whispered harshly.

'Sebastian cannot sack me. And I will come to fuck you whenever I please, you old whore.'

He pushed her face down into the mattress, lowered his shorts and repeated the act that had first brought him to her bed.

* * *

No amount of snorted coke was going to stop her shaking. She sat at the breakfast bar, a mug of coffee beside her and a slice of toast untouched. At least the house was quiet. She didn't know where Sebastian was and hadn't heard from Shelby or Surrey; the only person she could hear in the house was a contract cleaner dusting in the lounge. There was no sign either of the man she now feared more than anyone. She'd taken paracetamol and snorted coke, but the pain between her legs persisted, and when she'd finally eased from her bed, she noticed bloodstains on the sheets. But her mental anguish was so much worse. What was she to do? Would it do any good to tell Sebastian what Ernst had done to her? What had the Austrian meant when he said that Sebastian was not his boss? And did it have anything to do with Yana's death?

'You look like shit.'

Sebastian swaggered into the kitchen, going straight to the fridge and removing a carton of orange juice. He was dressed in a suit and looked ready for a busy day. Beatrice couldn't manage a reply when usually she could banter with her boss and come out on top. Her hair was a mess, she'd been crying, and she was still in her dressing gown.

'What's the matter, sweetheart? Cat got your tongue?'

He drank straight from the carton and stood awaiting her response. Tears welled in her eyes. How callous can one man be? He'd passed over the murder of his wife as if it were a minor hiccup in one of his business deals.

'Who the fuck are you, Sebastian?'

CHAPTER 47

Tara Grogan

'There was a girl on the other side of the landing,' said Jack.

'Can you describe her?'

'Really long hair, sort of ginger.'

Tara realised Jack was most likely describing Shelby Keibler.

'What was she doing?'

Jack shrugged. 'She was just leaning on the handrail and looking down into the hall. When she saw me, she moved away and went into one of the rooms.'

'Was it the room where Yana's bag was hanging on the door?'

'No. There was also a man.'

'Had he been with the girl you saw?'

'No, I passed him when I was coming downstairs again.'

'Did you recognise him?'

'No. He was one of the business types at the party, suit and tie.'

'Did you speak to him?'

'He asked me where the bathroom was, and I just pointed.'

Tara didn't think she would get much more from Carla and her sons, but she couldn't rule them out as suspects. Their contretemps with Sebastian had given them motive to hit back at the billionaire and his family.

She was relieved when Murray drove them out of Treadwater and back towards the city. On the way she asked Murray's opinion of the situation.

'There are plenty of people with a motive to attack Logan-Sharp,' he said. 'But we have no specific reason for someone to kill his wife.'

'I agree,' said Tara. 'But Logan-Sharp is the main person linked so far with Brady and Yana. He remains our prime suspect.'

'So, what next?'

'Until we have spoken to everyone who attended that party, we can't rule anything out.'

* * *

They found Dr Paul Renfrew in a modern building on the Liverpool University campus just off Abercromby Square. Students on the Environment and Urban Planning course were coming out of a lecture theatre, and as Tara and Murray squeezed by, they saw a man they presumed to be Renfrew speaking to one of the students. He looked inquisitively towards Tara, who was content to wait until the lecturer had finished his conversation.

A few moments later the student wandered off, checking his mobile as he went. The man smiled at Tara.

'Sorry to keep you waiting. Can I help you?' he asked and proceeded to gather papers from the bench between them.

Tara held up her warrant card. 'I'm DI Grogan and this is DS Murray. Are you Dr Paul Renfrew?' She noticed the instant change in the man's expression as if a veil of nerves had descended.

'Yes, how can I help you?'

Tara sensed an attempt at nonchalance but wasn't swayed by it. She could see a man suddenly ill at ease, about to face questions from a police officer.

'I believe you were present at the reception in the home of Sebastian Logan-Sharp a few days ago.'

'Yes. And you want to know if I had anything to do with the death of Logan-Sharp's wife?'

Tara ignored his attempt to cut to a single question. She wanted the full picture.

'Why were you invited to the party?' she asked. 'Am I right in thinking that you are engaged in a protest against Logan-Sharp's development plans?'

'Believe me, Inspector, it came as a surprise when I got the invitation. Having attended his reception, I now believe that it was an attempt by Logan-Sharp to undermine our protest. Mine was not the only protest group to be there. In the end all we got was a load of abuse from the man.'

Murray took a note of his arrival and departure times on the night of the party.

'Did you meet Yana Logan-Sharp?' asked Tara.

'I wouldn't describe it as meet, encountered perhaps.'

'Please explain, Dr Renfrew.'

He placed some papers into a pocket folder as Tara waited.

'The woman was very drunk, sloshed about the house all night. One minute she looked deep in amorous conversation with a bloke, the next she was slagging somebody off.'

'Which applies to you?'

He directed a smirk at Murray as if it was all lads together. To Tara's chagrin, Murray responded in like manner.

'Bit of both, I suppose,' the lecturer replied. 'She stumbled into me at one point, and I grabbed her in case she went head over heels on the stairs. She seemed to enjoy someone taking hold of her.'

'Did you exchange any words during your embrace?' Tara asked sarcastically.

'I can't remember exactly. I'd had a few drinks myself. She muttered something flirtatious. Something like "I'm getting all the attention this evening, but you'll have to get in the queue."'

'What did she mean by that?'

'I have no idea, Inspector. If you don't mind, I have a tutorial to prepare for this afternoon.'

'Did you see Yana again after your encounter on the stairs?' she asked, unconcerned about the man's schedule.

'Seems I was quickly forgotten. She was in the arms of another bloke before I'd reached the bottom step. Didn't see her after that.'

'Do you know this man?'

He shook his head.

'Why were you on the stairs?'

'I had gone to use the bathroom.'

Tara allowed the lecturer to leave and voiced her opinion to Murray.

'Seems like everything happened on that staircase.'

'And no one was inclined to use the downstairs loo.'

'Is there anyone left for us to interview? Our list of suspects is growing.'

CHAPTER 48

Tara Grogan

Tara's first impression was that Michelle Weller was a woman living on her nerves. And yet, Tara regarded her as a person to be admired. These days it took a brave soul to make any kind of stand against injustice. But Michelle Weller didn't immediately strike her as a leader of a protest campaign. She didn't appear confident, was plainly, if not poorly dressed, and she hadn't managed to smile nor even maintain eye contact and her gaze frequently dropped to the floor.

They met in a quiet corner of the reception area in the call centre where Michelle was employed. Tara and Murray stood by a huge window that overlooked the centre's staff car park, while Michelle kept her back to the reception desk where a colleague answered phones and greeted visitors. Tara always tried, initially, to put the person she was interviewing at ease. She believed it helped improve the response from witnesses and suspects. But Tara had a trembling woman before her. She briefly explained the reason for their meeting and then focused on Sebastian Logan-Sharp's house party.

'Did you meet Yana Logan-Sharp?' she asked.

'Not really. Someone pointed her out to me. She seemed quite drunk.'

'When was that?'

'Not long after I'd arrived.'

'Where exactly did you see her?' asked Murray.

Michelle appeared to flinch at Murray joining in.

'It was in that huge lounge, I think.'

'Did you see her any time later on?' asked Tara.

'I don't recall seeing her again. There were a lot of people coming and going.'

'What time did you leave?'

Michelle hesitated; her face seemed to cloud over. 'To tell the truth, I can't remember exactly. I'd had a few drinks, didn't notice the time. Paul Renfrew might remember.'

Tara looked at her quizzically.

'Dr Renfrew?'

'Yes, we left at the same time. We shared a taxi.'

'Did you go upstairs in the house at any point?' Murray interjected again.

Michelle shook her head. 'No. Can't think why I should have.'

Murray continued. 'Did you notice that Paul Renfrew went upstairs to use the bathroom?'

'Can't think why he should have done that. There was a bathroom downstairs in that great big hall.'

'Did you notice Renfrew being accosted by Yana?'

'No.'

Tara sensed the woman's growing agitation at Murray's barrage of questions, scarcely giving her time to answer. She tried to calm things down a little.

'I was wondering, Michelle, why you decided to attend a party at Logan-Sharp's home, given that you are leading a protest against him.'

'The invitation was a surprise to me, Inspector. I suppose I went out of curiosity, to get a little closer to the obnoxious man. Paul reckoned that protestors had been invited to get them onside or at least to try to cool their opposition to the development plans.'

'Did it succeed?'

'Not as far as I, or Paul, was concerned. We were faced with a thoroughly nasty billionaire who used the opportunity to belittle us. After my encounter with

Sebastian, all I did was binge on the free booze. I was quite drunk by the end of the night.'

'Did you notice Yana before you left?'

Michelle shook her head.

Tara smiled her understanding and thanked the woman, wishing her well in her campaign for women's rights. She noticed Murray's smirk as she did so. It didn't surprise her. A few years back, when she'd first joined Tweedy's team, Murray was less than pleased to have a woman as his boss.

'Right,' Tara chirped, when they returned to their car, 'Let's go speak to some football supporters. That should be more up your street, Alan.' She hoped she'd sounded sarcastic.

'Can't imagine any of these football guys having a motive to murder Logan-Sharp's wife,' Murray said as he drove them away.

Tara thought he sounded rather proud to defend their position.

'So far,' he continued, 'apart from the people working directly for Sebastian, no one knew Yana well enough to want to kill her.'

'That's exactly what we have to uncover, Alan, the motive to commit murder.'

'Just can't see it being someone associated with our football clubs.'

Tara smiled wistfully at Murray's manly attitude. She was well used to it.

'And why ever not?'

'Who wouldn't want investment in their football club, being able to buy the best players and hire the best managers and winning trophies?'

'What if you're associated with one of the clubs that is going to miss out on that investment? You might feel aggrieved then.'

'Enough to murder an innocent woman? Can't see it.'

'But perhaps as a way of getting back at the man with the cash?'

CHAPTER 49

Beatrice Howard

Beatrice had endured many different emotions in the time she'd worked for Sebastian, but until now fear had never been one of them. She'd had many arguments with her employer, disagreements on how business should be conducted, and bickering over the arranging of his diary. Recently, she'd decided that Sebastian needed to learn some of life's more compassionate lessons on how to treat people, particularly those he supposedly loved and who were a part of his life.

This morning, as she lingered in the shower wishing that mere soap and water could wash her life clean, she realised that her boss was beyond redemption. She thought she had been privy to all that went on in his life. She thought she knew his business inside out and even most of what occurred in private. But something was going on that Sebastian would not share with her. And that was dangerous. If he was heading for a fall, he could take her down with him, and she wouldn't know a thing about it until it was too late.

The Austrian bodyguard terrified her. She'd asked him questions he didn't like, and he'd raped her for doing so. It was a painful way to discover that Ernst was more than just a bodyguard. He had a hold over Sebastian. But if her boss wasn't prepared to tell her about his arrangement with Ernst, then to protect herself she must go on the offensive.

Maybe this Liverpool venture had never been a good idea. Was it really in Sebastian's best interests to be here?

And yet he had quickly become the one driving the project. She had known little about development opportunities on Merseyside and although she had done some research, she was swept along by her boss's apparent enthusiasm. She realised too that Ernst Eder had been hired by Sebastian around the time the project got underway. She had been involved in the recruitment of all of Sebastian's personal team – Shelby, Patrice and Gavin – but she hadn't been consulted about the hiring of Ernst. Now that made sense.

The success of the Merseyside project was now in doubt following Yana's murder. Beatrice considered whether it was better to forge ahead or to actively scupper the plans. Maybe Ernst had an interest in this project only and would have no further involvement with Sebastian if the deal collapsed. But would he simply depart, or would there be horrific consequences? She had already experienced his wrath.

Was Sebastian's life in danger from Ernst? Was hers? Surely, all suspicion for Yana's death and perhaps the death of Tommy Brady now fell on Ernst Eder.

Beatrice stepped nervously from the shower. She didn't feel safe in this room. It was primarily a family home – there were no locks on the bedroom doors. She was easy prey if the Austrian beast intended to repeat his assault.

Dressing quickly, she prepared to hurry downstairs. At least there she would be in the company of others – Sebastian, Patrice, Shelby and even Surrey. She must decide on how to move forward and get herself out of trouble. Maybe it was a case of deal, or no deal.

Beatrice sat on her bed, opened her phone and made a call.

CHAPTER 50

Tara Grogan

Tara felt that the afternoon's work had added little to her investigation, except perhaps to eliminate several people from suspicion.

Murray had spoken to those associated with Everton, and she'd delegated Wilson to speak with people who'd attended Sebastian's party and were linked with Liverpool. It was the rascal in her. She knew it would grate with both men having to deal with the rivals of the clubs they supported. She had gone to Wigan and Bleasdale to Tranmere. But when they'd gathered in the evening at St Anne Street, their reports were remarkably similar.

Board members from each club who had attended the party at the house in West Derby had nothing useful to impart. It seemed they had enjoyed the hospitality, a brief informal chat with Sebastian, followed by more food and drink. Apparently, there were no concrete business proposals discussed. None of the attendees had admitted to witnessing the heated confrontations between Sebastian and the other guests. No one specifically recalled meeting Yana at any time in the evening, although it was unanimous that her appearance was striking and she would have been hard to miss.

Also in attendance at the party were representatives of each club's supporters, those who had been vocal in their protests over rumours that Sebastian was intending to buy their club. It appeared that the twenty invited fans had availed of the food and drink, most got drunk and were then diplomatically encouraged to leave before they resorted to rival banter and their matchday chants. None of the detectives learnt anything regarding which of the clubs was favourite for a Logan-Sharp buyout.

Tara left the station for home with her thoughts centred on Sebastian's household, although the billionaire remained uppermost in her thinking. It promised to be another evening of having difficulty switching off.

* * *

The next morning, slowly warming to the prospect of another day at St Anne Street, she padded to the kitchen still in her pyjamas and slippers. Kate was preparing a packed lunch for Adele who sat munching Rice Krispies and listening to her mother explaining the contents of her lunch box.

'Morning,' said Tara. It sounded wearier than she had intended, not helped when she broke into a yawn.

'Morning,' Kate replied. 'There's another flipping car parked on the road.'

Tara shook her head in disgust.

'Do these people not have a life?'

'Are they reporters?' asked Kate.

'I assume so.'

Tara went into the hall and peered out of the window. A black SUV was parked across the road opposite her driveway. She could see the driver slouched behind the wheel. It seemed likely he'd been there for a while. What bothered Tara was that she didn't get the impression the man was a journalist. Unless he was an upmarket, perhaps well-paid, senior reporter. But it was an expensive-looking vehicle for any journalist to be driving. She hated this. She'd moved from the city to Hoylake for the peace and quiet, but this was her second murder case recently where an interested party had deemed it necessary to stalk her. There was no better word to describe it. Rogues or reporters, it didn't matter; it was stalking. The murder of Yana Logan-Sharp was a high-profile case, the biggest Tara had ever had to deal with. Now it seemed that she was to be thrust into the spotlight. Her thoughts were confirmed, it seemed, when she returned to the kitchen and Kate set the morning paper in front of her.

'You're famous.'

Tara examined the paper, already opened to reveal the relevant piece. It was page four, but that didn't help her unease. Directly beneath a picture of Yana Logan-Sharp strutting down a catwalk in Paris several years ago, was a recent photo of DI Tara Grogan standing by the front door of the house in West Derby where the former supermodel had perished. It was a surprisingly clear image of the police detective in slim jeans, leather jacket and heeled boots. What incensed Tara was the tagline above it.

'Who is the real super-model?'

Tara jumped from her stool. 'Right! I've had enough of this nonsense.'

Kate smiled and Adele stopped munching her cereal and twisted her head to watch her godmother storming out of the kitchen, the newspaper in her hand.

Tara stepped from her house and marched down the drive towards the parked car. It was difficult to view as more than comical because she still hadn't dressed. She walked out of one slipper on the driveway and hobbled across the road brandishing the newspaper. The driver sat upright from his slouched position when he saw her approach.

She was surprised that he hadn't simply driven off. Instead, he lowered his window and bid her good morning. Tara held up the offending article in the paper.

'Do you work for this rag?' she barked. She stabbed a finger at the picture.

The man, of around thirty with a square jaw and stubble, merely smirked.

'Can't say I do,' he replied confidently.

'Why don't you people just report the news instead of turning every event into a sleaze-fest? The murder of Yana

Logan-Sharp was a violent tragedy and you are just trivialising it.'

'Wasn't me, madam.'

'Then would you mind telling me why you're parked outside my house? And don't call me madam.'

The man grinned, said nothing further then raised his window. The engine started as Tara fumed in the middle of the road. He sped away, leaving her to note the vehicle registration. It was not the first time she'd ever had to do that. She thought about what Tweedy would say. He'd warned her of the hazards a case in the public eye would bring. Suddenly, she felt swamped by the pressure to get a result before she became a household name.

As she padded back along the drive, she read the report below her picture. Kate stood at the front door with a sympathetic smile. Tara only managed a nervous sigh. Another case was grinding away at her personal life.

CHAPTER 51

Sebastian Logan-Sharp

Sebastian threw his phone across the room. It hit a painting on the wall and clattered to the floor.

'Bastard!'

Beatrice, seated at the breakfast bar, looked up from her laptop.

'What's the matter?'

Sebastian's face was red, his eyes bulging, his fists clenched.

'What is it?' Beatrice tried again.

'I've had it with this fucking town.'

'Sebastian, if you won't tell me what's wrong, I can't help you.'

He glowered at his PA for a moment, contemplating whether to share the news. He was trembling. He doubted if Beatrice could help him with that.

'Where the hell is Ernst?' he said. 'I need to speak to him.'

Beatrice was glaring. By now she must know what was really going on, he thought. She'd been sleeping with the toerag for long enough. And for that reason, he no longer trusted his PA, if indeed he ever had done. Maybe she was a part of it. He shook his head trying to dispel the notion of having to fight the biggest battle of his life alone.

'He's in the other house,' Beatrice replied dryly. 'Shall I get him to come over?'

'No, I'll go myself.'

He stormed through the conservatory onto the patio and headed to the rear of the spare house. He found his bodyguard sitting comfortably in a lounger, feet up, smoking and talking on his phone. It wasn't in English. He struggled to calm himself before addressing Ernst Eder. When the Austrian noticed his approach, he cut his call and took a long drag of his cigarette.

'Hey, boss, what's up?' he said jovially.

Sebastian didn't know how to begin. Should he ask who he'd been talking to on his phone? Or should he merely state what he'd intended to say?

'Is there problem?' Ernst asked him, looking more concerned.

'I'll say there's a fucking problem. Cameron bloody Boal is digging his heels in. He's now refusing to meet our latest requirements for investing in the project. He's pulling out.'

'So, we can do without him. You get someone else.'

'Someone else?' Sebastian was apoplectic. 'There is no one else, sunshine. Not only are the Boals our last hope, but they're putting the wind up the other local outfits. I think they're all going to bail. We're screwed.'

Ernst rose casually to his feet as Sebastian slumped into a garden chair.

'*We* are not screwed, Sebastian, *you* are. You have pushed them too hard. You must now, as you say, sweeten the deal, convince the Boals to invest or you find someone to take their place. You know that Dulka does not tolerate weakness.'

Sebastian gazed at the man now towering over him. He jerked in pain as Ernst stubbed his cigarette into the back of his hand.

'Whatever you do, you must do it now,' said the Austrian with an ominous sneer. He strolled off across the lawn and was soon talking again on his mobile.

Sebastian rubbed at the burn on his hand. When he rose to walk back to the house, he saw Beatrice standing with arms folded watching from the doorway. Again, he wondered what she knew and how much she had overheard.

CHAPTER 52

Cameron Boal

Cameron felt relief – more than he'd known for weeks. Yes, a day on the golf course had improved his mood. The fresh air and a half-decent round had relaxed him. Even his father seemed to be off his case. At last James had seen right through the slimy tearaway. After all, Logan-Sharp was nothing but a boy from the gutter that was the Treadwater Estate. When his father told him to make the call, he could have hugged his old man.

He had relished the brief conversation with Logan-Sharp. He'd never trusted him and had always doubted his motives for returning to Liverpool. He still didn't know what was behind it, but as soon as he'd said the word 'withdraw' to the billionaire, he knew he'd inflicted a lot of pain. Suddenly absent was the cocky attitude and the lord-of-the-manor display he'd witnessed on previous meetings. Cameron knew that the withdrawal of his father's company from the Merseyside Delta Development project had caused Logan-Sharp severe problems, but he couldn't imagine just how serious they were going to be.

As he birdie-putted on the eighteenth green at Royal Liverpool, he reckoned that he was in the clear as far as the police were concerned. That pretty detective with the sweet face and tight ass had not come calling again. And to him that meant they remained unaware of his dalliance with Yana at the party. Even Sebastian hadn't mentioned anything, suggesting that he knew nothing of what his wife had got up to in his own house. Cameron felt he was in the clear.

Now he could forget all about Sebastian Logan-Sharp, his dodgy scheme and his shameless wife. He couldn't help a thought for that sultry-looking PA, though. So much going on with her. He was grateful yet mystified by the call she had made to his father. Whatever she'd told him, it was enough for James to exit from the deal. He now viewed her in a different light. He wondered too if he might still have a chance of making it to her bed.

CHAPTER 53

Tara Grogan

Tara felt like several storms had come at once. Firstly, this morning there had been the car parked outside her house. Then on the drive to St Anne Street she was convinced another vehicle was following her. Surely it was too much of a coincidence for the car she'd first noticed when she pulled out of her road, drove to Wallasey and through the tunnel, to still be tailing her when she turned into the station. She glimpsed it in her rear-view mirror as it continued along St Anne Street. It was a less salubrious-looking motor than the SUV that had been parked in her road.

Then, later in the morning, when she and Murray had stopped for coffee at a Costa, they were set upon by several reporters and photographers shouting the name Yana Logan-Sharp and demanding to know the police take on the matter. Tara pictured the coming headlines and squirmed at the prospect of their work being castigated. She imagined the tabloid angles on the situation. They'd be more concerned with Tara's bra cup size and who she lived with, rather than the two cases of murder she was investigating. She wondered what the public would make of a picture of her drinking cappuccino at a coffee shop when she should be interrogating a billionaire. If they only knew.

Following their coffee break, a swift and efficient check of mobile phone records had led them back to the temporary home of Sebastian Logan-Sharp in West Derby. The reason for the checks was all over social media and likely to feature in the same papers alongside the pictures of her entering a coffee shop.

Several social media platforms displayed the image of former supermodel Yana Logan-Sharp lying dead in her bedroom. Someone had believed it served a purpose to post such an image. It was no longer sufficient for your name to be featured on news bulletins following your death at the hands of another. Nowadays the public appetite for private details had to be gratified by the posting of an undignified image of a murder victim.

When Bleasdale had first drawn her attention to the post, Tara's initial reaction was to think it was merely an old picture of the model lying on a bed. But the tag below the image stated it was the murdered woman and, zooming in on the body, Tara saw the wooden skewer protruding from Yana's abdomen. She recalled that when the medical officer had examined Yana's body, he'd found the skewer lying on the floor next to the bed. Beatrice had admitted removing it from the body. It was this detail that alarmed her. She must find the person who had taken the photo and posted it online. It seemed plausible that whoever had captured Yana in death had also caused it.

Wilson and Bleasdale had contacted the social media companies that had facilitated publication of the picture. Soon they had an IP address and a likely culprit.

They were met at the front door by Beatrice Howard. Tara thought the woman looked tired and drawn. From their previous meetings she had been impressed by the glamorous and businesslike demeanour of the woman. This morning, however, Beatrice was casually dressed in loose slacks and trainers, wore no make-up, and could not even raise a formal smile in greeting them. She led them to the lounge and quickly retreated from the room.

As she waited, Tara considered whether to bring the suspect directly to the station for questioning or to settle for an interview at the house. Either way, she'd now decided that the issue was merely a distraction from her finding the killer, because surely the murderer would not have been so stupid to post a picture of their victim online only for it to be traced back to them.

Tara got to her feet as the young woman came into the room.

'Good morning, Shelby. We would like to ask you some questions.'

Shelby, looking pale, stood before Tara in shorts and sports vest. She was barefoot and did not even look her nineteen years, her long red mane dishevelled as though she'd just been roused from her bed. She said nothing in response to Tara's greeting, plopped into an armchair, crossed her legs, and waited. Tara resumed her seat next to Murray and maintained her informal manner.

'Firstly,' she began, 'can you confirm that it was you who took this picture?'

Murray had a print of the image and passed it to the nanny. Shelby held the A4 page in front of her and seemed to study it. She handed it back but said nothing.

'Did you post this photograph of Yana on social media?' Tara asked more sternly.

Shelby still made no reply, but her gaze fell to the floor.

'We traced it to a mobile device registered to you, Shelby, so we know it was posted from your phone.'

'Why ask me then?' she snapped.

'I asked you to confirm it, that's all.'

'Sure, it was me. I took the picture of Yana, and I posted it online.'

'Did you kill her?'

'No way!' Shelby looked shocked as though she hadn't realised that someone would reach that conclusion. She sat upright, her eyes wide and staring at Tara.

'Then you must tell me when and why you took this picture.'

'It was Surrey. I'd gone to her room to check she was OK, but she wasn't in bed.'

'What time was this?'

'I don't know. Late. Everyone from the party had gone home. We always keep some lights on, downstairs and on the landing. I went looking for Surrey. At first, I thought she might have gone to the kitchen for milk and cookies, but she wasn't there. When I came back upstairs, I noticed the door to Yana's room was open. I thought Surrey might have gone to her mother, and I decided not to disturb them. Heaven knows, the child got little attention from Yana. But as I reached the door of my room, Surrey came running out of her mother's and rushed into my arms. I asked her if she was OK. She said that her mummy wouldn't wake up. So, I got Surrey back into her own bed and settled. Then on my way back to my room I thought I should check on Yana. If Surrey had disturbed her, I knew I should apologise. I'm supposed to take care of the child and to make sure this kind of thing doesn't happen.'

'You went into Yana's room?' asked Tara.

'Yeah.'

'What did you find?'

Shelby gave a shrug as if to say the answer was obvious. Tara thought her attitude was rather soulless.

'It was dark in there, but I whispered to see if Yana was awake. She didn't answer. I had my cell with me, so I took a picture of her on the bed. Then I left.'

'Why do that?'

Another shrug.

'Seemed like a cool idea. Take a picture of the drunken wife of a billionaire as she sleeps.'

Tara glimpsed Murray's expression. He looked bemused by Shelby's behaviour.

'But Yana wasn't merely sleeping, was she?' said Tara. 'She was already dead, Shelby.'

'I didn't know that, did I?'

'But didn't you realise when you looked at the picture you had taken? Yana had been stabbed with a wooden skewer. It was clearly visible. And next morning when Yana was found and later when we arrived, you must have known that she was already dead when you took that photograph.'

The young woman shook her head in profuse disagreement.

'What did you hope to gain by posting it online?'

'Just thought it was cool, that's all.'

'I am going to ask you again, Shelby, did you kill Yana?'

'No.'

Tara was not convinced by Shelby's attitude. She wondered what a criminal psychologist would make of the performance. The nanny showed no empathy for the murdered Yana. Murray took over, while Tara gathered her thoughts.

'If you weren't responsible for Yana's death, who do you think would have wanted to kill her?'

'That's easy,' she replied.

'Really?' said Murray.

'Yeah. I thought you guys would have realised by now. Sebastian killed Yana.'

'Why do you think that?' asked Tara.

Shelby smiled. In other circumstances it may have appeared endearing, but Tara was growing disconcerted by the young woman's state of mind.

'Sebastian didn't love her. He's in love with me. He wants to be with me, but Yana was getting in the way.'

'But Sebastian and Yana were intending to separate. Why would he decide to kill her?'

'Divorce would not have been enough to get rid of a bitch like her. She had to die.'

'Did Sebastian tell you that he killed his wife?' asked Tara.

'No, but I saw him.'

'You saw him kill Yana?'

'No, but I saw him going into her room and I saw him when he came out again.'

'When exactly was this?'

'It was when I checked on Surrey before I first went to bed.'

'Did he see you?'

'Yeah, sure. After he'd been in Yana's room, and he saw me, he came to mine, and we made love. He'd gone back to his own room by the time I got up to check again on Surrey.'

'Why didn't you tell us about this when we first met?' Tara struggled to hide her incredulity at Shelby's revelation.

The woman merely shrugged in response.

'Can you tell me what you know about Tommy Brady?' asked Tara.

'I'm sorry, I've never heard that name before.'

CHAPTER 54

Tara Grogan

'Tweedy will go spare,' said Murray. 'And the press is going to have a field day.'

'What do you expect me to do, Alan?'

They waited in the lounge, while Beatrice went to fetch her boss.

'The nanny has told us that Sebastian was in Yana's room,' Tara said. 'It fits with the approximate time of death, and he had motive.'

'It could have been the nanny. She was in the room and admitted taking the picture of the victim. And she's nuts, claiming that Sebastian loved her.'

'Why is that so strange?'

'You can see she is infatuated with the man,' Murray said. 'There's something odd about her.'

'I believe there is just one person responsible for killing Yana and Tommy Brady. Sebastian has motive for killing both. You heard Shelby. She had no clue about Brady. We have to bring Sebastian to the station now, and I think we'll get enough to charge him with both murders.'

Murray looked doubtful as Sebastian strode into the lounge. He again was not pleased to see Tara in his home.

'What the hell do you people want now?'

Beatrice had followed him into the room. She looked as though she knew what was about to unfold.

Tara got to her feet, but Murray spoke. 'Sebastian Logan-Sharp, I'm arresting you on suspicion of the murders of Yana Logan-Sharp and Tommy Brady.'

The billionaire threw his head back and laughed heartily at Murray's formal tone as he recited the rights of the individual being arrested.

'You people are fucking nuts,' Sebastian said. 'I've told you I didn't kill anybody. My lawyers will tear you to shreds, love. You'll be lucky to be selling knickers at an Ann Summers party when they're done with you.'

Tara raised her eyebrows at the cheek of the man. How rude could he possibly get, she thought. She nodded to Murray who produced a pair of handcuffs.

'Surely there's no need for those, Inspector,' said Beatrice.

Tara didn't reply and allowed Murray to place their suspect under restraint. He then marched Sebastian out of the room.

'May I come along?' Beatrice asked.

'I'm not sure what that will achieve, Ms Howard. Unless you intend to act as his legal representative, you will not be allowed to speak with him.'

Nevertheless, Beatrice followed them from the house and was met by Gavin Westport waiting by their car and texting on his mobile.

Several reporters were hanging around by the gates as Tara and Murray drove through with Sebastian in the back seat. Tara no longer cared about the pictures taken or how quickly the news of the arrest would break. She did wonder what Tweedy would say but reckoned she could handle it. She now had a witness that saw Sebastian enter his wife's bedroom for a period long enough for him to put a pillow over her face and smother her. She already knew about Sebastian visiting the home of Tommy Brady on the day he died. Sebastian had a motive for killing his wife, and Tara believed she could establish one for Brady's murder too. As they drove to St Anne Street, she was content with her decision to arrest the billionaire.

* * *

Before Sebastian's solicitor arrived, Tara and Murray went over the questions they would put to their suspect. Tara was jubilant that Tweedy had not raised an objection to the arrest of Logan-Sharp. The news had already leaked. Reporters had witnessed the billionaire's departure from his home in the back of a police car. Photographers had been waiting by the entrance as the car rolled into St Anne Street station. Tara pictured the headlines. They would all be about the murder of Yana and how her husband was responsible. She hoped that she didn't feature in any of the reports. The billionaire would be tried and convicted online and in the press. It was succulent news for public consumption. And yet Tara had a slightly different agenda. The Yana murder inquiry could wait for a short time while she first dealt with the death of Tommy Brady.

The solicitor, a member of Logan-Sharp's legal team for his business ventures whilst in Liverpool, was shown into the interview room. He didn't strike Tara as a man used to attending police stations to represent clients in criminal matters. She guessed he was of the corporate variety – expensive suits, plush office, and a pool of juniors all working the legal end of Sebastian's business empire.

Phillip Stratton, a trim-looking man with short brown hair, prominent nose, and narrow mouth, shook hands with Tara and Murray. Then Tara noticed that when Stratton greeted Sebastian, it seemed they hadn't met previously because he introduced himself to his client and explained his position in the law firm. Sebastian looked as though he couldn't care less that Stratton was there to represent him. He was just another lackey. Tara allowed them ten minutes in private.

Sebastian had accepted the offer of tea and when it was brought into the room by a young female constable, he had something to say.

'You haven't any Scotch to go with it, love?'

Tara hoped that soon the man's bravado could be peeled away. She wanted to get under his skin. From previous encounters she believed it would be the best way. Get him riled and he would say more than he'd intended. She wasted no time in going through the preliminaries of a police interview, then as a first attempt to agitate her subject, she let Murray ask the first question.

'Tell us why you went to visit Tommy Brady,' he said.

It was as if someone had just plugged him into the electricity mains. Phillip Stratton didn't get the chance to advise his client to offer no comment. Sebastian just blew.

'What the fuck is this? I came here to talk about the bastard who killed my wife, and you're asking me about Tommy fucking Brady.'

It was clear to Tara that Sebastian had not listened to what was said at his home before coming to the station. The man was under arrest as a murder suspect; he was beyond a mere witness assisting with police enquiries.

'We would appreciate an answer to DS Murray's question, Mr Logan-Sharp,' she said.

Tara thought he was about to dive over the table and grab her by the throat. The man's eyes bulged in their sockets. He slammed his palms on the table and tea splashed from his cup.

'Typical bizzies. Never change, do you? I'm the frigging victim here. My wife has been murdered and you're pissing in the wind, love.'

He looked sternly at his brief, perhaps expecting him to take control of the situation. But Stratton already seemed out of his depth.

Murray continued as if the outburst hadn't happened.

'So, please explain why you decided to visit Tommy Brady'

Sebastian looked incredulous and then finally resigned. Stratton attempted to whisper instructions, but Tara reckoned that few people could get away with telling Sebastian what to do.

'I told you before,' Sebastian said. 'I was catching up with an old mate.'

'What prompted you to renew contact?' asked Murray.

'It was my first time back in Liverpool for years. I have already told you this.'

'Who made the initial contact, you or Tommy?'

'Why? Does it matter?'

'Was the meeting arranged to discuss business?'

Tara opened a loose-leaf folder and produced an A4 sheet containing printouts of several emails. She slid it across the table in front of Sebastian. He gave it a cursory glance as Tara elucidated.

'These are several emails exchanged between you and Tommy Brady. We retrieved them from his computer. They are dated three weeks prior to your arrival in Liverpool. In the first one, Tommy Brady requests a meeting with you to discuss a business proposal.'

Sebastian threw his gaze to the ceiling and scoffed. Tara was not put off.

'Your first reply was dismissive, wouldn't you say?'

'Too right. I told him to get stuffed.'

'But Tommy Brady persisted, didn't he? In this final email, he advises that it would be in your best interests to meet with him.'

Sebastian fumed at her, but Tara was well used to men trying to intimidate. She'd seen them come and go – some to prison and several to their graves. She matched his stare and waited.

'OK, OK! If I tell you this crap, will you please get on with finding the lowlife who killed Yana?'

'Don't you think it's too much of a coincidence that two people connected with you have been murdered within days of each other? I would appreciate your co-operation with investigating Tommy Brady's death and maybe I can find the person responsible.'

'OK, OK! Tommy contacted me when he heard I was coming back to Liverpool. He said that he had a deal for me. So, I went to see him.'

'What did you discuss?' asked Tara.

Sebastian smirked.

'It was the same old Tommy. He hadn't changed. Still playing with his computers and junk. And, of course, all he wanted to talk about was the good old days. I said I didn't have time for reminiscing. So, he told me about his business idea. It didn't sound useful and, besides, funding a start-up for a computer app is not my thing these days. He explained it all, but I told him I wasn't interested.'

'Did he ask you for money?'

'Yes, of course, it was the only reason he'd wanted to see me. He wanted me to invest in his idea.'

'But you refused?'

'No way was I giving him a penny. He'd blow it all in a couple of weeks. Tommy was no businessman. Can I go now? I've told you about Tommy. I have work to do, that's if I still have a business after you bringing me here for all the world to see.'

He got to his feet and straightened his jacket.

But Tara was far from finished.

'Please sit, Sebastian. We are not done.'

He flapped again but eventually resumed his seat, drumming his fingers on the table.

'I'm wondering why you even bothered to meet Tommy,' said Tara. 'Surely, he had explained a little of his idea when he first contacted you. There must have been something of interest for you to spare the time from your busy schedule to visit him.'

'Like I've already said, I was catching up with an old friend.'

'He was hardly that, Sebastian. Your ex-wife told us that you and Tommy had an acrimonious parting years ago. You hounded him out of his own company and left him penniless. Doesn't sound like the kind of relationship you would be keen to revisit, nor Tommy for that matter. So, what really made you go to his house?'

'I wouldn't believe a word Carla told you. She's another bloody leech.'

'Why did you *really* visit Tommy Brady? It's a simple question.'

Sebastian slammed his fist on the table, his face glowing.

'Because the toerag was trying to ruin me!'

CHAPTER 55

Tara Grogan

'Tara,' said Tweedy when his DI entered his office. 'I thought you should be party to this before we go any further with Mr Logan-Sharp.'

Tara gave her boss a curious look followed by a cold stare at the stranger seated by her boss's desk. She thought it must be important for her to have been called out of an interview with a murder suspect.

'This is Simon Jackson,' Tweedy said.

The man rose immediately, smiled at Tara, and reached out his hand. He wore a grey tailored suit, had an athletic build but was not terribly handsome. Tara responded, and he squeezed her soft hand in his.

'How do you do?' he said in a cheerful voice with a cultured southern accent.

'I'm fine, thank you,' Tara said. 'So, now you have decided to visit my workplace rather than staking out my home?'

Tweedy's expression changed to one of surprise.

'What's this, Tara?'

She didn't reply and still appeared mystified. Jackson filled the gap.

'National Crime Agency,' he said with confidence, resuming his seat. 'Financial Intelligence Unit.'

She wasn't any more satisfied by his introductions.

'Mr Jackson has requested that we desist from interviewing Sebastian Logan-Sharp,' said Tweedy.

'And why is that?' Tara asked curtly. She felt her irritation rising.

'I'm afraid it is not a request,' said Jackson. 'We are instructing you to release Sebastian Logan-Sharp immediately.'

'But we are in the middle of a murder inquiry,' she protested. 'Sebastian Logan-Sharp is our prime suspect for the murder of his wife.'

Jackson sat back in his chair. 'Our inquiry takes precedence over that.'

Tara looked to her boss in alarm. 'Sir, this is ridiculous. I have witnesses to a row between Logan-Sharp and his wife, a few hours before she was killed. I have a witness who saw him enter her bedroom around the time she died. He has motive for killing her. He is already under arrest.'

'Well then, you have all that you need,' said Jackson. 'Just keep it under wraps until we conclude our operation. He's all yours after that.'

'But, sir? Surely a murder inquiry takes precedence over a financial investigation?'

'Our hands are tied over this, Tara,' Tweedy responded.

'The order comes directly from the office of the Home Secretary,' said Jackson. 'Your investigation has strayed into an operation of national importance.'

Tara fumed.

Jackson glanced deliberately at his watch.

'You need to be quick, Superintendent. The longer this takes, the more damage it could do. You must release him immediately. The press is already speculating over why he's been brought here. Bad publicity could scupper the deal he's been planning in Liverpool. Get him out of here now and not a word to the media, please. And another thing, stay away from his house.'

'Why are you so interested in him?' asked Tara.

It was Jackson's turn to look peeved. 'You are not entitled to know that. Please just get on with it. I don't have all day to debate things with you.'

Tara shook her head. 'Right, fine. Before I do anything, would you mind telling me why you were parked outside my house?'

Jackson shrugged frivolously. 'Operational reasons, DI Grogan. Reasons that I cannot divulge at this stage.'

Tara glared at him before referring to her boss for his comment. Tweedy responded with a sympathetic grin but said nothing.

Tara, red-faced, said nothing more and bounded from the room.

CHAPTER 56

Tara Grogan

Murray had remained in the interview room with Sebastian and his solicitor. They appeared to be having a nice convivial chat about football when Tara walked in. The scene did not help her mood.

'You may leave now, Mr Logan-Sharp,' she said sourly.

'Great!' Sebastian retorted, getting to his feet. 'Thanks very much for pissing on my day, love.'

'It's DI Grogan,' Tara said, 'please remember that. I have no doubt we'll meet again soon.'

'Hope not. I won't sleep soundly knowing the likes of you are supposed to be protecting us.'

Tara grinned sardonically. Sebastian stomped from the room leaving Stratton to ask all the questions. The solicitor placed notes into his briefcase as Tara looked on. She wanted to speak with Murray and waited for Stratton to leave.

'I trust you will have no further need to speak to my client?'

'On the contrary, Mr Stratton,' Tara replied, 'your client will remain of interest to us, and you may tell him that I would prefer he remains in Liverpool for the time being.'

She smiled glibly and the solicitor departed saying nothing more.

'What's going on, ma'am?' said Murray as they made their way upstairs. 'You don't seem happy with how that ended.'

'It wasn't the interview, Alan. Logan-Sharp is our chief suspect for two murders. But we have just been shackled.'

'I don't understand.'

By the time she'd reached her desk she'd explained the situation to Murray and tried her best not to sound bitter. Too many times she had shouted her frustrations when something had hindered her work. On this occasion, she believed, she already had her man. All she could do was continue gathering evidence and build her case, and when the National Crime Agency was finished with Sebastian Logan Sharp, she would re-appear in the billionaire's life and show him the error of his ways.

Over coffee in the canteen, Tara gathered her thoughts and tried to cool her temper. It was frustrating when all roads still pointed to Sebastian Logan-Sharp, and she was weary of seeing Murray demolish a fry-up.

Returning to the office, she called Bleasdale to her desk and asked her to fetch the information collated on all attendees at the house party in West Derby. Wilson and Murray were instructed to bring the files of forensic evidence amassed so far on the murders of Tommy Brady and Yana Logan-Sharp. With her team assembled, Tara suggested a private meeting room for them to thrash out a way forward. She even suggested coffee and doughnuts. Before they got started, Tweedy came to see them.

'At this time, folks, we need to remember that we are not the only organisation in this country committed to protecting the public. It may seem that our investigation has been suspended but that is far from the truth. We are free to continue our inquiries into these murders, but we must do it without compromising our colleagues who are involved in an equally challenging operation.'

Tara couldn't disagree, it was just that at times she found it difficult to emulate Tweedy's obliging nature. When he had left the room, she got down to business.

'John, anything further arising from the post-mortem on Yana?'

Wilson opened the manila file in front of him and glanced at the first page within. 'Not much that we hadn't already surmised from the scene, ma'am. Cause of death is confirmed as suffocation. The victim had a single puncture wound to the left side of her abdomen that perforated her small intestine. It's likely that the skewer found on the bedroom floor had been used to inflict the wound. The absence of bleeding suggests that it was removed after the victim's death. This fits with the statement given by Beatrice Howard that she had removed it when she found Yana dead. Her blood alcohol level was 223 milligrams of alcohol per 100 millilitres of blood, more than twice the legal driving limit. Confirms many of the comments from guests at the party that she had been drunk that night. There was also evidence that Yana had taken drugs. Cocaine metabolites were identified in her blood and urine, and traces of powder were detected in nasal passages. No proof that the victim was deliberately drugged prior to suffocation. She was either asleep or was incapacitated from drinking and was unable to fight off her attacker. There was no evidence to indicate a struggle or a sexual assault.'

'Any fingerprint or DNA evidence to help identify our killer?' asked Tara.

Wilson shook his head. 'Fingerprints lifted from the scene have been matched to several members of the household,' he said, 'all of whom could have plausible reasons to be in Yana's room. Forensics are still working through DNA analysis. Matches so far are the same as for fingerprints.'

'Talking of fingerprints, ma'am,' said Bleasdale, 'Sebastian Logan-Sharp's prints were collected during his arrest. They are a match to prints lifted from the hall, living room and the upstairs room where Tommy Brady's body was found. They weren't present on the murder weapon.'

'Well, we know that Sebastian was at the house on the day Brady was killed,' said Tara. 'He was in the middle of explaining why he'd gone there when we had to break off the interview. Alan, was anything of interest said after I left the room?'

Murray looked up. 'No, ma'am. Logan-Sharp seemed to calm down when you were called away. He took his brief's advice and offered "no comment" to my questions.'

Tara winced. It was no real surprise. She returned to the murder of Yana Logan-Sharp.

'Did you get any reason why, according to Shelby, Sebastian went to Yana's bedroom?'

'I'm afraid not, ma'am,' Murray replied.

'Is there any CCTV security at the house in West Derby?'

'No, ma'am,' said Wilson. 'I asked Beatrice Howard about that. She told me that they were aware of the lack of internal security at the house when they rented the property. There is an intercom at the gate, and burglar alarms inside the house, but little else.'

'Doesn't help us,' Tara said, gloomily.

They fell into silence for a short time and availed of the doughnuts. Tara directed their thinking to the extensive list of attendees at the house party.

'There is no easy way to do this. We will simply have to re-focus our efforts on the people who attended that party, but steer clear of Logan-Sharp's household in case we compromise the higher investigation.'

It was sinking in just how much they were hampered in having to avoid the temporary home of Sebastian Logan-Sharp. The scene of a serious crime, the centre of a police inquiry, and yet they could no longer visit it. Tara was also intrigued at how the inscrutable Simon Jackson had so quickly become aware of Sebastian's arrest. Perhaps he was a devotee of a social media platform.

CHAPTER 57

Michelle Weller

Michelle visited the cemetery every week. The flowers she brought didn't last much longer than seven or eight days. Roses, especially, wilted quickly and in the variable springtime weather, daffodils didn't fare any better. Mostly, she bought whatever was on offer in the supermarket: carnations, chrysanthemums, daisies, lilies and sometimes dahlias, which were her favourite. She removed the dead stalks from the holder set in the headstone and inserted the fresh blooms. She always came prepared with a bottle of water and a cloth that she used to wipe down the polished pink granite. There was usually bird mess to be cleaned off. When her work was done, she stepped back and read the gold-lettered inscription as if for the first time. Sometimes she read aloud.

'Weller Edward, died 24 March 1999, aged 40 years. His beloved wife Marjorie, died 7 June 2013, aged 52 years.'

Between the name of her father and her mother was a third name. She always read it last, but the words were frequently lost in her sobs.

A warm breeze streaked through her hair as if the spirits of the dead swirled around her. She wiped a tear from her eye. Nothing strange in that. There were always tears. If she was lucky, they came only once a week as she stood in the cemetery. There were times, though, when they came in the night, lying alone in bed and even as she worked at the call centre. Sometimes life and death just wouldn't leave her alone.

Strolling along the main drive of the cemetery, her mind turned to the things she had witnessed at that damned party. She thought also of Paul Renfrew. By the time she'd reached the bus stop on Watts Lane, she was having serious doubts about their date. At least he'd merely called it a get-together for a drink. He'd suggested they discuss how to pool their resources in the fight against Sebastian Logan-Sharp. She wondered if he was hoping to make it back to her bed and this time for something they would remember the next morning. Romance was not something she craved. Loving a man had not featured in her thinking for years, although there were occasions when she'd considered love in the arms of a woman. But she didn't feel comfortable about such things. She had not been raised to think like that.

Paul had been quite charming and persistent. She finally agreed to meet him in town for a drink. When she'd given in, he swiftly upgraded the meeting to dinner at a restaurant. She wasn't so sure about that. Restaurants, like romance, hadn't been major ingredients of her social life.

She got off the bus in Lime Street and walked to a chain eatery that specialised in serving Portuguese-style flavoured chicken. She'd insisted on nothing fancy, and Paul had obliged. When she got there, he was waiting outside browsing his phone.

'Hello,' he said.

She smiled weakly, and he kissed her on the cheek. It was enough to embarrass her, and then sheepishly she followed him inside. Once they'd sat down it was a relief to have a menu to study without the need for small talk. After all, this man had already spent a night in her bed, sleeping beside her. Who knew what he thought about that. Aside from his dedication to environmental issues she knew nothing about Paul Renfrew.

Once they'd ordered food and both sat with soft drinks the small talk inevitably began.

'What have you been up to since we last met?' he asked.

The question sent a shiver down her spine. It sounded over inquisitive. What exactly did he mean by that? She stared without reply. But he seemed to notice her unease.

'I meant in general, how've you been?' he said, smiling.

She thought he looked nice, better than when they'd got drunk at the party. He wore a green polo shirt and jeans and despite his beard smelled of a fresh aftershave.

'I work shifts at a call centre,' she replied. 'There's not much else going on.'

'What about your protest group? Any more plans to get at Logan-Sharp?'

'It's all gone a bit quiet. Besides, we're not exactly a big organisation. Just a committee of twelve.'

'That's not so bad. If you get too big you run the risk of losing control of your own agenda. At least, as far as Sebastian Logan-Sharp is concerned someone did us a favour.'

Their eyes met briefly. His were smiling, hers, she felt, were darting nervously. What did he mean?

'Yes,' he continued, 'the murder of his wife has certainly put the proverbial cat among the pigeons.'

She felt his eyes remain on her but couldn't look. What the hell was he getting at?

'Do you think it's been enough to send him packing?' he asked.

'I hope so,' was all she could manage in reply.

CHAPTER 58

Beatrice Howard

It was a humid night, and it was impossible to sleep. The room was stuffy, and Beatrice lay on the bed in her slip without even a sheet to cover her. She longed to be back in London. To begin a new chapter in her life. A life minus Sebastian Logan-Sharp. Somehow, she'd found the conviction not to snort any more coke, and to avoid beasts like Ernst Eder in future. Neither of those resolutions was any comfort as she lay in the semi-darkness, her curtains and window open to get some fresh air, a full moon casting a faint glare over the garden. The third decision she'd made, however, caused the greatest consternation. She realised she had probably ruined the man she'd served for the last fifteen years.

Her first call to James Boal, she knew would result in his withdrawal from the development project, and he'd wasted no time in doing so. Beatrice could see that James Boal was honest, a man of integrity. She didn't think the same of his son Cameron, although, she realised, he'd justifiably harboured reservations over participation in the scheme. When she'd told James Boal that the entire business model for the project was shored up by dirty money from drug and people-trafficking cartels in Europe, the Liverpool businessman had gasped in horror. He had thanked Beatrice and promised not to reveal her part in his decision to withdraw from the project.

Her second call had been to the chairman of one of the four football clubs that had been under consideration for a buyout. Gaining similar assurances of her anonymity, she'd left the man in no doubt of his course of action. He promptly warned his counterparts in the other clubs that they should avoid further contact with Sebastian Logan-Sharp.

With that done she had lain low, avoided her boss and Ernst Eder and waited for the solid matter to strike the fan. It had not been as difficult as she'd first envisaged to bring the project crashing down. After Ernst had threatened and raped her, she did some digging on the Austrian. He had an unsettling hold over Sebastian, and her boss was reluctant to confide in her. If the Logan-Sharp business was rotten then she was not going to be implicated when the whole thing came crashing down.

It only took a brief internet search and a couple of phone calls to get an idea of what was really going on in the life of Sebastian. She wondered why she hadn't investigated sooner.

Her online search began with Yana Logan-Sharp, the supermodel who'd emerged from rural Hungary to become a global fashion icon, only to opt for apparent domesticity with her marriage to Sebastian. Beatrice avoided the recent speculative social media posts following Yana's murder, except for one photo on Instagram that piqued her interest and led to her calling an old friend in London. The picture appeared to have been taken more than five years ago, before Yana married Sebastian, since the legend below the image stated her maiden name Bartos and not Logan-Sharp. It showed a rather exclusive gathering, abroad, judging by the sunshine and the luxury yacht. Yana was the central figure wearing a white bikini and draped over a couch on the deck of the boat. Seated next to her was a man Beatrice didn't recognise, but the legend stated the name Victor Dulka. He looked around forty with dark hair and a toned body. But this man did not immediately interest Beatrice. It was the figure standing behind Dulka that intrigued. He wasn't cited in the legend, but she was convinced it was none other than Ernst Eder.

She found nothing online beyond what she already knew about the Austrian, that he was a former elite soldier who had ventured into personal security. But she was horrified to learn of the reputation of Victor Dulka, a Serbian billionaire with apparent links to criminal fraternities across Europe. At that point, she'd called her old friend Cecilia Lacourt, a French journalist based in London.

'You must not involve yourself, Beatrice,' Cecilia warned. 'Very bad news.'

'The thing is, Cecilia, it might already be too late.'

'Then you must stop immediately. It has not been proven, but Dulka has been associated with the Mafia in Italy, and criminal gangs in Albania and Romania. It is rumoured that he is behind the biggest people-trafficking organisation in Europe and with that comes drugs also. His fortune is not legitimate, but he has ingratiated himself with respectable wealthy people and several governments.'

Cecilia did not have to say much more. Beatrice could fill in the blanks. Dirty money had to be washed clean to make the owner appear respectable. Now she realised that Sebastian and his building project on Merseyside had been intended for such a purpose. What better way to launder money than to funnel it through a massive development project. But Sebastian wasn't going to settle for that; he had intended to buy a football club and use it to wash even more dirty money. The one remaining question was how deep was Sebastian in cahoots with Dulka? Beatrice reckoned that he must already be out of his depth, and that's why he had been freaking out over the smallest hiccups in their plans. Sebastian was running scared of Victor Dulka. And it seemed likely to her that Ernst Eder took his orders from the Serbian.

Rather than drifting into sleep, Beatrice continued to process all that she had so recently learnt. She hoped that by wrecking their plans she could get herself out of this dangerous environment. Perhaps she might also rescue Sebastian, that's if he wanted to be helped. But her fear intensified when she thought again about Ernst.

Rising from the bed and without switching on a light, she pushed the stool at her dressing table across the door. It was feeble protection if he came for her again, but it might be enough to alert her, if she was sleeping, and allow her vital seconds to lift the carving knife she'd taken from the kitchen to defend herself.

After a visit to the en suite she returned to her bed and lay down once more, hoping for sleep to come. What seemed like only a few minutes later, as she grew drowsy and her eyes were closing, there was a knock on the door. Straightaway, she reached to the bedside table and grasped the knife.

CHAPTER 59

Tara Grogan

'There are three cars this morning,' Kate announced as she came into the kitchen. 'You're definitely getting famous.'

Tara smiled at her friend then winced at the comment; she couldn't decide how to react.

'They wouldn't be wasting their time sitting outside if they knew I'd been stopped from investigating Logan-Sharp. It's him they're interested in, not me.'

Kate scooped the morning paper from the table and playfully read aloud the latest commentary on Tara's murder case.

'The attractive baby-faced detective inspector – ooh! – remains tight-lipped regarding rumours that the death of former supermodel Yana Logan-Sharp may be linked to the murder of a local man named Tommy Brady.'

'Oh no! I was dreading that,' said Tara. 'A clever journalist has finally made the connection. This won't go down well with that fella from the National Crime Agency.'

'Why is that?'

'I may have forgotten to share that particular piece of information with Mr Jackson.'

'He probably already knew about it.'

'Maybe, but I suppose I should expect a call from the nice man later today.'

Tara heard car engines starting up as she stepped outside. This morning there would be a convoy on the drive to St Anne Street.

* * *

Entering the detectives' room, Tara expected to hear immediately of the consequences of the press linking the murders of Yana Logan-Sharp and Tommy Brady. But she wasn't met with a request from Tweedy to speak with him, and thankfully there was no sign of Jackson spitting teeth and demanding to know why he had not been told about Brady. She did find, however, a note on her desk with a name and phone number upon it. Wilson came over.

'Ma'am, you just missed the call by five minutes.'

'Any reason given?'

'No, ma'am.'

She settled into her seat, picked up her desk phone and dialled the number. It was answered promptly.

'DI Grogan, thank you for returning my call.' The voice sounded uneasy.

'What can I do for you, Beatrice?'

'I can't talk here. Can we meet? Somewhere in public?'

'Of course. Is everything all right? You sound upset.'

'I'm fine. I have something to discuss with you, that's all.'

Tara suggested a Starbucks in Paradise Street at Liverpool One in an hour, and having agreed, Beatrice ended the call.

Tara had intended to spend the morning with Wilson, Murray and Bleasdale in advancing the investigation in view of the embargo placed on them by Simon Jackson. Now she was intrigued as to why Sebastian's PA had requested a meeting.

The storm she had imagined waiting for her when she'd arrived at St Anne Street finally showed up as she was preparing to leave for her meeting with Beatrice Howard. She watched with glee as Simon Jackson marched through the detectives' room heading straight for Tweedy's office. The super was just the person to deal with irate questions over why the NCA had not been informed of the connection between two murders. Tara checked the time on her phone, rose quickly, and whispered to Bleasdale that she was on her way to a meeting if anyone should come looking for her. She smiled and looked towards Tweedy's office. Bleasdale grinned her understanding.

'OK, ma'am. See you later.'

* * *

The coffee shop was busy with customers, and from the doorway she couldn't see Beatrice. She ordered a cappuccino, and as she waited at the counter, Beatrice entered the shop and gazed around. Tara raised her hand to catch the woman's attention then pointed to a table she'd had her eye on.

'Can I get you anything?' Tara asked.

'Just a flat white please.'

Beatrice headed swiftly for the free table. It all seemed rather clandestine. Joining her, Tara smiled but was intrigued by the woman's appearance. She looked exhausted; her face was pale, and she seemed to have aged since the last time Tara had seen her. But what struck Tara most was that her eyes lacked the confidence she had noticed when she'd first met the PA. The woman's gaunt image seemed complete by the absence of her business clothes. She wore a white T-shirt and jogging trousers, both of which hung loosely on her trim frame.

Beatrice sipped her coffee then managed a thin smile.

'I'm sure you're wondering why I asked to see you, Inspector.'

'It has to be something important; I realise that you have a busy schedule.'

The woman gazed around the shop and even turned and looked out of the window behind her.

'Are you sure everything is all right?' Tara asked.

Beatrice forced a pensive smile, but Tara saw a woman emotionally disturbed by something.

'Do you need help?' Tara asked. 'We can speak in confidence.'

Beatrice wrung her hands, but before she could respond she broke down in tears, using her bare forearm to wipe her eyes. Tara reached her a napkin. The professional woman that Tara had first encountered at the house in West Derby had vanished. When Beatrice blew her nose, Tara noticed specks of blood on the napkin. Sympathy, and copious amounts of it, were needed. Reaching over the table, she took Beatrice's hand in hers.

'Let's ignore the fact I'm a police officer,' she said softly. 'Tell me, as a woman, why you're so upset.' Tara felt Beatrice quivering as she struggled to compose herself.

'I hardly know where to begin,' she sobbed. 'I hadn't realised how much all this has got to me. I had intended to pass on information this morning and that would be all. I'm sorry, I don't know what's wrong with me.'

Tara gently squeezed Beatrice's hand and smiled, although she remained mystified.

'Tell me just as it comes, Beatrice. We'll make sense of it all later.'

Beatrice looked helplessly at Tara as tears rolled down her face. 'I've been raped.'

CHAPTER 60

Carla Smith

The damned smoke alarm had gone off again. When would Jack ever remember to switch on the extractor before using the toaster? She turned over, hoping for one last doze before surrendering to the day and dragging herself from the comfort of her bed. The beeping hadn't stopped. Surely, one of her sons would have the sense to wave a tea towel beneath the alarm in the hall ceiling. Frustrated and now wide awake, she rolled onto her back. The noise stopped.

Carla lay with her arms spread wide. At times like this she longed for a man beside her, someone to give her a cuddle. Ever since her quarrel with Bobby she had been veiled in renewed loneliness. She hadn't felt this bad for such a long time; always too busy raising her boys to worry about herself. She was certain of one thing, though, and that was to expect more of the same for the rest of her life. But she realised it was recent events that had her feeling uneasy. After the last visit from the bizzies she felt there was something that Jack hadn't told the police and wasn't telling her either. What else had happened at that party? She wondered if it had something to do with Bobby. Had Jack tangled with his dad a second time that night? Her sons had been busy with their exams; there hadn't been a good moment to raise the subject again.

After the clash in the living room, she had gotten way too drunk to make sense of anything. Then she thought perhaps that something more occurred when Jack had ventured upstairs. He'd told the policewoman about asking

Yana where the bathroom was. Carla hadn't contradicted her son's account in front of the bizzies, but she knew it wasn't true. Jack and Lee had already used the downstairs loo several times during the evening. In fact, Jack had found it as soon as they'd arrived at the house — he said he was bursting for a pee. So, Carla wondered what her son had got up to when he'd gone upstairs. She remembered that Jack's eyes had nearly popped from his head when he'd first seen Yana. Despite her drunken state, Yana looked stunning and virtually stark naked in that blue dress. Jack, more so than Lee, could not stop his gawping. It didn't help matters when Yana had attempted to flirt. Carla wondered if her son had followed Yana into her bedroom. If so, what had he done?

She showered and dressed, relishing the silence in the house. Evidently, there had been no further mishaps with the toaster. As she stepped down into the hall, she noticed that the postman had already been. Several envelopes were scattered on the floor. Most of it was junk mail as usual, but amongst it was a plain, handwritten envelope addressed to her. She dumped the other letters on the sofa then ripped open the envelope. As she pulled out a single piece of folded paper, another dropped to the floor. She read the brief note in her hand.

> *Dear Carla,*
>
> *I don't assume for a minute that you'll believe this comes from Sebastian (Bobby). We both know that he would never have a change of heart on this scale. But I, for what it's worth, think that you and your sons deserve something. I will understand perfectly if you decide to rip this up and throw it away. But please think about it. I can assure you that Sebastian will never know. I hope you make good use of it.*
> *Beatrice (Sebastian's PA)*

Carla retrieved the second piece of paper from the floor and turned it over. It was a cheque from a company named Logan-Sharp Enterprises, signed by Beatrice Howard and made out to Carla Smith for the sum of one hundred thousand pounds.

'What's up, Mum?' asked Jack.

Carla clutched the letter to her breast.

'You look like you've seen a ghost,' he said.

Her thoughts swirled from elation through sadness to gratitude. When she managed to speak, it was with a sense of reality and fear.

'Jack. I want the truth. You need to tell me what happened between you and Yana Logan-Sharp.'

CHAPTER 61

Tara Grogan

'I realise it's my word against his, Inspector. Even if I did press charges, he could easily deny rape because we'd had sex a few minutes earlier.'

'That does not excuse violent behaviour. We can at least put your allegations to him under police caution. Are you willing to tell me his name?'

Beatrice dabbed her eyes with the napkin and continued to glance around the coffee shop. She seemed nervous of people coming and going.

'Ernst Eder,' she whispered, 'Sebastian's so-called bodyguard.'

Tara tried to maintain a neutral expression. For some reason, she'd been expecting to hear Sebastian's name. Somehow, she would not have placed this woman with the arrogant bodyguard.

'Is your relationship serious and ongoing?'

'Neither. It was just sex.'

Suddenly, and before Tara could respond further, Beatrice dismissed the subject.

'Sorry, that's not the main reason for my wanting to meet you,' she said. 'But it does have to do with Ernst.'

'What do you mean?'

'I believe he killed Yana.'

'Why do you think that?'

'I can't prove it yet, but I think that Ernst is more than a mere bodyguard. He has a hold over Sebastian. I believe he works for a man who controls what Sebastian does. This whole business enterprise on Merseyside is a front for something illegal. I've already tried to pull the plug on the deal. I've advised potential investors not to get involved. Sebastian isn't aware of what I've done.'

'Do you know the name of this person?'

'Victor Dulka. He's a Serbian oligarch, rumoured to be involved in drug and people smuggling. Of course, he maintains a very public and philanthropic image and ingratiates himself with the rich and famous.'

Beatrice removed her phone from her handbag and quickly retrieved the image she had saved. She turned the screen to face Tara.

'That's Dulka. You can see Ernst Eder standing behind him.'

Tara gazed at the photo but was drawn immediately to the image of Yana Logan-Sharp seated next to a handsome man. She would not have recognised Ernst Eder but for Beatrice confirming that it was indeed the Austrian.

'Yana knew this man?'

'It seems so, but neither she nor Sebastian had ever mentioned him to me. I've been Sebastian's PA for fifteen years, and in all that time I've never come across Victor Dulka. Seems that I've been kept out of that loop. It explains those occasions when I was not required to accompany him on business trips.'

'But what motive could Dulka have to sanction Yana's murder?'

'It must be connected to this Merseyside project. I don't know, maybe Yana did something to threaten the deal, or she has upset Dulka in some way. Or maybe she was killed to keep Sebastian under their control. I know that Ernst and Sebastian had private conversations, and when I asked about them Sebastian wouldn't tell me anything. But he was really wound up after each time he'd spoken with Ernst.'

Tara's mind was flooding with questions and the name Simon Jackson was uppermost. Was this what the NCA were investigating? Was this the reason why she'd been told to steer clear of Sebastian?

'What about Tommy Brady?' Tara had difficulty with Beatrice's story. There was too much supposition and little hard evidence.

Beatrice looked blank in response to the question about Brady. 'I don't know,' she said. 'It might have nothing to do with it.'

Tara frowned. She was convinced there was a single perpetrator and motive for the two murders.

'Have you told Sebastian about your theory?'

'I've been so frightened in the house since Ernst raped me.'

The admission brought further upset and Beatrice fell silent, her shoulders heaving in sobs. Tara again took hold of the woman's hands and gently caressed them in hers.

'Beatrice, I realise this is difficult. If you prefer, we can talk somewhere more private.'

Beatrice nodded, and without fuss Tara rose from the table and led the woman from the shop. Her first thought was simply to reach her car and drive to a place where they were not likely to be disturbed and where Beatrice would not feel uneasy. That, she decided, ruled out a room at St Anne Street station. But the drive from the city, via the tunnel to New Brighton seemed to relax Beatrice, and soon she was recounting her association with the Austrian bodyguard. She explained about asking him who he really worked for and why he had a hold over Sebastian. His reaction, she struggled to say, had been to rape her.

'When he'd finished, he threatened to come to my room whenever he pleased. There are no locks on the bedroom doors. I slide a stool across at night just to give me warning if he was to burst in. And I keep a knife on the bedside table. I would gladly use it if I had to.'

Tara glanced sideways at Beatrice then quickly returned her eyes to the road.

'Has he come back?'

'No. Last night there was a knock on my door. It was very late, and in crept Sebastian, knocking over the stool. I was so wound up. If he hadn't spoken first, I would have stuck the knife in him.'

'What did he want?'

'He was looking for my advice.'

Beatrice laughed. It felt peculiar to Tara, considering the gravity of their conversation.

'He finally explained what had been going on with Dulka and Ernst. I've never known Sebastian to be frightened of anything or anyone, but last night he was shaking. He was terrified, and was in no doubt, Inspector, that Ernst or someone else connected to Dulka had killed Yana.'

'What did you say to him?'

'I suggested we both come to you. I realise that we might well be in trouble regarding Sebastian's business practices but none of it is worth dying for.'

'So, why didn't he come with you today?'

'He ignored my advice, flatly refused to consult the police. When I came downstairs this morning he was gone. There's only Shelby, Surrey, Patrice and me in the house.

'What about Ernst?'

'I think he has abducted Sebastian.'

CHAPTER 62

Tara Grogan

Tara dropped Beatrice at the house in West Derby, advising her to secure the property as best as she could and to call immediately if she heard anything from Sebastian or Ernst Eder. By the time she'd reached her desk at St Anne Street, she had the familiar feeling of her day closing in around her. On one hand, she had her investigation of two murders to pursue, on the other she realised she must update Tweedy on what she'd learnt from Beatrice. That would mean, however, that Tweedy would be obliged to contact that pompous man from the NCA, Simon Jackson. It was a sad reflection on the modern world when financial crime took precedence over murder and rape.

Nevertheless, Tara was professional and informed Tweedy of the latest developments. Less than twenty minutes elapsed before Simon Jackson marched into the operations room en route to Tweedy's office. Nerves jingled in her stomach at the thought of being summoned again. She had no desire to speak or listen to Jackson. Seconds later, her desk phone rang, and she jumped. As feared, her presence was required.

Her colleagues Murray, Wilson and Bleasdale were busy with the tasks she had assigned since her return from meeting Beatrice Howard. Murray was researching Victor Dulka and his association with Ernst Eder. Wilson was collating the evidence gathered on Yana's murder and researching her connection to the Serbian oligarch. Tara was intrigued that Yana had been in the same photograph as Victor Dulka and Ernst Eder. She felt it strange that all three had then been associated with Sebastian Logan-Sharp. Certainly no coincidence, she thought. Bleasdale concentrated on reviewing the murder of Tommy Brady. Tara still had no suspect other than Sebastian for the killing. If, as Beatrice claimed, Ernst Eder had murdered Yana, what motive was there for him to have killed Brady? It didn't make sense, unless Brady, in trying to re-engage with Sebastian, had been considered a threat.

Jackson had a smug grin on his face as Tara entered Tweedy's office. He didn't even acknowledge her. It was Tweedy who spoke first.

'Tara, I've informed Mr Jackson of the latest developments regarding Sebastian Logan-Sharp. He has some questions for you.'

'Yes, sir,' Tara replied, taking a seat.

Jackson immediately asked his first question.

'When exactly did you hear that Logan-Sharp had fled?'

'This morning, around ten. His PA told me.'

'Did she tell you why he left?'

'He was frightened, apparently. He felt threatened by Ernst Eder and whatever linked him with Victor Dulka.'

Jackson's eyes widened on hearing the Serb's name. Tara decided to say her piece.

'I have little interest in the situation regarding this man. My concern is that Logan-Sharp has done a runner, when he was my prime suspect for two murders and, owing to your interest, I was forced to let him go.'

She noticed the pained expression on Tweedy's face. She had been less than tactful, and her boss knew it. Yet again she'd gone too far. It was becoming her habit to step beyond what her rank permitted. Jackson merely smirked.

'I wouldn't be overly concerned about the whereabouts of Logan-Sharp,' he said.

'And why is that?' said Tara.

Another smirk.

'We have our ways, DI Grogan.'

He may well have his ways, she thought, but right now it was of little benefit to her.

'And what of Ernst Eder, do you also know where he has gone?' she asked. 'He has questions to answer regarding an allegation of rape.'

Jackson could not have looked less interested. He ignored her comment and turned to Tweedy.

'As discussed, Harold, please leave Sebastian Logan-Sharp and Ernst Eder to us. We can deal with them back in London.'

Tara seethed. It seemed her investigation was irrelevant.

'You know that Logan-Sharp is in London?' she asked.

'Not quite,' Jackson replied, getting to his feet and straightening his suit.

'How? How can you know? We've only just told you that he'd left Liverpool.'

It was that irritating smirk again. Tara fumed. She hated that I-know-something-you-don't-know look.

'There was an incident on the M6 early this morning. Someone ran Logan-Sharp's car off the road. It went over the barrier onto its roof.'

'Was he injured?'

'Several shots were fired, and Logan-Sharp was hit once in the arm. He was saved from further injury by his driver.'

'How do you know all this?' Tara asked again.

'Logan-Sharp's driver is one of our officers.'

CHAPTER 63

Shelby Keibler

Patrice was preparing breakfast for Shelby and Surrey, but this morning something didn't feel quite right. The house was abnormally quiet. Surrey picked her way through an omelette but was more interested in pulling her slice of toast apart. Shelby didn't care so long as she was quiet. Lately, the child had taken to singing as she ate, such an irritating thing to do.

Despite the calm in the house, Shelby endured a blinding headache. It was self-inflicted, she knew, resulting from the bottle of champagne she'd swiped from the fridge before going to bed. She wondered where she'd gone wrong with Sebastian. He hadn't come to her room last night. There'd been zero replies to her texts. Why was he ignoring her? After all she'd done for him. With Yana out of the picture, surely it was only a matter of time before he realised that he couldn't do without her, even if she were only to continue looking after Surrey. At least she could still give herself to him. And she knew she was great at sex. She knew how to make an old guy like Sebastian feel good.

After breakfast she played swing ball in the garden with Surrey. She kept an eye on the house, looking out for activity and waiting to speak to Sebastian. Only Patrice worked in the kitchen. The dude had never interacted with anyone else in the household. Maybe it was a French thing, or perhaps he knew better than to get involved with the dysfunctional family of a billionaire. He said little but sure was an awesome cook.

There was no sign of Beatrice either. She hadn't come down for breakfast. Even Patrice was puzzled that no one had eaten any of the food he'd prepared. And where was Ernst? She hadn't seen him or Gavin, and the car was gone.

After she'd managed to get Surrey settled in her playroom with a video game, she wandered through the house. If the bedroom doors were closed, she could knock and listen before venturing inside. But it only took a couple of minutes to discover that Sebastian and Beatrice were not in their rooms. She went via the conservatory to the spare house. The back doors were open, and she called out. She didn't wish to be confronted by the huge Austrian guy, but at least he might know what was going down. She saw Patrice who was now chilling on a sofa in the lounge and watching TV. He shrugged a 'don't know' to her asking if anyone else was in the house.

She sent several more texts to Sebastian and one to Beatrice. It was lunchtime before she received a reply from the PA. 'Back soon,' the message read. There was still nothing from Sebastian.

In the early afternoon, Shelby was at last greeted in the kitchen by a pale and anxious-looking Beatrice.

'I need to have a word, Shelby,' she said rather seriously, grabbing a beer from the fridge.

Shelby closed the lid of her laptop and prepared to listen to what Beatrice had to say. The woman sat down opposite her at the table, nursing the bottle of beer in her hand.

'We would like you to continue looking after Surrey, at least for the foreseeable future.'

Shelby felt some relief on hearing that piece of news, but she hadn't dismissed the confusion in her head about what was going on.

'Where is Sebastian?' she asked.

'I have no idea. He left during the night. I don't know where he's gone or what he's doing.'

It was a dismissive answer, but by the look on Beatrice's face Shelby guessed it was an honest one.

'What's going on, Beatrice?'

The woman looked her in the eyes. It seemed that she was choosing her words carefully. But that wasn't going to help Shelby. She wanted to know everything. She'd worked so damned hard to win Sebastian over and to show him that he didn't need Yana.

'As I've already said, Sebastian has been called away. I don't know how long he will be gone. I would guess that it could be weeks or even months before we see him again.'

'Are we to stay in Liverpool?'

'Yes, for now. There is still business to be taken care of.'

'But I really need to speak with Sebastian.'

Beatrice frowned at her.

'I know you've been screwing him, Shelby. Believe me, that is all it was. You will never feature in Sebastian's life.'

Shelby jumped to her feet, her face red and angry.

'Yes, I will. I love him.'

'No, you don't. You're just a silly girl looking to get ahead.'

'And you're just a drug-snorting whore!'

Beatrice stared hard. Tears welled in her eyes and Shelby could see the woman struggling to remain composed.

'Whatever you think I am, Shelby, I'm trying to stop you from becoming the same.'

CHAPTER 64

Cameron Boal

His hands trembled as he read the note for a second time. A single printed sheet carried a disturbing threat.

> *I know what you did to Yana. It cannot go unpunished. You will pay me, or I will tell the police what I know.*

The note had arrived through the post. He had no idea who had sent it. In the past couple of days, he had finally begun to relax. His father had pulled the plug on their participation in the Merseyside Delta project, and he'd since learnt that the entire scheme was likely to collapse. There had been no further visits from the police asking him about that damned party. He'd thought he was in the clear. And now this.

Removing a bottle of Balvenie from a mahogany cabinet, he poured a generous measure into a crystal tumbler. Even after taking a mouthful, he felt no easier. The questions piled up. What should he do about it? Who sent the bloody thing? Should he tell his father? Should he come clean to the police? He poured a second glass of Scotch and slumped into his desk chair, throwing his head back and shutting his eyes. How did this person even know what happened between him and Yana?

Ignoring his ringing desk phone, he struggled to recall who might have seen him with Sebastian's wife. He supposed it could have been anyone at the party who had stepped into the garden and gazed toward the patio where he and Yana were kissing. But what did it matter? The worrying issue was who saw him entering or leaving Yana's bedroom. That person was most likely to be the blackmailer. But that thought didn't help either. It still could have been anyone at the party.

There was a light tap on his door, and he sat up to see Joyce coming into the office. She held a large, padded envelope in her hand, smiled weakly, and didn't seem surprised to see him languishing by his desk. Joyce was used to his laziness.

'This came for you,' she said, placing the envelope on the desk.

Cameron snatched it up. He just knew it was going to be bad.

'Who brought it?'

'Courier. It was signed for at reception.'

He started to rip it open then waited for Joyce to leave before removing the contents. Inside was a red tote bag and a single sheet of paper. His hands shook again as he read the note.

> *Instructions for payment.*
> *£250,000 in used notes no higher than £50. In red Liverpool bag. You have 2 days. Have it ready. Instructions will follow.*

Suddenly the whole thing seemed ridiculous, the stuff of Hollywood movies. If only he could speak to this moron, he'd put them straight. There was no way he was going to part with that much cash.

CHAPTER 65

Tara Grogan

Tara needed some fresh air to clear her head. She needed
to reset, and St Anne Street was not the place in which to
do it. She was fuming with that supercilious man Jackson,
angry too with Superintendent Tweedy. Her boss had sat
back and allowed the NCA to stamp all over her
investigation.

Her team continued to uncover fresh information that
might prove useful, but she wasn't up for discussions right
now. She needed a serious talk with herself. Before leaving
work, she telephoned Beatrice Howard with the news that
Sebastian was in hospital in Stoke-on-Trent, being treated
for a gunshot wound to his left arm and for minor cuts
and bruises resulting from the crash. She reiterated her
advice to maintain security at the house and not to admit
any vehicle, particularly one that may contain Ernst Eder.

Arriving home early for her, she was delighted to find
Kate and Adele already there. Adele had just completed
her homework and sat at the breakfast bar with juice and
cookies.

Since Kate was already preparing dinner, Tara took
Adele for a walk to the beach. It was a calm afternoon as
they strolled close to Royal Liverpool Golf Club, but
Tara's mind was in turmoil.

Yet another case was in tatters. If Simon Jackson was
to be believed, at least Sebastian had failed to make a clean
escape. She was bemused to learn that the man her
colleagues had referred to as 'Gavin the driver' was an
undercover NCA officer. That fact may have aided

Jackson's investigation but had obstructed hers. She might have guessed that Gavin Westport was more than just a driver. Thinking about it, the man had behaved like a Simon Jackson clone with his demeanour and that condescending attitude to her questions. But what if Westport had sat idly by outside Tommy Brady's home while Sebastian had gone in to kill him? Complicit in murder? Tara would have said so. Might he not also have done something to prevent the death of Yana? Surely the NCA knew what Ernst Eder was capable of. Had they not watched him as carefully as they had Sebastian? The major concern for Tara was whether Merseyside Police would ever get Sebastian and Eder to face charges, or if two murders and a rape would be swept beneath a case of international fraud?

Her attention switched to her god-daughter. They chatted about school and the new teacher she would have, come September. Adele held Tara's hand and hardly paused for breath as she recounted her day. First it was maths then reading, games outside, music and finally writing. Tara couldn't help it; as Adele chatted, her mind again returned to work.

She could readily believe that the Austrian bodyguard, under orders from Victor Dulka, had murdered Yana. Perhaps it was done to intimidate Sebastian, or maybe Yana had crossed the Serb. What continued to puzzle her, however, was the death of Tommy Brady. Her interview with Sebastian had been aborted by Simon Jackson's intervention. She never got to ask how Brady intended to ruin the billionaire. According to Gavin Westport, Eder had not entered Brady's house when they'd visited with Sebastian, although he could have returned later and committed the murder. Tara could not make sense of it. She assumed that it was Eder, acting on orders from Victor Dulka, who had forced Sebastian's car off the road and then fired shots.

When she next jumped to the present, she realised that they'd strolled quite a distance from home. It was further than planned.

'Come on,' she said. 'We'll be late for dinner and your mummy will be cross.'

They walked quickly, and when they reached home Tara noticed it was the first time in days that someone was not keeping watch on her from a car. Tomorrow, she intended to tidy up loose ends in her investigation. Questions still needed answers. Some issues still niggled; things didn't make sense; other scenarios had to be eliminated. It was all she could do whilst denied access to her main suspects.

CHAPTER 66

Paul Renfrew

Paul had a wall-mounted TV in his office. Usually, it was left on mute with BBC, CNN or Sky News playing. Lectures were now finished for the summer and examinations were in full flow. Upon his desk sat a pile of papers that required marking. As he steeled himself for several hours of monotony and dross, he glimpsed a lead line scrolling the bottom of the TV screen on regional news.

> *Merseyside Delta Development project falters as investors withdraw support.*

He reached for the remote and enabled the sound. Fifteen minutes later, he heard the newsreader mention the name Sebastian Logan-Sharp. Paul looked up from his marking. He could hardly believe what he was hearing and, smiling to himself, he picked up his phone. He composed a text with a link to the news item and sent it to all members in the Merseyside Environmental Justice WhatsApp group. Then he gathered the examination papers, locked them in a filing cabinet, grabbed his jacket and left the office.

* * *

'Have you heard the news?' he asked quite cheerfully. He stood before her on the doorstep holding a bunch of garage-bought flowers and a bottle of Prosecco.

'What's happened?'

'It's Logan-Sharp. Someone has tried to kill him. He's been shot. And it seems his project has been scrapped.'

'Oh,' said Michelle. 'I hadn't heard.'

'It's bloody fantastic! We did that!'

'Shot him?'

'No, of course not! Someone else did. But we let him and his investors know that they couldn't walk all over us. That there are people who really care about what scum like him are doing to the environment.'

'But that wasn't anything to do with me. I was protesting about his treatment of women.'

'Well then, we did it together.'

'But he isn't dead, is he?' said Michelle.

'No, there seems to be no end to the man's good luck.'

Michelle looked rather perplexed by the news.

'Aren't you going to invite me in?' He held up the bottle of wine. 'These are for you.' He handed her the bunch of mixed flowers. 'I thought we could celebrate.'

Without speaking, she opened her door wider then padded back inside leaving him to follow.

'You don't seem so happy to hear about Logan-Sharp,' said Paul as he opened the Prosecco.

Michelle set two tumblers on a cluttered dining table.

'Sorry,' she said, 'I don't have proper champagne flutes or even wine glasses.' She hadn't responded to his comment.

'Doesn't matter.' He poured the wine, handed a glass to Michelle and raised the other one. 'Here's to seeing the back of that rogue. Cheers!'

They clinked glasses and Paul smiled like all his dreams had just come true.

'I could order pizza,' she suggested rather sheepishly.

'That would be great. I seemed to have worked up an appetite.'

Removing his jacket, Paul draped it over the back of a dining chair. He couldn't stop himself from revelling in the news. But he sensed that Michelle was unmoved by the situation, while he couldn't let it rest.

Michelle ordered the food, and they settled in her living room, every bit as untidy as the rest of the house with books, magazines and empty coffee mugs dotted around. When she switched on the TV, he realised she was struggling again with conversation. He couldn't help smirking when the news appeared, and in seconds a local bulletin covered the collapse of the Merseyside Delta Development project and reported the attempt on Sebastian Logan-Sharp's life. Paul, however, had his eyes on Michelle as she watched. He couldn't understand her lack of elation.

'Is he going to be charged with the murder of his wife?' she said at last.

'No idea. I suppose that nice-looking detective will get to the bottom of all that. Doesn't matter to our campaigns though.'

'I was hoping he would be.'

When their food arrived, Michelle produced a bottle of cheap red wine and as they ate and drank, the subject finally moved away from Sebastian Logan-Sharp. They watched more television, finding a thriller movie on Netflix, and Michelle retrieved a half-bottle of gin from the back of a kitchen cupboard. By the end of the movie, Paul felt quite giddy and stood up to go. Michelle was sprawled on her sofa. She grinned rather drunkenly.

'You can stay if you like,' she said.

After it was over, Paul slumped beside her on the bed and Michelle lay on her back staring blankly at the ceiling.

His hand glided softly over her naked midriff.

'I've been meaning to ask you,' he began. 'That night at the party when we both got smashed. Where did you go that time? It was just before we left. I saw you upstairs going into one of the bedrooms?'

CHAPTER 67

Carla Smith

Carla had ditched the vape and gone back to the fags. Her nerves were shot to pieces. She hadn't slept for three days, worrying that the bizzies would come calling again. She prayed that she had raised her boys in the right way and that what Jack was telling her was the truth. Sure as hell that clever cop would get to the bottom of it all. The woman picked up on every little detail and wouldn't let go until she got it right. She reminded Carla of that American TV detective in the tatty raincoat who always had one more question to ask. Colombo, he always got to the truth and found the murderer. What if her Jack somehow had gone into Yana's bedroom, his stepmother, for goodness' sake? That detective would eventually find out.

Carla groaned. She'd just cut in too far on her client's silky blonde hair. The young mum in her twenties gave her a concerned look in the mirror.

Carla smiled, said nothing, carried on cutting and carried on being distracted. Work was not the place for her to be right now. She had been thrilled initially at receiving a cheque for so much money, but she was unsure what to do next. Bobby would go nuts when he found out what Beatrice had done. How could he not notice one hundred grand missing from his account? What would her own bank have to say when she tried to lodge the damn thing? More questions. Then she wondered if the money was even legal, legit as they called it on TV, Beatrice had stolen it, so of course it wasn't legit.

Her heart jumped in her chest. She peered through the salon window. She'd thought it, and now it was happening. That damned cop was getting out of a car. Carla craved a fag. What the hell was she going to ask this time? And what should she tell her? That her son was possibly a murderer?

The salon door was pushed open, and DI Grogan strode in.

'What have I done this time?' Carla faked nonchalance.

The detective smiled as if she was well used to smart-arse comments as she went about her job.

'Sorry to bother you at work again, Carla. I just have one question I'd like to ask you.'

And there it was, that Colombo moment, one more bloody question. Carla set down her scissors. She would make a complete mess of her client's hair if she were to cut and talk at the same time. She led the detective to the back room and felt herself shaking as she awaited the question.

DI Grogan produced a piece of folded paper from her bag. When she opened it up, Carla saw that it was a printout of a photograph.

'I meant to ask you sooner.' She handed the picture to her.

Carla took one glance and immediately recognised the image.

'It's a wedding picture,' the detective explained. 'Tommy Brady's wedding to Esther.'

'Yes, I know,' Carla replied.

'I just wondered if that was you as a bridesmaid?'

'Yep, that's me. Long time ago. A lot slimmer then. Why are you asking?'

'The other bridesmaid looks familiar but I'm not certain. Do you remember her?'

'Yes, of course. That's Michelle. Esther, Michelle and I used to be great mates.'

'Michelle?'

'Michelle Weller. Another old chum from school.'

'And she knew Tommy Brady?'

'Yes. Tommy, Esther, Bobby and me. All rogues together.'

Carla watched as the cop seemed to be thinking what to say next. Then DI Grogan cocked her head to the side.

'The party at Sebastian's house,' she said, 'do you recall seeing Michelle there?'

Carla nodded.

'Yes, I spoke to her early on, but as I told you before I'd had a lot to drink by the time I left. Michelle seemed to have had a few too many as well. She was with some bloke. I didn't know him. Now that I think of it, he was the guy who tried to break up the row between Bobby and my boys.'

'Did you see either of them again before you left the party?'

'I don't remember.'

There was no way Carla was telling the cop anything further of what occurred in the hall and staircase of the house. She couldn't risk the wily detective asking more questions of her Jack.

CHAPTER 68

Tara Grogan

'Explain why we are doing this?' said Murray as he and Tara waited in a queue of traffic at a busy junction on Queens Drive. 'Only, I thought we already had our murderer.'

Tara didn't care for his sarcasm. Murray would probably claim to be playing devil's advocate.

'I know, I know,' she bit back. 'Ernst Eder is the most likely suspect, given that he works for a Serbian oligarch with dubious credentials, who apparently controls Sebastian Logan-Sharp. And if Jackson had been more forthcoming with information, we would have known the culprit from day one.'

'But you still think it's useful to question a university lecturer who is an environmental protestor?'

'Yes, I do.'

'Why?'

'Because some things don't make sense, Alan! As usual, people, when we've interviewed them, have thought it wise to hold back on the supply of information. I spent yesterday evening considering those who I still think have more to tell.'

'And this guy Renfrew is one of them?'

'Yes. According to Carla Smith, the guy who tried to break up the fight between Sebastian and his sons was with Michelle Weller, the women's rights activist. Weller told us that she was in Renfrew's company during the party. So why didn't Renfrew mention he tried to break up the fight? I also want to speak to the Logan-Sharps' nanny again.

Carla's son Jack described seeing a woman matching the nanny's description on the landing at the time he saw Yana entering her room. Why didn't Shelby Keibler mention that? Carla identified Michelle Weller as an old friend in Tommy Brady's wedding photograph. And Weller had attended Sebastian's party. I think it's worth checking the link between Michelle Weller, Sebastian and Tommy Brady. Have I said enough, DS Murray?'

'Plenty, ma'am.'

Murray seized the opportunity to ease their car across the junction as the lights changed in his favour. Tara tried to breathe easier after her rant. But it had been worth it. All too often she had been cast as the pedant, chasing obscure leads when it seemed the solution to her case was the obvious one. Better to explain her thinking now, she mused, before her colleagues started grumbling about their workload.

They inquired at the reception desk in the Department of Geography and Planning for the whereabouts of Dr Paul Renfrew. On their previous visit they had been directed to a lecture theatre.

'He should be in his office,' said a middle-aged receptionist in a chirpy voice. 'But I don't recall seeing him come in this morning. Hold on and I'll check.'

Tara and Murray waited as the woman attempted to call the lecturer's office.

'Sorry, there's no answer,' she said a minute later.

'That's OK, thank you,' Tara replied. 'We can try to reach him at home,' she said to Murray as they were leaving the building.

Murray shrugged. It seemed he remained unconvinced of the need to speak with Paul Renfrew. Tara ignored his truculence; she was well used to it.

Since Sebastian Logan-Sharp was currently in hospital, Tara saw no reason to abide by Jackson's instruction to stay away from the twin houses in West Derby.

'May as well speak with Shelby Keibler before we head to Renfrew's home; it's on our way.'

Murray, without further comment, drove as requested from the university to the temporary residence of the billionaire. The gates to the grounds were closed just as Tara had advised Beatrice. When she announced her arrival through the intercom it was the PA who answered. A few seconds later the gates slowly opened, and Murray drove through, pulling up outside the primary dwelling of the Logan-Sharp entourage. Beatrice opened the front door and seemed quite pleased to welcome her visitors.

'Inspector Grogan. How can I help you?'

'Good morning, Beatrice. Have there been any developments from your side?' Tara thought the woman looked brighter than when they'd last met.

'Sebastian will be in hospital for several days and then I think he'll return here before heading back to London. Apparently, the National Crime Agency have been investigating him. I've not heard anything from Ernst. I will soon have to return to London and begin looking for another position.'

'You're no longer going to work for Sebastian?'

'I think it's time I moved on.'

'It might be best if you remained in Liverpool until we know for sure what is going to happen with your employer.'

'I suppose I can do that.'

Beatrice led her visitors into the spacious lounge that had become quite familiar to Tara.

'We would like a word with Shelby, if she's available.'

'I'll fetch her, she's playing with Surrey upstairs.'

As Beatrice went in search of the nanny, it occurred to Tara how much more accommodating the PA had become. Perhaps the presence of police officers made her feel more secure and satisfied that something was being done to resolve her situation. A minute later, Shelby entered the lounge and grinned nervously as she was again faced with two detectives. Beatrice did not return and presumably was keeping an eye on Surrey while Shelby was interviewed.

Tara began with her questions even before the nanny had flopped onto a sofa.

'It has come to our attention, Shelby, that you may have witnessed the point when someone, the murderer perhaps, entered Yana's bedroom. What can you tell us about that?'

'Don't know what you mean.' She folded her arms and sat defiantly upright.

'We have a witness who saw you on the landing at the time Yana went into her bedroom, it seems, for the last time before she died. Why didn't you mention seeing Yana at that point?'

The young woman shrugged but said nothing.

'I want the whole story from you, Shelby, and it has to be the truth. Right now, I have every reason to believe that you killed Yana. You had motive, you were in her room, and you took a picture of the dead woman.'

'Doesn't mean I killed her.'

'It means I can arrest you as a suspect.'

'But Beatrice said that it was Ernst. He's tried to kill Sebastian; doesn't that prove it? You should be looking for him instead of coming after me.'

'The truth, Shelby, right now!'

Tara realised she was faced with a young woman far away from home and nursing an unhealthy infatuation with her boss, but she didn't like her attitude.

'Save your tears, Shelby. Answer my question please or I will arrest you for obstructing a police inquiry.'

'OK, OK, I'll tell you.' Shelby reached for a tissue from a dispenser on the coffee table and dabbed her eyes.

Tara was unmoved by the sudden outpouring of emotion.

'I was watching the party from the landing for about ten minutes,' Shelby began. 'I saw Yana struggling to make it upstairs. She was really off her head, almost fell a couple of times. There was a young guy, took hold of her arm and helped her reach the top. I heard him say he was looking for the bathroom.'

'Did you recognise him?' Tara asked.

'I had never seen him before, but he was quite young, not one of the business guys. Beatrice told me that Sebastian has two sons and they'd been at the party. I guess this guy might have been one of them.'

'What happened next?'

'Yana muttered something to me as she staggered by. I couldn't make out what she said, but I'm sure it wasn't pleasant.'

'Did she do anything before going inside?'

'Oh yeah! She left her bag hanging on the door handle. Dumb.'

'Did you see anyone enter the room after Yana?'

Shelby laughed. Suddenly she seemed to relish telling the story she had previously been reluctant to share.

'Sure did. The young guy came out of the bathroom. He smiled at me and asked me if I'd seen Yana. I pointed to the door with the bag hanging on it.'

'Did he go in?'

'Yep. But if he did anything with Yana it didn't take very long. Couple of minutes tops. When he came out again, he headed downstairs, but some guy stopped him to ask something. I guess he was looking for the bathroom too because he went straight there. When he came out, he looked around for a second. He smiled at me then went directly to Yana's room.'

'Do you have any idea who that man was?'

'Not really.'

'What do you mean, not really?'

'Well, I didn't know him, but when he came out of Yana's room, I suppose he was in there a few minutes longer than the first guy, he was going downstairs, and an older man called to him from the hall.'

'What was said?'

'The old guy called him Cameron, I think. I didn't hear anything else. After that I went to check on Surrey.'

CHAPTER 69

Tara Grogan

Tara and Murray discussed the revelation on the journey to Paul Renfrew's home.

'Do you believe her?' Tara asked.

Murray grunted.

'There's a lot going on with that girl,' he said. 'I think she's capable of making up all sorts.'

'Including her affair with Sebastian?'

'I suppose it's hard to believe that Sebastian would resist a woman coming on to him, especially if it's a young woman with an infatuation. I'm sure the PA and him have shared a moment or two.'

Tara thought of Beatrice and her relationship with the Austrian bodyguard and wondered whether she might also have had a romantic history with Sebastian.

'It's a strong motive for Shelby to want Yana out of the way,' said Tara. 'But it doesn't make any sense when you pair it with the murder of Tommy Brady.'

Murray stopped the car outside a modern detached house in Norris Green.

'No car in the drive,' he said.

'I imagine that an environmental campaigner may not even possess one. More likely to own a bike.'

Murray shrugged his indifference.

Tara got out of the car and walked to the front door. After pressing the doorbell, she waited a few seconds but got no reply. She tried again then peeked through the front window. The interior was quite pristine, minimally furnished with a suite, television, and well-stocked bookcases. After a third attempt on the doorbell, she headed back to the car. Having checked the rear of the property, Murray appeared on the driveway.

'Not at home and not at work,' said Tara. 'I'm sure we'll catch up with him soon.'

* * *

Back at her desk, Tara obtained the contact details for Simon Jackson from Tweedy. She recalled seeing the man's card on her boss's desk. Tweedy had no objections to her calling the NCA officer. When she dialled the number of a mobile, for some reason she was surprised that it was answered straightaway.

'Jackson,' was the curt greeting.

'This is DI Grogan, Merseyside Police.' She hadn't warmed to the man and preferred to keep her tone formal.

'What can I do for you, Detective Inspector?'

'I would like an update on Sebastian Logan-Sharp please.'

Tara pictured Jackson, loitering in his car in a residential street, keeping watch on another unsuspecting individual of interest to the NCA. She sensed the smugness of the man pinging from the nearest phone mast.

'Of course, you would. Well, let me see. He remains in hospital under our guard for the time being.'

'You have him under arrest?'

'I didn't say that.'

'Then what?'

She realised she sounded abrupt, but this man seemed to enjoy being difficult.

'What's the phrase you regular plods use? Helping with enquiries, isn't that it?'

'You do understand that he remains a suspect for two murders, and we would like the opportunity to question him again.'

'All in good time, DI Grogan. Thanks for your call, oh and thanks also for eventually sharing the connection between Logan-Sharp and that other individual. Brady, wasn't it?'

Tara could almost taste his sarcasm.

'Tommy Brady is a victim of murder,' she replied.

'Whatever. Nice talking to you, DI Grogan.'

'Hold on, Mr Jackson. What about Ernst Eder?'

'What about him?'

Tara seethed. Jackson was a pompous cad.

'Do you have him in custody?'

'No,' Jackson replied, stretching the word to breaking point. 'I would say that if you do not have him in your sights then he is probably lying low somewhere in central Europe. Austria, for example.'

'But is he responsible for shooting Sebastian Logan-Sharp?'

'I would think so, although we might have difficulty in proving it.'

'Thank you, Mr Jackson, you've been very helpful.' Not, she thought, and cut the call before he could respond.

She sat for a while trying to breathe easier after the irritating exchange with Jackson. Bleasdale, having heard Tara's side of the call, looked over with an understanding smile.

'There are times when none of this is worth it,' said Tara with a sigh. 'We should just head off on a round-the-world trip.'

'I'm with you, ma'am,' Bleasdale replied.

Tara lifted her bag and stood up.

'Alan! Let's go.'

CHAPTER 70

Cameron Boal

I bet you thought I was joking, Silly boy. Take the bag with the cash to Bootle cemetery, the gates at Linacre Lane. Put it behind the tree on the right as you come through the gates. Then leave. If I see you hanging around, I'll tell the police what I know. If you decide to bring the police to the cemetery, I'll see them first. Do it tomorrow morning, ten o'clock. Don't be late.

He still hadn't notified the police. What could he tell them that wouldn't land him in a heap of trouble? He was surprised they hadn't already discovered that he'd been in Yana's bedroom. Anyone, including his own father, could have seen him that night. But this blackmailer, surely it had to be Sebastian. Although, why a man worth over a billion quid would care to extort a couple of hundred grand from him, he could only guess. Maybe it was his warped revenge for them pulling out of the deal. Or maybe it was Sebastian's way of telling him that he knew what he and Yana got up to at his damned party. The confusing thing for Cameron was that he'd heard about Sebastian getting shot, in which case who was going to collect the money if he decided to go through with the arrangement? Then he wondered if Sebastian's sultry PA was behind it all. That would make sense. She had probably noticed everything that happened during the party.

Cameron was still holding the ransom note when he saw the pair of detectives walk into the outer office to be greeted by Joyce. It seemed the cops had finally come for him. So, was it already too late for his blackmailer? At least if he was arrested, he would not have to part with a quarter of a million quid. Now that the cops were here, he no longer had a decision to make. Besides, he had done nothing about getting the cash together.

The pretty detective stepped into his office looking quite sombre. He supposed that just because she was beautiful didn't mean she had to walk around smiling and pouting all the time.

'I'd like to ask you some more questions, Mr Boal,' she said in a serious tone.

'What about?'

Still holding the ransom note, he snatched the opportunity to sit. She joined him by his desk.

'We have a witness who claims to have seen you entering Yana Logan-Sharp's bedroom on the evening she was killed. Would you care to explain?'

'Who is this witness?'

'I can't share that with you, I'm afraid.'

Cameron drew a deep breath then pushed the note across the desk towards the detective.

'Your witness may well be trying to blackmail me,' he said.

DI Grogan studied the note then passed it to her companion.

'Have you any idea who sent this?' asked Murray.

Boal suddenly felt the tension ease. The cops were interested in the blackmail and now apparently less so about him having been seen going into Yana's bedroom.

'I would have guessed it was Sebastian,' he replied. 'Surely, he's the only one with the balls to try such a thing.'

'And why would he wish to blackmail you?' asked Tara.

'Well, for one thing he's probably furious with us, Dad and me, for pulling out of his development project.'

Cameron watched both detectives for a reaction, but they remained silent. Foolishly, he filled the gap.

'I assume he is your witness?'

'Are you now admitting to going into Yana's bedroom during the party?'

His stomach tightened. He'd just made a huge mistake. The woman cop was staring right at him.

'Look, I didn't want to cause trouble. Yana came on to me when we were in the garden, and she invited me up to her room.'

'Why didn't you mention this before now?' Grogan asked.

'I thought it best to stay out of it. We had a few drinks together then she told me she was going to bed. She asked me to join her. She told me to give her a few minutes and she would leave her bag outside the door so I would know which room.'

'And then?'

'I went upstairs, saw her bag hanging from the door handle and I went in. That's when Sebastian must have seen me. But honestly, nothing happened.'

'Did you kill her, Mr Boal?' Murray asked.

'No! I swear! Absolutely nothing happened. When I went into her room, I could see she had passed out on the bed. I tried to rouse her, but she was well out of it, so I left.'

'Was she already dead?'

'No. At least, I don't think so.'

He saw the disbelieving looks on their faces, but the woman cop switched to the blackmail note.

'How much contact have you had with the person who sent this?'

'That's the third one.' Cameron opened a desk drawer and pulled out the previous notes and the red bag enclosed with the second one. 'There has been no direct contact.'

He watched as both cops examined the notes.

'Our witness who saw you going into Yana's room is not Sebastian Logan-Sharp,' said Tara. 'Do you remember seeing anyone, either when you entered Yana's bedroom or afterwards when you came out?'

Cameron shook his head.

'No one I can remember. There were people coming and going on the stairs. One young lad directed me to the bathroom. I'd had a lot to drink, and I was worried about the deal. If I'd been sober, I probably wouldn't have gone to Yana's room in the first place.'

Tara got to her feet.

'That's all for now, Mr Boal. We'll be in touch if we have any further questions. In the meantime, please do not leave the city.'

'That's it?' Cameron said, aghast. 'Aren't you going to do anything about the blackmail? I don't have that kind of money to throw away.'

She was smiling at him, or was she laughing?

'Let's see, your blackmailer said they would go to the police with what they know if you don't pay up. But am I right in thinking that you have now told us everything that happened regarding Yana?'

'Yes, I have.'

'Then why concern yourself with this blackmailer? They no longer have any leverage over you. Unless you haven't told us the full story.'

'I swear, Inspector, I've told you the truth.'

'Then you have nothing to worry about. Please, don't consider going to the cemetery tomorrow. If we may have the notes and bag, we'll take care of things.'

Cameron handed her the tote bag and felt a peculiar relief as the cops departed.

CHAPTER 71

Tara Grogan

'Can you believe that man? Why didn't he tell us about his flirtation with Yana when we first met him?'

'You think he's still hiding something?' said Murray. He was driving to the location of the last subject of Tara's unfinished business.

'Perhaps, but what irks me is why people, apparently innocent people, believe they can improve a situation by withholding information. I'm sick of it, Alan. At times I wonder if we should simply allow crimes to go unpunished. Then we'd soon see who wants to speak the truth.'

Murray kept his eyes on the road and said nothing. Tara stewed in the silence, vacantly observing the passing streets of houses and businesses, each holding their little insignificant secrets.

They entered the grounds of the call centre, a prefabricated structure of grey panelling that revealed nothing of the nature of business conducted inside. Murray didn't waste time searching for a space and stopped right outside the main door. Tara went in alone. The young receptionist seated in front of a computer screen looked up and seemed to recognise her from the previous visit. She smiled warmly. Despite the apparent recognition, Tara still produced her ID and asked to speak with Michelle Weller.

'Yes, Detective Inspector Grogan, I'll call her down.'

A couple of minutes later, while Tara gazed from the window to the dull surroundings of the car park and a blank wall of the neighbouring business unit, she heard footsteps behind her and turned to face the unassuming figure of the women's rights campaigner.

'Hello, Michelle, sorry for dragging you away from your work but I'd like to ask you some more questions.'

Michelle's expression didn't flinch from a dull stare lacking a smile.

'Is that all right?' Tara asked, having received little response.

'Yes, I suppose.'

'I'm sure you've heard by now that Sebastian Logan-Sharp has been injured during an attempt on his life?'

Michelle still said nothing. Tara felt her attitude strange. Here, she thought, was a woman who was constantly uneasy with life, as if every meeting, every conversation was somehow a threat. Maybe such a demeanour stemmed from a past, unpleasant experience. Been there, got the T-shirt, Tara thought.

'When we last spoke, Michelle, I got the impression that although you were campaigning against Sebastian Logan-Sharp and his reputation for treating women poorly, you didn't know the man personally. But recent information has come to me suggesting that you knew him quite well a long time ago. Would you like to tell me about that?'

Tara detected a sneer as the woman shifted her weight from one foot to the other.

'I don't know what you mean.'

It was a feeble retort. Tara opened her bag and removed the copy of the wedding picture that she had shown to Carla Smith. She held it out for Michelle to see.

'You were a bridesmaid at Tommy Brady's wedding.'

'So?'

'You knew Tommy, Esther, Carla, and Bobby Smith, aka Sebastian Logan-Sharp. All of you were friends at school.'

'That was a long time ago.'

'But Tommy has been murdered, and then Yana. When we first spoke, you didn't mention that you had known Tommy and Sebastian.'

Michelle suddenly assumed the impertinence of a stroppy teenager.

'You didn't ask me about Tommy before.'

'OK, fair enough.'

'Anyway, it was Bobby who killed them.'

'How do you know this?'

'I just know; It said so online.'

'Have you anything you want to tell me, Michelle?'

'No.'

CHAPTER 72

Michelle Weller

Summer didn't seem an accurate term to describe the weather. Michelle gazed from her lounge window at a grey sky, and puddles of rain on dull tarmac. She had risen early. She'd scarcely managed to sleep except for that portion due to her nervous exhaustion. Besides, a two-seater sofa was a poor substitute for a comfortable bed. An attempt to eat breakfast floundered at the first slice of toast. The butter was off. After today, she told herself, things would be different. If all went well, she could leave this house, get out of Liverpool and perhaps move south. Cornwall or Devon. Who knows; after all she had been through, she might feel brave enough to venture to France or Spain. She'd never been abroad. Looking out on a dismal day, the opportunity to live in a place where the sun was always shining was a heartening prospect.

Pulling on a waterproof anorak over her hoodie, she lifted the car keys from the kitchen table and prepared to leave. She lingered by the front door for a moment, drinking in the silence of the house she'd lived in since she was a teenager. Only a few pleasant memories came to mind. Mostly, they were of her parents. The more recent ones were of lonely nights in front of the telly, or occasionally a friend dropping by and them looking uncomfortable at how she was living. There was nothing to keep her here any longer. Her work was almost done. A final glance to the top of the stairs and then she opened the door and stepped into the rain. Today, she would not be going to that boring call centre.

It had been years since she'd driven, but she at least had to try. Today's task would be easier using a car. She climbed into the Skoda and gazed at the dashboard. There were a lot of things she didn't recognise, modern gadgets that they put in cars nowadays. She inserted the key, switched on the ignition and the engine came to life. It took a moment to locate the wipers and the indicators, but with that done, she slipped into first gear and eased her foot off the clutch. The car jerked forward and stalled. She tried again, stalled and then braked to stop from rolling into the car in front. After three attempts she finally got moving along her street without changing from first gear. Thankfully, the basic skill she had learnt years ago began to surface. She could steer, she could brake, and eventually, she could change gear. What else did she need?

She'd thought out a route in her mind and felt pleased that she reached the cemetery without incident. Her stomach fluttered as she drove past the entrance on Linacre Lane. At the first opportunity, she turned the car around and headed back along the road. This time she slowed down and peered at the cemetery gates. It was just as she'd hoped. Deserted. She repeated the exercise three more times and, on each occasion, saw no one. If he had done as she'd ordered, Boal should have already left the bag at the tree to the right of the gates. She drove past one more time, then, seeing all was clear, finally drove into the cemetery.

Glancing to her right, she spotted the red bag beneath the tree. It was tempting to just stop the car, get out and scoop the cash, but she was suddenly gripped by fear. There had to be someone watching. If it wasn't Cameron Boal, then it could be the police. Her heart thumped in her chest, and she almost stalled the damn car again. But she drove on to the middle of the cemetery and soon stopped by the grave she visited every week. The weather had already taken its toll on her latest flower arrangement. She hadn't brought any this morning but sat for a while reading and re-reading the inscription on the headstone as she always did. This morning, however, she also kept watch for activity at the entrance gates.

Thirty minutes went by as the rain cleared away and the sun threatened to break through the cloud. There was little movement. Several cars entered and proceeded to graves well away from her position and from her prize. Michelle watched them all. She still couldn't summon the courage to approach the bag or even to give up and drive away. Instead, she drew comfort from her family grave.

A short while later, a funeral cortège filed in and drove out to the newer graves on the left side. Surely, she thought, if someone was watching the bag, they would reclaim it soon because no one was going near it. Nerves jingled with every possibility. If she didn't act soon, a stranger or a worker at the cemetery would find it and then what? But she let another twenty minutes pass before she finally had the nerve to start the car and move toward the tree and a quarter of a million pounds. But before she got there, her courage waned again, and she drove on by, out through the gates without even a glance at the red bag.

She drove along Linacre Lane twice before her adrenalin finally surged, and she re-entered the cemetery. The bag was still there, but as she came to a halt this time, she glimpsed a car behind the caretaker's hut. How could she not have seen it before? Fortunately, she didn't stall and roared onwards until she again reached her family gravestone. When she gazed in the rear-view mirror, she saw someone leaving the car by the hut and walk towards the tree. It was bittersweet relief that she hadn't attempted to collect her prize. She could see that damn Detective Inspector Grogan holding the red bag in her hand. Michelle's instinct was to drive away before she was challenged. She felt eyes were upon her, but surely, she hadn't drawn suspicion. All she had done was come into the cemetery to visit a grave.

She remembered there was another set of gates at the Menai Road end of the cemetery. Michelle steered the car further along the central drive but a minute later was faced with a pair of locked metal gates. She couldn't go back. Not now. That cop might still be waiting for her. She pressed her foot hard on the accelerator. The wheels spun on the tarmac as, much too slowly, she released the clutch. Closing her eyes, the car shot forward. It smashed into the wrought-iron gates, the lock and chain giving way, and rolled across the road. Both her feet slipped off the pedals; the car bounced on a kerb and stalled. Michelle screamed in despair. It had all been for nothing, but at least she'd escaped.

CHAPTER 73

Tara Grogan

Her morning ended in frustration. Convinced that the blackmailer would turn up to claim their illicit prize, she'd waited in the cemetery. She had her own idea as to who it could be but didn't share it with Murray. She couldn't bear hearing him scoff again. Besides, it was only another loose end to clear up. It probably had nothing to do with apprehending a killer.

But no one came anywhere near the red bag that she'd filled with newspapers. As she'd finally gone to retrieve it, Murray called to her from the car. When she reached him, he explained that he'd just run a check on the registration of a vehicle that had entered the cemetery a few minutes earlier. It wasn't the first time they'd noticed it. They had seen it parked in the centre of the graveyard for a while before it had driven out. Only when it returned a few minutes later, had they become suspicious.

'It belongs to Paul Renfrew,' said Murray.

Tara gazed to the middle of the cemetery where she'd noticed the Skoda a few moments earlier. It wasn't there now.

'Did it drive out again?' she asked.

Murray shook his head.

'Didn't come this way.'

They waited for a couple of minutes, but when the car did not re-appear, they drove further into the cemetery, pausing roughly at the spot where the Skoda had been parked. They both climbed out and wandered among the headstones, looking for a reason perhaps why the car had been sitting at this location. It didn't take long for Tara to discover a grave that instantly shed light on the identity of her blackmailer. She read the inscription.

'Weller Edward, died 24 March 1999, aged 40 years. His beloved wife Marjorie, died 7 June 2013, aged 52 years.'

Engraved between the two names was another, 'Baby Alice, born asleep 21 November 2006.'

Returning to their car, they ventured to the far end of the cemetery, still on the lookout for the Skoda. But their searching came to a surprising and disappointing end when they came upon the smashed gates.

* * *

Back at St Anne Street, feeling rather foolish for having let their blackmailer slip away, Tara's thoughts lingered on why Michelle Weller had the use of Paul Renfrew's car. Were Renfrew and Weller both involved in blackmailing Cameron Boal? She hadn't identified the driver at the cemetery, but it must surely have been Michelle. It was no coincidence for the car to have stopped by a gravestone inscribed with the name Weller.

* * *

An hour later, with a search underway for Michelle and Paul, Tara and Murray were called to a house in Bootle. A SOCO team were already examining the property. The detectives were immediately directed to the master bedroom.

Even Murray, a man well used to seeing a horrific crime scene, gasped at the sight before them. Tara's eyes watered at the carnage before her. If the body on the blood-soaked bed was indeed Dr Paul Renfrew, it would take DNA or dental records to confirm it.

'Multiple, and I *mean* multiple, stab and slash wounds,' explained Brian Witney, standing over the double bed. 'Frenzied in the extreme.'

Tara stared at the bread knife embedded in the victim's chest. It seemed inconsequential compared to the butchery surrounding it. Hardly a single area of the man's body was unscathed; head, face, chest, abdomen, genitals, arms, and legs had been sliced open.

'This is several days old,' said Witney. 'With the recent warm weather and the enclosed room, the body has already begun to putrefy.'

That much was already obvious as Tara at last breathed fresh air in the street outside the house. An incident tent had been erected over the front door of Michelle Weller's home. Gazing around, Tara was struck by the location. She was standing only a few houses away from the home of Tommy Brady, a fact she had somehow missed.

'Not for the faint-hearted, Alan,' she said to her colleague who was wiping his mouth and nose with a tissue.

'Or even the likes of us, ma'am.'

It was another gruesome image for them to process. She stepped closer and gently squeezed his arm.

He handed her a framed picture.

'I found this in the living room. It was just lying on the floor next to the sofa.'

Tara saw it was the same image she had been carrying around of Tommy Brady's wedding and had shown to Michelle Weller only the day before. Then she recalled the space on the grubby wall inside Tommy Brady's home. Perhaps she was holding the very picture that had once hung there. She wondered about Michelle.

'I think she's gone off the rails completely,' said Murray.

'We need to find her quickly.'

* * *

At the station, they spent the afternoon building a profile of Michelle Weller and her motives for committing murder. Tara sat in Tweedy's office as they anticipated news of Weller's arrest, now that a major hunt was underway.

'What I can't understand–' Tara sighed through her frustration '–is why should Michelle kill Paul Renfrew if they were both involved in blackmailing Cameron Boal?'

'But has this got anything to do with the other murders?' said Murray.

'I think it has, although I don't understand how Michelle's opposition to Sebastian Logan-Sharp led to the death of Tommy Brady.'

'But why,' said Murray, 'when we had so many reported sightings of people on the landing in Sebastian's house, did none of them involve Michelle?'

'There was such frenetic activity during that party, it's an easy oversight,' said Tweedy.

Wilson knocked on the glass of the door and came into the office.

'An interesting point that we didn't pick up, ma'am,' he said.

'Not another one,' Tara groaned.

'During the initial investigation surrounding Tommy Brady, our uniform house-to-house inquiries recorded the name Weller. Apparently, she had reported seeing a large black car outside Brady's home on the day of the murder. It was confirmed as being registered to one of Logan-Sharp's companies.'

'Thanks, John.'

Tweedy looked sympathetically towards his senior detective.

'I suggest you go home, Tara. Alan too. It's been a horrendous day. Until we have Michelle Weller in custody you should get some rest. I'll keep you posted if there are any developments.'

'Yes, sir, thank you.'

When Tara had returned to her desk and prepared to leave, Murray came over.

'Fancy a drink before going home, ma'am?' he asked. 'Take the edge off our day.'

'Thanks for the offer, Alan, but I would like to go straight home, stretch out in front of the telly with a large glass of wine and something funny to watch.'

'No problem, have a good night, ma'am.'

Murray headed out, but as Tara attempted to follow, Bleasdale called her over.

'Ma'am, some news for you.'

'Have they found Weller?'

'No, ma'am. Sebastian Logan-Sharp has been discharged from hospital and has returned to Liverpool.'

'How do you know?'

'The super has just circulated an email. He'd been informed by that man Jackson from the NCA.'

'So, Sebastian mustn't be under arrest. Thanks, Paula. See you in the morning.'

By the time she'd reached her car, Tara was in a quandary. Should she go home as Tweedy advised? Or grab the opportunity to speak with the irascible billionaire about his past, and specifically, his association with Michelle Weller? As she drove from the station, she decided that she must speak to Logan Sharp right away

CHAPTER 74

Tara Grogan

Approaching the twin houses in West Derby, she found the electric gates wide open. She pulled up at the front door of the main residence. There were no other vehicles, and she assumed that Gavin Westport would no longer be working for the billionaire. Stepping from her car, she felt the heat rising from the tiled driveway. The sun was still high and, after the morning's drizzle, the weather had gradually improved.

She rang the doorbell and, as she waited, her mind processed the list of questions she intended to put to Sebastian. Perhaps, if he'd been more forthcoming from the outset, at least one death, Paul Renfrew's, might have been prevented. But Sebastian had never even hinted that he had known Michelle Weller from years ago. Then again, it would hardly have seemed relevant, not when early suspicion for the deaths of Tommy Brady and Yana had centred on Sebastian himself.

Tara spied her through the glass. Shelby, a smiling, happy-looking nanny, skipped to the door. She pulled it open and for the first time did not appear disappointed to greet the visitor.

'Hi,' she piped. 'Sebastian is in the backyard.'

Tara smiled at the young woman's obvious joy.

'Thank you, Shelby. This won't take long.'

Tara entered the hall, and Shelby closed the door then bounced off to join Surrey at the breakfast bar.

Sebastian was seated on the patio with his feet up on a lounger, his left arm in a sling. Tara couldn't decide whether he was pleased or irritated to see her again. Probably the latter. Next to him sat Beatrice, casually dressed and holding a bottle of beer. She smiled pleasantly at Tara and got to her feet.

'Inspector Grogan. Can I get you a drink?'

'Some water would be great, thank you.'

Sebastian still hadn't uttered a word as Beatrice went inside to fetch the drinks.

'How are you feeling, Mr Logan-Sharp? I hear you've had a lucky escape.'

'No thanks to your lot,' he sneered.

Tara let his comment slide. His recent experience hadn't soothed his manner. It would serve no purpose to aggravate him any further, however; she still needed answers and they were perhaps best obtained without antagonising a wounded man.

'If you don't mind, I would like to ask you some questions.'

'You never let it drop, do you? I've spent the last couple of days answering a hundred questions about my financial affairs, and no one is doing anything about catching that Austrian brute who killed my wife.'

'I can't speak for the National Crime Agency, but I can assure you that we have continued with our investigations into your wife's murder.'

'And what have you come to tell me?'

Beatrice returned with two bottles of beer and a glass of water. She handed the water to Tara and set a beer on a glass-topped table beside her boss.

'Please have a seat, Inspector,' said Beatrice.

Tara sat down on a wrought-iron chair facing Sebastian.

'I would like to ask you about Michelle Weller,' she began.

Sebastian could not have looked more incredulous, but he never had the chance to respond. A high-pitched scream of a child came from within the house. The noise of chairs moving over wooden floors and sounds of struggle followed soon after. By the time Tara and Beatrice jumped to their feet they were faced with a terrifying scene. Even Sebastian had struggled out of his seat. Beatrice screamed.

'Hello, Inspector Grogan. I'm glad you're here. I've been hoping to meet you again.'

Michelle stood inside the conservatory, the door open to the patio. She had a firm grip of Surrey's hair, the child sobbing, her eyes pleading for rescue. To Michelle's left, Surrey's young nanny had slumped to her knees, watching serenely as her own blood dripped to a puddle on the floor, her fingers unable to stem the flow from the gash at her throat.

'I've been looking for you too, Michelle.'

'You've caused me a lot of trouble.'

Beatrice gasped when Michelle brandished the knife she held in her right hand.

Tara stepped forward to help Shelby.

'Leave her!' screamed Michelle. 'Silly girl got in my way! Stay back or I'll do the same with the child.'

CHAPTER 75

Tara Grogan

'There's no need for this, Michelle,' said Tara, feebly raising her hands to calm the situation.

'Tell that to him,' Michelle snapped, glaring at Sebastian.

The billionaire, it seemed, had no bluster to impart.

'Please, let Surrey go,' Beatrice cried. 'She's just a child. She's done nothing to hurt you.'

'But her father has!' Michelle fixed her manic gaze on Sebastian.

'Me?' he said. 'What the fuck did I do?'

'Michelle, we need to fetch an ambulance for Shelby,' said Tara, edging towards the stricken nanny.

Michelle put the knife to Surrey's tiny neck. 'Back off or I swear I'll cut her.'

'OK, OK!' Tara halted but did not back away. 'Tell me what you want, Michelle. I can help you.'

'I want him to pay for what he did to me.'

'What did I do?' Sebastian blurted, a picture of innocence.

Tara winced. He wasn't helping. He needed to stay quiet, or this woman was going to kill his young daughter.

'Tell me what Sebastian did to you, and I can help you out of this?'

'The whole story if you want it, Inspector,' said Michelle.

She still wore the anorak over her hoodie, black leggings, and trainers. Tara reckoned that she must be hot in so many clothes. But now was the time to keep the woman talking. Just keep her talking.

'Can we start at the beginning?' Tara asked. 'Why Tommy Brady?'

Michelle sneered and shifted on her feet, still holding the carving knife to Surrey's throat.

'That's not the beginning,' she said.

'OK then, you tell me when it all began.'

Michelle shook the child, to stop her whimpering.

'It's OK, Surrey,' Beatrice tried. 'This lady just wants to talk to us. We'll be finished soon and then we can have some ice cream.'

'What is it they say in the movies?' said Michelle. 'I can tell you but then I'd have to kill you.' She smiled a sickening smile.

Surrey screeched.

'It's OK, Surrey,' said Tara. 'You're safe. This lady won't hurt you.'

Michelle grinned at her hostage. Tara detected a hint of empathy, as if the girl meant something to the woman.

'Surrey is such a lovely name. Do you know, Inspector, my mother named me after The Beatles' song. She used to sing it to me while she did the ironing. She knew all their songs and told me that one day I would find a man just like Paul McCartney, and I'd be rich and famous. She was half right, I suppose. Not rich but maybe now I'm famous.'

Tara tried to think how best to disarm Michelle and rescue Surrey. But the woman hadn't dropped her guard. The knife remained at Surrey's young neck.

'I'm sure you love her very much,' Tara said.

'Loved. She's dead now.'

'I'm sorry.'

'You don't have to be. But that's not where it all started for me.'

'So, tell me.'

'That picture you showed me, the one of Tommy's wedding... That very night is where it began for me. Did you notice that one person was missing from the picture?'

'You mean Sebastian, or Bobby as he was back then?'

'That's right. He was Tommy's best man, and while that picture was being taken, he was off booking a room at the hotel.'

'Oh shit,' Sebastian groaned. The billionaire had shifted and now stood behind Beatrice.

'For him and Carla?' Tara asked.

'No, sadly not. He could have had Carla anytime, he told me. She was his fiancée. But it was me he wanted.'

Tara heard Sebastian grunt then clear his throat. She prayed he would stay quiet. Michelle wasn't deterred. Her eyes were keenly set upon Tara's.

'He had booked a room for the two of us. I told him I wasn't interested. In those days I wasn't even sure if I was interested in any man, if you know what I mean? But during the wedding party he put something in my drink. Do you remember now, Bobby?'

The billionaire seemed incapable of a reply. Then he managed to utter, 'This is bollocks.'

'When I was well out of it, Bobby played the perfect gentleman and helped some of the others carry me to the room and put me to bed. He quite happily told me all this the next morning lying beside me. Of course, that was after he'd raped me at least twice.'

'Did Carla know?' asked Tara.

'This is a load of crap!' Sebastian snapped.

Fortunately, Michelle no longer seemed incited to harm Surrey. The talking had calmed her down. She'd lowered the knife but still had a firm hold of the child.

'If she did, she never ever mentioned it to me,' said Michelle. 'And, of course, she married him.'

'But why kill Tommy?'

'Hold on, Inspector, you're jumping way ahead. I thought you wanted the whole story.' She put the knife back to Surrey's neck and the child screamed again.

'I'm sorry.'

Tara looked desperately at Shelby who had now slumped to the floor unconscious.

'A few weeks later,' continued Michelle, 'I told Bobby that I was pregnant, and that the baby was his. He just laughed in my face. Can you believe that? I told him I was keeping it no matter what. He said he could have me killed if I ever suggested to anyone that he was the father. Shortly after that, he buggered off, leaving Carla pregnant with her twin boys. Such a nice man, don't you think?'

'Did you have your baby?' asked Tara, although the recent memory of what she'd read on the gravestone was all the answer she needed.

Tears streaked down Michelle's face. She sobbed and dropped to her knees.

'Alice was the most beautiful little girl you ever saw. Born asleep, Inspector.'

'Michelle, I'm so sorry. I understand what that must have been like.'

'How would you know?'

Tara was crying too. 'My baby son was stillborn.'

Michelle's eyes widened. She was still on her knees, and she'd lowered the knife from Surrey's neck.

Tara seized her chance. She dived forwards, landed on the woman and knocked Surrey across the room away from immediate danger. Beatrice swept up the girl in her arms. Michelle screamed hysterically, but Tara had pinned her to the floor, the knife lying beside her.

'Sebastian! The knife!' Tara yelled.

The man stepped forward and lifted the weapon but seemed at a loss over what to do next.

'Call an ambulance!' Tara shouted.

CHAPTER 76

Tara Grogan

'Tell me why you killed Tommy.'

Tara sat next to Murray, across the table from Michelle Weller and her allocated duty solicitor. She felt it necessary to have the story completed, to get her answers before another sunrise. Michelle looked pale and suddenly a woman ten years older. Her eyes were bloodshot and she had two staples in a cut to her left temple, the result of being jumped upon by Tara.

'Poor Tommy,' she replied, sniffing tears. 'It was too good an opportunity. Tommy and I were old friends, you know. I hadn't seen much of him in recent years even though we lived in the same street. He was mostly in his room with those damn computers, and I worked shifts. But that Sunday, I saw Bobby going into Tommy's house. Could hardly believe it. Didn't think I would ever see him back in Liverpool, and suddenly there he was, visiting his old friend. I wondered what was happening. I waited for Bobby to leave, then I went over to speak with Tommy. On the way, I was struck with an idea on how to get back at Bobby, after all these years. So, I killed Tommy. He knew nothing, Inspector. He hardly took any notice of me dropping by. He didn't even see me standing behind him with the knife. My hope, you see, was that Bobby would get the blame.'

'Such a waste of life, Michelle. If only you had left Tommy alone to complete his work.'

'What do you mean?'

'Tommy Brady was just minutes away from destroying Sebastian's business. There was no need for you to have killed him.'

Tara watched as Michelle's expression clouded in confusion.

'And were you attempting to implicate Sebastian in the murder of Yana?'

'Yes, I suppose, although I hated the woman anyway. Didn't know her, but I hated her all the same. Trash married to trash. At that party she was pissed out of her head, and she was rude to everyone. Just a money-grabbing whore.'

'And that was your reason to kill her?'

'That and the hope that Bobby would be blamed for her death too. I really wanted him to suffer. Given the chance, I would have killed him, but seeing him put away for life seemed even better.'

'Tell me what happened.'

'From the hall, I saw Yana struggling to climb the stairs. One of Carla's boys was giving her a hand. When he came down, he stopped halfway to speak with Cameron Boal. I saw him pointing upstairs and then I watched as Boal went firstly to the loo, then afterwards go to Yana's room. I could see everything just by climbing the first few steps on the staircase. Boal wasn't in Yana's room for long, though. So, I guessed that she had sent him packing. That's when I seized the chance to go and tell Yana what a lowlife her husband was. When I ventured into the room, I saw she had passed out. All I did was make it permanent. I had a skewer in my hand from eating the party food. I needed somewhere to put it, so I stuck it in her. She opened her eyes and gasped at me. Then I pressed a pillow into her stinking face and held it there until she'd stopped moving.

'In a way, I'd done your job for you, Inspector. I even told the police about the car outside Tommy's house. I thought when Bobby was arrested, that would be it. He would get blamed for Tommy and Yana. But then you fools let him go.'

Tara stared at the woman. She was facing yet another killer, calmly describing their act of murder. Apart from a few selfish tears, there was little sign of remorse in the woman. She was content with her work. And there was still a third victim to discuss.

'Why Paul Renfrew?'

'I could give you several answers to that question, Inspector. But he was a man. That is more than enough.'

Murray shifted uncomfortably in his chair but didn't speak.

'Were you both attempting to blackmail Cameron Boal?'

'No,' she said, sounding amused, 'that was just me. I'd remembered seeing Boal going into Yana's room. Since the police were making a mess of getting Bobby, I decided that I needed a fresh start. I thought it would be easy to get money from the man who'd tried to have a good time with Bobby's slut. I only used Paul's car to get to the cemetery.'

'But you had to kill him first?'

'Paul had seen me going into Yana's room. His mistake was telling me about it. And since he couldn't resist my bed, I'm afraid I just got rid of all those years of anger.'

Tara glanced at Murray. Her mind had filled with the vision of the bloodied corpse of the environmental campaigner lying on Michelle's bed. Viciously killed because he'd befriended a disturbed woman with murder on her mind.

CHAPTER 77

Tara Grogan

The papers were sated with news and backstory, all of it featuring the 'Scouse billionaire' as he'd been named. Tara learnt nothing new.

Simon Jackson, to her surprise, had thought it prudent to contact Tweedy and explain that Sebastian Logan-Sharp would face lesser charges of corruption in exchange for assisting the NCA and its European counterparts in exposing the activities of the Serbian oligarch Victor Dulka.

Tara had no desire to ever meet Sebastian again. She had saved the life of his daughter but did not expect to hear any words of gratitude. She believed that despite Michelle Weller facing a triple murder charge, there might be some justice, too, if Sebastian Logan-Sharp could be held to account for rape. But she couldn't see that happening. There were people who sailed through life unscathed and never held accountable for their deeds. Sebastian Logan-Sharp was such a man. It was a bitter fact of life.

Adele huddled close to Kate on the sofa with a Disney movie on television. Tara absorbed all that she could from the papers regarding her investigation. She descended to introspection of her own conduct. What had she done wrong? What had she missed? Could she have prevented any of the murders and avoided the traumatic events experienced by young Surrey?

The last thing she'd done after interviewing Michelle Weller and before leaving the station, was to read a technical report from the Met regarding the content of Tommy Brady's computer. Most of it was jargon and beyond her, but the gist of the conclusions was that Brady had gained access to all of Sebastian Logan-Sharp's financial accounts. He might well have been on the verge of stealing the billionaire's entire fortune. Whether he would have done so was something they would never know.

She made coffee and had bought doughnuts for Sunday breakfast. Little things done to get back to normality.

Sitting alone at the kitchen table, she read a lengthy text from Beatrice. Despite the tragedy surrounding the life of Sebastian Logan-Sharp, it seemed that a little good had sprouted forth. The woman that Tara had at first regarded as cold, cynical and aloof had a heart after all. The message explained that the former PA had engaged a lawyer to fight for custody of Surrey Logan-Sharp. Sebastian had continued to deny paternity. If successful, then Shelby, when she'd recovered from her near fatal injury at the hands of Michelle Weller, would be hired to help raise the young girl. Beatrice was now looking for a fresh career path. Tara replied and wished her well.

For a second, she pondered a walk to the beach then thought better of it and jumped onto the sofa beside her best friend and god-daughter.

CHARACTER LIST

DI Tara Grogan – Liverpool detective of serious crimes.

DS Alan Murray – Tara's closest assistant.

DS John Wilson – Newly promoted officer in the team at St Anne Street station.

DC Paula Bleasdale – Youngest member in Tweedy's squad.

Detective Superintendent Harold Tweedy – Senior officer in charge of squad.

Dr Brian Witney – Medical officer – pathologist.

Kate – Tara's closest friend.

Tommy Brady – Council worker and computer geek.

Sebastian Logan-Sharp – aka Bobby Smith – Liverpool born self-made billionaire.

Yana Logan-Sharp – Former supermodel and Sebastian's wife.

Surrey Logan-Sharp – Yana's infant daughter.

Beatrice Howard – Sebastian's PA.

Shelby Keibler – Surrey's American nanny.

Ernst Eder – Sebastian's bodyguard.

Patrice Allard – Sebastian's personal chef.

Gavin Westport – Sebastian's driver.

Simon Jackson – Investigator for the National Crime Agency.

James Boal – Liverpool-based property developer.

Cameron Boal – Son of James Boal. Works for his father's company.

Dr Paul Renfrew – University lecturer and environmental protestor.

Michelle Weller – Campaigner for women's rights.

Carla Smith – Sebastian's ex-wife.

Lee Smith – Carla's son and twin brother to Jack.

Jack Smith – Twin brother of Lee.

Victor Dulka – Serbian oligarch.

If you enjoyed this book, please let others know by leaving a quick review on Amazon. Also, if you spot anything untoward in the paperback, get in touch. We strive for the best quality and appreciate reader feedback.

editor@thebookfolks.com

ALSO IN THIS SERIES

AN EARLY GRAVE (Book 1)

A tough young Detective Inspector encounters a reclusive man who claims he holds the secret to a murder case. But he also has a dangerous agenda. Will DI Tara Grogan take the bait?

THE DARING NIGHT (Book 2)

Liverpool is on high alert after a spate of poisonings, but DI Tara Grogan is side-lined from the investigation. Yet when she probes into the suicide of a company executive, she becomes sure she has a vital lead in the case. Going it alone, however, has very real risks.

THE SILENT VOICES (Book 3)

When bodies turn up on a Liverpool council estate, DI Tara Grogan goes undercover to get inside information. But she risks everything when the cover story she adopts backfires. Can she work out the identity of the killer before she is exposed and becomes a target?

LETHAL DOSE (Book 4)

Investigating the death of a journalist, DI Tara Grogan stumbles upon his connection to a number of missing women. Is it possible the victim was actually a serial killer? Tara closes in on the truth but can she evade a fatal jab?

LETHAL JUSTICE (Book 5)

When a body is found, cruelly crucified on a makeshift wooden structure, DI Tara Grogan suspects it is the work of a secretive religious cult. Focusing on this case and with her guard down, she becomes once again the target of a man with murder on his mind, among other things. Will the wheels of justice turn quick enough to save her from an awful fate?

LETHAL MINDS (Book 6)

Following a murder, a drugs feud in a notorious Liverpool estate is kicking off when a missing woman's body is found in the Irish sea. DI Tara Grogan has her attention divided, and someone with a grudge to bear has her in his sights.

DEADLY CONVICTION (Book 7)

Shortly after leaving prison, Stephen Lloyd is beaten up and killed. DI Tara Grogan quickly becomes convinced the murder was due to his past crimes but on digging further, she discovers evidence that he was subject to a miscarriage of justice. The trouble is, those responsible for his wrongful conviction are still very much alive and kicking.

All FREE with Kindle Unlimited and available in paperback.

MORE FICTION BY THE AUTHOR

THE MOURNE MOUNTAIN MURDERS

Father and daughter Sidney and Ursula make an unusual private detective team. But hitherto they've survived the tough streets of Belfast. Yet when curiosity gets the better of them and they probe into a murder, they'll attract the unwanted attention of a nasty criminal gang. Can they outwit the mob, or are their days numbered?

BOUND TO RUN

A romantic getaway in a remote Lake District cottage turns into a desperate fight for survival for Alex Chase. If she can get away from her pursuer, and that's a big if, she'll be able to concentrate on the burning question in her mind: how to get revenge.

THE WIFE'S BOYFRIEND

Charlie Geddis is thrown out by his wife but, determined to win her back, decides to prove that her new boyfriend, a property developer with a lot of assets, is in fact a lying crook. In the process, he becomes embroiled in a web of bribes, infidelities and possibly a murder.

All FREE with Kindle Unlimited and available in paperback.

OTHER TITLES OF INTEREST

THE DI JORDAN CARR SERIES
by Diane Dickson

Being a policeman in Liverpool certainly has its challenges, and perhaps more so when you are a six-foot-tall black man. Yet despite surprising some people by his appearance, Detective Inspector Jordan Carr tends to shrug off any consternation it provokes. He has a sympathetic persona, a calm demeanour, and a quiet but determined resolve to get to the truth and not cut corners. This commitment often places him at loggerheads with his superiors, and it's not difficult to imagine that some simmering racist sentiment might lie behind the friction, but Carr puts his victims first and justice for them overrides any of his personal struggles. This wins him respect among his peers and makes his team a force to be reckoned with when faced with the serious cases that policing Merseyside presents.

All FREE with Kindle Unlimited and available in paperback.

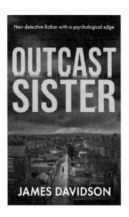

OUTCAST SISTER
by James Davidson

London detective Eleanor Rose is lured back to her old city
of Liverpool by Daniel, an ex-boyfriend and colleague who's
in danger. It's against her better instincts, as she has no
desire to confront her past. But when she gets there, he's
nowhere to be found, and as she retraces his steps, Eleanor
gets caught in a dark web of deceit, corruption and violence.
Her half-sister, who never forgave her for leaving, seems
involved too. Will their path cross? Will she find Daniel?

FREE with Kindle Unlimited and available in paperback.

Sign up to our mailing list to find out about new releases, special offers, free books and more!

www.thebookfolks.com

Printed in Great Britain
by Amazon